THE LAST MONSTER

HAVE YOU EVER WONDERED HOW BOOKS ARE MADE?

UCLan Publishing is an award winning independent publisher specialising in Children's and Young Adult books. Based at The University of Central Lancashire, this Preston-based publisher teaches MA Publishing students how to become industry professionals using the content and resources from its business; students are included at every stage of the publishing process and credited for the work that they contribute.

The business doesn't just help publishing students though. UCLan Publishing has supported the employability and real-life work skills for the University's Illustration, Acting, Translation, Animation, Photography, Film & TV students and many more. This is the beauty of books and stories; they fuel many other creative industries! The MA Publishing students are able to get involved from day one with the business and they acquire a behind the scenes experience of what it is like to work for a such a reputable independent.

The MA course was awarded a Times Higher Award (2018) for Innovation in the Arts and the business, UCLan Publishing, was awarded Best Newcomer at the Independent Publishing Guild (2019) for the ethos of teaching publishing using a commercial publishing house. As the business continues to grow, so too does the student experience upon entering this dynamic Masters course.

www.uclanpublishing.com
www.uclanpublishing.com/courses/
uclanpublishing@uclan.ac.uk

Also by Dan Walker

SKY THIEVES
DESERT THIEVES
THE LIGHT HUNTERS

DAN WALKER

uclanpublishing

For Frankie, the beanpole.

The Last Monster is a uclanpublishing book

First published in Great Britain in 2022 by
uclanpublishing
University of Central Lancashire
Preston, PR1 2HE, UK

978-1-912979-77-6

1 3 5 7 9 10 8 6 4 2

Set in 10/16pt Kingfisher by Nicky Borowiec.

A CIP catalogue record for this book is available from the British Library.

Printed and bound in Great Britain by Clays Ltd, Elcograf S.p.A.

"You ask me what Light is? Light is everything. Every single thing. The very fabric of our world is made up of this force – people, trees, the chair I am sitting on, this pen I am writing with. Few can access Light, control it. You are one."

Professor Majeson Medela

· CHAPTER 1 ·

It all began with a cat.

It was a black, fluffy cat, with orange patches that made it look like a bear that had fallen into a jar of marmalade. The cat was high in an enormous oak tree, in the middle of a gloomy, Light-projected wood, right in the centre of Dawnstar's training wing.

Below, were the three younger members of Squad Juno – Lux Dowd, Brace James and Fera Lanceheart III. Brace, a tall, buck-toothed boy with more enthusiasm than sense, whispered so that their squad leader, Ester Nova, wouldn't hear.

"What do we think her trick will be, then?"

"I think it'll turn into a Monster and attack," said Fera, her face lit by silver moonlight.

"No way, she did that the other week."

Lux, Squad Juno's Healer, watched the cat closely, its edges flickering where they touched the air. Since Dawnstar's chief

1

Inventor, Tesla, had installed his latest device in the training wing – a Light-projector capable of recreating any environment – Lux, Fera and Brace had suffered training sessions in all sorts of places. Throwing Light-casts underwater had been difficult, but nowhere near as hard as throwing them while jumping between clouds in a storm.

Today's session was different again. A cat up a tree. Simple. But, like all of Ester's easier training drills, there would be a catch.

"I think it'll jump when we try to grab it," said Brace decisively. "That'll be her trick. It jumps and we fall on our faces."

The cat jumping probably was Ester's most likely plan, but it wasn't one Lux liked the sound of. He'd have to throw a Light-cast to catch whoever climbed to fetch it. And the absolute *last* thing he wanted to do at that moment was throw Light.

"Maybe the trick is that there is no trick," he suggested hopefully.

Brace and Fera looked at him like he'd just told them to eat their socks.

Lux knew his idea made no sense. But his friends could throw Light as easily as they brushed their teeth. It wasn't so easy for him anymore. Not after the previous year in Kofi, when he'd lost his grandpa; when that new, powerful purple energy had exploded out of him.

"You're worrying again, aren't you?" asked Fera, watching Lux play nervously with the sleeves of his Light Hunter uniform.

"I'm not."

"You are," added Brace. "You've got your *I'm a scared mouse* look."

"All right, I'm worried," Lux admitted. "But you're not the one who keeps leaking weird purple energy."

Brace and Fera exchanged a meaningful glance. "No, but we *are* the ones who keep saying we trust you," said Fera. "We know you won't hurt us."

"Again," said Lux.

A breeze shook the trees, causing the black cat to hunker against the branch. Ester, sitting on a nearby log, tapped her dark metal Gauntlet. "Three minutes. Not that I'm trying to hurry you or anything."

"Come on, Lux," whispered Fera. "If we're going with the plan that the cat'll jump . . . we are going with that, aren't we?"

The boys nodded.

"Then we need you one hundred percent focussed, not worrying about purple energy and exploding. Besides, nothing's happened for months now."

This, at least, was true. The first few weeks after his explosion, Lux's new powers had leaked out of him like water from a tap. But the last few months had been better. Maybe it *would* be all right.

"Oh, okay," he said reluctantly.

"Woohoo!" cried Brace. "I vote Fera climbs the tree while I set up a little staircase of Light-arrows. Lux, you have your *Catch* ready for when she jumps."

"Why am *I* climbing the tree?" Fera demanded.

Brace looked nervously at the gnarled oak, which was as tall as a house. "Well, you know . . ."

"He hates heights," Lux reminded her.

3

"I hate his jokes, doesn't mean I can avoid them." But Fera shook her head grumpily, giving in. "If any of your Light-arrows slip, I'll cook your backside with a *Flame*," she told Brace.

The three young Light Hunters moved into position beneath the tree, ignoring Ester, who was watching them carefully, an amused twinkle in her eye.

It was Brace who threw his Light first, conjuring his bow in a bright blue flash and firing a staircase of arrows, which fizzed where they bit into the bark.

"I'm going out on the branch," said Fera. "If we're right, it'll leap out about . . ." She cast around, choosing the right spot. "Here."

A nervous bubble popped in Lux's stomach, but he did his best to ignore it.

Hugging the tree, Fera climbed using Brace's Light-arrows. The archer cheered her on, only once firing a shot past her ear as a joke.

Soon, she was level with the cat, which was clearly wondering why one of the humans was up its tree. The wind picked up slightly, bending the branches. Then, suddenly, a great rush made Fera lose her footing.

"Oi!" Brace shouted at Ester.

"I never said I'd make it easy." She sat back on her log, looking satisfied.

The wind continued to blow as Fera shifted carefully onto the branch, her body throwing a long, lean shadow.

"You ready?" Brace asked Lux.

Was he? He knew how to throw a *Catch*, of course. He'd been

4

doing that long before he joined the Light Hunters. But his new powers . . . that purple energy . . . if it came, there was nothing he could do.

Think positive, he thought.

Fera was just a yard from the cat now. She turned her head ever so slightly, showing Lux she was ready. Then she pounced.

The cat sprang away instantly, soaring into the air with a bright blue flash. Fera pushed herself off the branch, following the light.

Adrenaline burned through Lux. He joined his fingers, ready to cast the *Catch*. But instead of a blue crackle of Light, he heard a soft throbbing noise, and saw purple threads creeping along his arms. He felt hot and cold at once.

No, no, no, he thought, panicking.

Fera was about four metres high now, over the ground. Her expression changed to one of terror as she saw the purple energy pouring out of Lux, and she reached frantically for something to hold onto. Brace conjured his Light-bow, aiming it at her, but realised there was nothing he could do. Ester, too, leapt up, preparing her Gauntlet, but she had nothing that could break Fera's fall.

It was all down to Lux.

Pressing on a rising sickness, he joined his fingers again, concentrating hard on his *Catch*, imagining Fera bouncing off it like a cloud. He breathed, willing everything he had into his Light.

But it was no good.

The purple energy grew.

Lux met Fera's eyes as gravity pulled her down and he watched in horror as she fell, fell, fell, landing with a muted *thud* on the sodden floor.

· CHAPTER 2 ·

In Dawnstar's training wing, there was a whiteboard above the main entrance that detailed the number of accidents that had occurred in the previous week: hunters falling off climbing frames, running into training dummies. It was a new initiative from Legau Moreiss, one of the oldest Light Hunters there. "Show the rug rats how many people get hurt and maybe they'll be more careful!"

There were plenty of injuries to fill the board. Many, Lux had seen with his own eyes. But he'd never witnessed anyone hit the ground like Fera.

She impacted like a stone, face first, her arm bent awkwardly. There was a horrible *whumphh* noise as all the air rushed out of her. Then she was breathing like a saw cutting through wood.

"Oh man!" said Brace.

He helped her up as Lux stood still, feeling guiltier than he ever had in his life.

Ester knelt beside Fera, comforting her as she regained her breath. The younger girl looked shocked, covered in Light-projected mud and twigs.

"Lux, can you heal her?" asked Ester.

He wanted to say yes, but he wasn't sure. *Heal* was the first cast he'd ever learned; he knew it off by heart. But he'd known *Catch* off by heart too, and that hadn't exactly gone swimmingly.

"It's broken, I think." Ester guided Fera's arm so that it was resting in her lap. The woods were quiet now, apart from the faint shouts of other Hunters training nearby.

"I . . . I don't think I should," said Lux.

Brace nudged him. "Go on."

"No!" Lux pulled away. It was easy for Brace to try and talk him into it – he wasn't the one leaking dangerous energy.

"It's okay," said Ester. "Just a quick *Heal* and she'll be right as rain."

Lux shook his head and walked to the tree. Ester shot Brace a warning look, stopping him from bringing him back. She indicated for him to lift Fera instead. "Take her to the hospital wing."

"But . . ."

"Brace!"

He helped Fera up and started to walk her away.

"It's all right." Fera looked over at Lux, "I'll be fine. Accidents happen." She winced in pain. "Gets me back for that time I froze you with my *Snow*."

Fera waited for a response, but Lux said nothing. She allowed Brace to walk her away and soon they'd disappeared in the dark.

Ester gathered her things. There was a loud click as she pressed a button on her Gauntlet and, in a bright flash, the Light-projected woods faded. Lux found himself standing under the soft light of Dawnstar's training wing.

"Help me clear up," she said.

Their leader was well known for her moods when one of her squad members disobeyed an order, so Lux followed her to the edge of the training wing. There, she found two sweeping brushes in a cupboard.

The training wing was enormous, filled with equipment and tools to prepare Light Hunters for Monster battles. It was late afternoon now, and long beams of sunlight were falling through the high window.

Lux swept where they'd been training, thinking things over. Although his new powers had been rumbling all year, Fera's fall was the first time he'd actually hurt somebody since they'd first appeared. He felt awful – even worse that he hadn't healed her afterwards.

Both Lux and Ester spoke at once.

"Want to talk about it?"

"Ester, I didn't mean to—"

Lux put down his brush. Ester patted a wooden bench for him to sit.

Lux had known Ester Nova – Squad Juno's nineteen-year-old Tech – for just over a year and a half, ever since she'd arrived at his grandpa's clock repair shop disguised as a house-lady. That she'd turned out to be a Light Hunter – part of the ancient order trained to defeat Monsters – had been nothing short of astonishing.

"What happened?" she said.

"I don't know," said Lux quietly. "I was worried about it, but I didn't feel different to normal. Then Fera jumped and it just kind of came on."

Ester played with her Gauntlet. "You didn't tell me you'd been feeling it again."

"I didn't want to worry anyone."

"Dad will have to know."

Ester was talking about her father, Artello Nova, the leader of Dawnstar. Lux got on well with the old man, but that didn't mean he wanted him finding out.

"I can keep it under control," he said. "I've just got to stop using Light for a bit."

"A Light Hunter who doesn't throw Light?" Ester raised a questioning eyebrow.

The other Hunters in the training wing had finished now and were packing away. They waved as they disappeared. Lux just about managed to wave back. It was cold without Tesla's Light-projector running, and he shivered.

"I was going to give you this tonight at the celebration evening," said Ester, "but maybe now's the time instead."

She reached into her pocket and pulled out a fabric badge. It was black, with gold stitching, and felt rough to the touch. In the centre was a golden star.

"Your grandpa's," she said, pressing it against the other badges on Lux's arm. He had four now – his Healer badge, and three to show the Monsters he'd defeated. "Dad and I were going through his old things. It's his Luminary badge. I thought you might want it."

Lux's grandpa had died the previous year, after spending ten years in Daven, raising Lux and fixing clocks and watches. But before that he'd been the Light Hunter Luminary. Seeing his badge now . . . Lux felt an overwhelming sense of pride.

"Dad doesn't mind you wearing it. As long as you don't show off to the other squads."

"Thanks, Ester."

Somewhere in the distance, a door slammed shut. Lux was about to carry on sweeping, but Ester took his brush and guided him towards the exit.

"Go on, I'll finish up. Rest. You'll need your strength for all that food tonight."

Lux managed a weak smile.

"Your grandpa would have been proud, you know?"

"I know," said Lux, although he wasn't sure he believed it anymore.

And with that he walked out of the door.

· CHAPTER 3 ·

Back in Daven, when Lux was suffering endless, boring days with his teachers at school, he would argue with Maya, his only friend, to try and get out of attending school parties. Maya loved them – the dancing and singing, the buffets so big you could go back for seconds. But Lux hated them. So, when Fera and Brace had raced up in Dawnstar's library a month earlier, telling him it was soon to be the Light Hunters' annual celebration evening, his heart had sunk faster than a wrecked ship. Now the night was upon them, he wanted to go less than ever.

Dawnstar's dorm rooms were arranged in a star shape, with five corridors each containing six rooms. Squad Juno's was between Squads Celan and Belex.

It was dinnertime when Lux left the training wing and walked the quiet corridors to their room. Normally, most Light Hunters would have been in the dining hall grabbing something to eat or reading in the library, but that evening they were getting ready. Lux slipped by the double doors that marked Dawnstar's Intelligence wing and down a level to the dorms themselves. Shining green lamps highlighted metal signs, labelling each room. Squad Juno's was slightly bent where Brace had hit it with a Light-arrow.

A creak of the door and Lux was inside.

The room was only slightly bigger than his bedroom back in Daven, yet it contained three beds (squad leaders had their own rooms further down the corridor.) Lux's corner was relatively tidy by his standards, with his grandpa's two *Clockmaker of the Year* certificates pinned above his bed and the only surviving picture of his family in pride of place on his bedside table.

Brace's corner was far messier, with wooden games and puzzles spread across his bed and so many Monster pictures on the wall that it looked like an art classroom. Fera's corner was by far the tidiest. Her notebooks were all stacked neatly by her bed, next to the Monster figurines she collected whenever they were out on a mission.

Lux was surprised to find the light on and music playing from a radio. He was even more surprised to see Brace back from the hospital, eating a sandwich he must have stolen from the kitchen. The wonderful fresh bread smell made Lux's mouth water.

"Ahoy!" said Brace, lifting his sandwich in greeting.

"You're back?"

"Yeah, well, the Healers won't let me spend too long there after I set the bin on fire that time."

Lux dumped his things, sliding his grandpa's Luminary badge

that Ester had given him between the pages of a book to keep it safe. He changed out of his uniform, hanging it in the wardrobe.

"Is she okay?"

"Broken arm," answered Brace, taking another bite of his sandwich. "Nothing they can't fix. They've cast *Heal*. Should take a couple of hours to settle. She said she'd meet us at the skyship hangar for the party. She'll be in a sling, but I told her it'll make her look cool."

Lux collapsed in relief. He'd known, of course, that Dawnstar's Healers would fix Fera. Still, it was good to know she was all right.

"Is . . . she angry?"

Brace smirked. "You're worried."

"No, it's just—"

"I'm only winding you up. No, she's not angry. Not with you, anyway. She will be with me when she finds out what I've done with this though."

Lux turned to see what Brace was talking about. He lifted a pretty blue dress he'd taken out of Squad Juno's shared wardrobe. On the back was a yellow piece of paper that said 'Kick Me.'

"That's mean."

"No worse than what she did the other day."

Brace was referring to a training session in which Fera had left a couple of *Bolt* casts in his boots.

He was avoiding talking about the incident in the training wing. Lux appreciated it.

"Listen, we'd better start getting ready if we want to arrive for the start of the party. We've only got half an hour."

"I don't think I'm going."

"What?"

"I might just stay here." Lux avoided his friend's gaze.

"But . . ." Brace was speechless, trying to make sense of what he was hearing. "But I need you. I'm finding out if I've got on the pilot training track, remember? And Fera. Her leadership thing. You can't not come!"

The fact it was his friends' big night was part of the reason Lux *didn't* want to go. They were about to move up at Dawnstar, while he was stuck, unable to control even the most basic of healing casts.

Before he could answer, a smiling face appeared in the doorway. "Hello Dawnstar! Guess who's back?"

Lux's best friend, Maya Murphy, burst into the room, grinning, her cheeks bright red from the cold. She was a short girl with blonde hair, and she was carrying two stuffed fabric bags, which she dumped on the floor. She sat down, removing her shoes and wiggling her toes.

"And how are we? I'm glad to have made it in time. That walk up from the village is a beast! I got so lost I thought I'd end up back in Daven. Speaking of which," she slapped Lux's leg to make sure he was listening, "you should see it there now, how much it's changed. They've got Light everywhere. Even the street lights are powered by it. It's like Mrs Piper said it was when she was young . . ."

Maya trailed off, looking between Lux and Brace, who were staring at her. "What?"

"Nothing," said Lux. "It's nice to see you. So Daven was fun?"

15

"Everyone at the orphanage thought I was the best because I'm a Light Hunter Inventor. They gave me so many sweets." She handed him a packet of bon-bons from one of her bags. "I saved you some too." She tossed one to Brace. "Although you already owe me two bags. Don't ever say I'm not nice. So, are we all ready for tonight? I got a dress."

Lux and Brace exchanged a glance.

"Oh my giddy aunt!" cried Maya. "Is someone going to tell me what's happened?"

"There was an accident. In training," said Brace. "Fera broke her arm."

Maya looked puzzled. "So? That happens all the time."

"It was my fault," said Lux.

"Oh," said Maya, understanding. "But you healed her, right?"

Lux turned off Brace's radio and looked out of the window, where the sky was turning dark pink.

"He says he's not going tonight," said Brace.

Maya jumped like she'd sat on a *Flame*. "Excuse me?"

"Don't start," said Lux. "It's been a rubbish day—"

"I don't care if you dropped one of Tesla's teleporters on your toe, we are *going* to that party."

"Maya . . ."

"Lux, we've talked about this. In spite of what you think in that little head of yours," she knocked a couple of times on his forehead, "you cannot control everything that happens in the world. All you can control is *your* intentions. Your grandpa told me that, so you should know it better than anyone!"

Maya popped a boiled sweet in her mouth to calm down.

Outside, Lux saw a bird gathering twigs. He knew Maya was right, although that still didn't mean he felt good about Fera. But he also knew that with Brace and Maya bugging him, his chance of avoiding the celebration evening were about as small as his chances of beating Tesla in an argument. Easier to give in now.

"All right," he said, turning into the room. "I'll go. But I'm having a bag of sweets first."

· CHAPTER 4 ·

Artello Nova was a man who knew more about Light than anyone. As Dawnstar's current Luminary, he was thoughtful and patient, especially with the younger Light Hunters, who thought of him as a kindly grandfather. But there was one thing Nova hated, and that was lateness. "If you're one of mine then you're on time," he would say.

And so it was that, with Nova's words ringing in their ears, Lux, Brace and Maya raced to get changed in time for the celebration evening.

Dawnstar provided every Light Hunter with a costume for such occasions. It resembled their normal uniform, except it was black, with gold edges and white sleeves. Because it looked so bad, few of the younger Hunters wore it even when they were supposed to. Instead, they mixed and matched their own colourful clothes with badges of which they were particularly proud. By the time Lux and the others were ready, they resembled a bunch of garden flowers.

"Nice hat," said Brace, referring to a bowler placed jauntily on Maya's head.

"Nice face," she fired back.

The corridors were busy now, with dozens of Light Hunters wandering in groups. Lux was reminded of the annual fair that came to Daven.

"Shoot!" he said, suddenly remembering. "I forgot something."

"Your sense of style?" said Brace.

"You guys go ahead. I'll meet you there."

Lux battled the tide back to Squad Juno's room, where he found his grandpa's Luminary badge and pinned it to his arm, admiring it in the mirror.

The corridors were much quieter on the way back. He glanced at his watch and saw that it was 6:58 PM, two minutes before the party was due to start. He recalled Artello Nova's anger when Squad Juno was late for a Monster meeting and hurried up.

Rounding the corner into the corridor outside the skyship hangar, he bumped into Fera and Legau Moreiss.

"I told this Monster," he heard Legau say, "it's you or me and—"

The older Light Hunter stopped his story, barely avoiding bowling Lux into the wall. "Careful, this isn't your training session," he said grouchily.

"Sorry," said Lux.

There was an awkward silence, during which Legau looked between Lux and Fera. He could tell there was something they needed to discuss.

"Two minutes, then inside," he said, leaving them in the Light-lit corridor.

When he was gone, Fera screwed her foot into the floor nervously. "Hey."

"Are you . . . all right?" said Lux. "I'm sorry about earlier. I don't know where it came from."

"It's fine, I'm all fixed." Fera lifted her arm in its sling, forming a *Flame* cast. "Still hurts but should be good enough for tonight. Where are Brace and Maya?"

"Inside."

"Well, my healing friend, shall we?" she said brightly, holding out her other arm for Lux to take.

Happy that she seemed to have forgiven him, Lux did his best to smile, took Fera's arm and they made their way inside.

· CHAPTER 5 ·

Dawnstar's skyship hangar was normally an echoing, cavernous space, with criss-crossing Light-bridges and massive skyships. But on the night of the celebration evening, it was transformed.

There was Light *everywhere*: the walls, ceiling, chairs, tables and particularly on the long stage that had been erected on the floor. Blue, yellow, red, green, white – the Light flashed, reflecting in the eyes of all the Hunters. Balloons hung from walls and a giant buffet table was filled with every sort of food. It smelled absolutely amazing. Dawnstar's annual celebration evening had long been known as something special, but for Lux it was like walking into a royal feast.

Because a few squads were away fighting Monsters, not every Light Hunter was present. Those who were sat at tables according to their squad, squad leaders having a table of their own near the stage. Lux and Fera spotted Brace and Maya (whom Artello

Nova had allowed to join Squad Juno's table that evening as an exception) sitting in a corner.

"There you are," said Maya, greeting them. "I was beginning to think a Monster had got you. Hi Fera."

"No Monster," said Lux. "Just got a bit waylaid."

Maya and Brace made space for them to sit. There were plates on the table with silver knives, forks and spoons, as well as a red candle that smelled of strawberry.

"So exciting," said Maya, grinning. "I can't believe how amazing it all looks. Are you nervous?" she asked Fera and Brace.

"I know Legau's not going to choose me," said Brace. "So I'm not."

"You don't know that," said Fera.

"He called me a 'blitherin' idiot' the other day. He hates me. Besides, it's easy for you to say. You'll get on the leadership track, no problems."

"Fat chance."

"Oh, you two are so negative," said Maya. "And what's up with you now, Lux? You look like someone's stolen your ice cream."

Lux thought about telling her that it wasn't just your everyday accident that had hurt Fera earlier. But it was supposed to be a fun night; he didn't want to be the one to ruin it.

"Come on, let's get some food," he said.

Together they gathered up their plates and headed to the packed buffet table, where they filled them with sandwiches, breadsticks, dips, crisps, and dozens of little bits and bobs of which Lux didn't even know the name.

"Brace, could you have *fit* any more on there?" said Fera, lifting a sandwich off his plate that he'd covered in a layer of dip and crisps.

"Let me have my fun."

Each day at Dawnstar, the cooks fed hundreds of people, so that often their meals were little more than meat and mash, pie and chips. But the food at the celebration evening was *fantastic*. The members of Squad Juno gobbled it down, so that by the time they'd all finished, they had to lean back in their chairs just to breathe.

"So, what's the running order?" asked Lux.

Brace slid a leaflet from beneath his plate and slapped it on the table.

⚡ DAWNSTAR'S CELEBRATION EVENING ⚡

YOUR LUMINARY, ARTELLO NOVA, INVITES YOU TO AN
EVENING OF FUN, FOOD AND FESTIVITIES IN THE SKYSHIP HANGAR
ON THE LAST DAY OF THE MONTH, SEVEN O'CLOCK SHARP.

RUNNING ORDER:

BUFFET
⚡
SPEECHES
⚡
AWARDS AND PROMOTIONS
⚡
DISCO

As if on cue, there was a knocking on the microphone. They turned in their seats to see Nova on the stage, dressed in his usual blue robe.

"Ahem. Can you all hear me?"

A cheer from the younger Light Hunters.

"Good. Well, it falls to me to welcome you all to another Light Hunters celebration evening. I am pleased to see you've taken our request to dress in your ceremonial outfit seriously."

Lux looked around and struggled to find a single Hunter in their black costume.

"Never mind. I hope you've all enjoyed the food. And I hope too that you've left some for Tesla and Legau. They get upset when there's nothing left for them."

The two older Hunters, sat together on a table near the front, sent up a loud, "Yes!"

"I don't think I will be telling you all anything you don't know when I say it's been the busiest year in our history. The Fire-Drake attack in Ringtown, the Light leakage in Leverburgh and, of course, the events in Kofi one year and six days ago today."

The crowd fell silent, leaning to see Lux, who stared at the strawberry table candle intently.

"But all of that is behind us," Nova went on brightly. "We have new Monsters to fight, new problems to solve and . . ." he paused, as if he was revealing a secret, ". . . those all-sought-after awards and promotions."

The young Hunters erupted, throwing their hands in the air, or banging their knives and forks on the table. Lux caught Fera and Brace's eyes. They looked nervous.

"And so, without further ado, I hand you to my friend and the grumpiest man at Dawnstar, Legau Moreiss!"

When Lux had first met the old Light Hunter, he figured Legau was grumpy because of the injury he'd recently sustained to his leg. But it had turned out, as the months had passed, that he was just plain grumpy. He scowled like other people breathed.

"Let's not mess around and just get straight on with the nominations," he said once he'd climbed to the stage, glancing at the papers in his hand. "So, those nominated to join the Intelligence team are as follows . . ."

Legau read a short list of names, inviting each up to receive a little certificate. The audience clapped.

"*So* glad I'm not doing this," said Maya. "I think I'd burst." She glanced at Fera and Brace, who looked close to bursting, and smiled awkwardly.

Soon, it was time for Brace's announcement: the Pilot training track. Brace had wanted to be a Pilot his whole life, despite his fear of heights. He spent most of his time in between missions in the library learning all he could about flying. Lux would have had him as a definite for the track. There was only one problem. The person who ran the course was Legau Moreiss.

"Here goes," said Brace.

On the stage, Legau turned his notes, squinting to see the small writing. "So, the Light Hunters who'll be joinin' me on pilot trainin' this year . . ."

Brace put his hands nervously beneath his legs.

". . . Millerson. Wilson. Danim. That's all."

Brace's face dropped like a stone. His surname, James, hadn't been on the shortlist.

"Moving onto the technical Inventor's track," said Legau. "Though why anyone would want to work with Tesla is beyond me . . ."

Lux touched his friend's shoulder, but Brace shrugged him off. He tried a smile, so wobbly that it threatened to turn into tears, then he shoved himself out of his chair and hurried to the exit.

"I'll go," said Fera.

"You can't," said Maya. "What about your announcement?"

Fera gave her a sceptical look. "With the kind of day we've had, do you really think I'll get it?"

For once, Maya had no reply.

"Besides, Squad Juno sticks together, right?"

Lux thought of everything that had happened that day. "Yeah," he said, getting out of his seat and making his way to the door. "Let's go and find him."

· CHAPTER 6 ·

Growing up in the little seaside town of Daven, Lux's favourite sweets came from a tiny shop called *Mrs Miggin's Sugar Rush*. As his grandpa had once told him, there wasn't a sad heart that couldn't be lifted by Mrs Miggin's sweets. Unfortunately, in her collection she'd brought earlier that day, Maya didn't have a single bag from Mrs Miggin. And besides, once they heard the news that Fera truly *didn't* get onto her leadership track either, Lux wasn't sure that even Mrs Miggin's sweets would have cheered them up.

Instead, they sat in Squad Juno's room, discussing their bad luck until eventually Maya disappeared and one by one the others drifted to sleep.

In the morning, Lux woke to find Fera already gone and Brace leaning over his bed, reminding him they were meeting Tesla in his lab that morning for a special mission.

Leaping up, he got changed into his Light Hunter uniform, transferring his grandpa's badge from the clothes he'd worn the night before. Then he and Brace hurried through Dawnstar, following the shining blue line that guided them to Tesla's lab.

The others were already there – Fera slumped over a wooden lab bench, Maya working on a bronze spherical object and Ester and Tesla discussing something next to his glass Light chamber.

Dawnstar's chief scientist had barely changed in the year since Lux had met him. He was still rake thin, with a grin that couldn't help but make you smile, even when he was telling you off.

His lab, however, was very different. This was mainly thanks to Maya, who'd brought along her infamous messiness from Mrs Piper's orphanage when Tesla had made her his assistant. The lab no longer resembled a bomb-site, but rather a meteor wreck.

Taking pastries from a plate Tesla had provided, Lux and Brace wandered to Fera, waving a hello at Maya.

"Feeling better?" asked Lux.

Fera was holding a letter and a photograph, reading carefully.

"Earth to Fera?" Brace finished his first pastry and doubled back for another.

"Oh, hi," she said, distracted.

Lux worried for a moment that Fera's arm might still be hurting, or that she was upset about not making the leadership track. But the way she was holding the letter told him it was something else.

"Still can't believe last night," said Brace, sweeping a pile of books off the counter and sitting on the wood. "Ridiculous."

"Yeah," agreed Fera.

"Legau is such a . . ." Brace looked at Ester and Tesla. "Well, I can't say it, but you know what I mean."

"Mmm."

"Are you all right?" Lux asked. He offered Fera one of his pastries, but she shook her head.

"It's nothing," she said, folding the photograph and letter and putting them in her pocket.

"The same 'nothing' Maya says is wrong when she's upset with me?"

"I can hear you," called Maya.

"I got a letter from home," said Fera, joining Brace on the bench.

"Oh dear," said Brace, stopping chewing.

"Oh dear?" Lux didn't know much about where Fera came from, other than that her family owned a farm – a whole village, really – and were very wealthy.

"It's my brother," she explained with a sigh. "Barny. He's just not very nice, that's all. He never wanted me to be a Light Hunter. Hated it when I first came. Now, he doesn't talk to me. Or sign these," she said, pulling out the letter again.

"Sorry, Fera. That must be rubbish."

She sniffed. "I'm used to it."

Lux didn't know how to cheer her up. So, while he waited for Tesla and Ester to finish their chat, he wandered over to say hello to Maya.

"Honestly, I could find better tools in Daven," she said, banging the screwdriver she was holding on the bench. "I really can't get this thing open."

"What is it?"

Maya was holding a bronze sphere about the size of her fist, formed of smaller jigsaw-like segments. On each was a relief carving of a mountain – one tall, pointed peak in the middle and a smaller one either side. Maya turned the sphere, showing Lux the other side. He was surprised to see one of the jigsaw pieces missing. He looked inside the gap and the sphere wobbled in Maya's hand.

"Careful!" she warned. "Tesla wants me to open it. I don't want you breaking it before I've even got started."

"Correct," said the Inventor, rolling towards them in his wheelchair. He'd finished his conversation with Ester. "I see you, Dowd, and I suggest you don't go near that object again if you want to stay in my lab. Now, gather around. You too, Zippy and Dippy." He was talking to Fera and Brace, who joined Ester near the glass chamber.

"It may come as a surprise that I asked you all here to do more than just annoy me. I requested a squad from Nova to do a job and for some reason he suggested you lot."

Tesla searched in a wooden box as he spoke. Out of it came Gauntlets, old lab coats, a pair of spectacles, a map, a skyship part and so many Monster figurines that Fera could have decorated her entire bedside table. Finally, the Inventor surfaced, carrying a pile of thin black discs threaded with Light.

"Guardians," he explained, showing them around. "Tiny ones.

Your job is to hike the meteor crater, putting these in the ground. Do that and you can take the rest of the day off."

Tesla grinned mischievously, knowing the offer he'd given them was about as appealing as cleaning every toilet at Dawnstar.

Brace took one of the discs and stuck it on the wooden bench. To their surprise, a Light-hologram of Tesla popped out, pointing an accusing finger.

"Zippy, Dippy – get out of here!" it squeaked, repeating the phrase.

"Nice," said Lux.

"My idea," said Maya proudly. "The big Guardians watch Dawnstar's main entrance. But we keep getting these reports of Monster spawn on the ridge. I thought I'd make these to scare them off."

"Zippy and Dippy," echoed Fera, offended.

"Well, you know . . ."

Tesla coughed, drawing them all back to the matter at hand. "Despite what Maya tells you, the contents of the Guardians are unimportant. What matters is that they watch the Monster spawn."

Tesla took Brace's disc, put it on the pile and handed it to Fera.

"I'd say you're the most sensible here – although that's not saying much – so I'm giving them to you."

Fera pocketed the discs.

"Come on then," said Ester, heading for the door. "The sooner we finish—"

"We're going *now*?" said Brace. "I thought it'd be after breakfast!"

Ester glanced at the empty plate of pastries, most of which were now in Brace's stomach.

"Oh," he said.

With a goodbye wave from Maya, Squad Juno marched out of the door.

· CHAPTER 7 ·

There were two main exits to Dawnstar – one at the front and one at the rear. To get in and out, Light Hunters needed a special ring – a shining silver band with a star-shaped head of Light. Tesla had given Lux his recently, and he used it now to open the circular entrance.

The stone platform outside was surrounded by giant cliffs. Ester tapped her Gauntlet and a thread of Light shot up and over the top. She pulled and it held.

"Grab on."

Lux helped Fera hold on with her recovering arm, then hooked on himself.

Brace stayed back. "I really think we should just steal a skyship," he said, looking queasily up at the tall cliff.

"Come on," said Fera.

Squeezing his eyes shut, he gripped Lux, then the four Light

Hunters shot into the air, the chill morning wind rushing past. In no time, they'd looped up over the cliff-edge and landed on the sandy rock.

"Ouch!" cried Fera, nursing her arm.

"Sorry," said Ester, reeling her Light-thread in. "It's sped up. I really should get Tesla to look at that."

There was a saying among the older Hunters at Dawnstar: "If you're out on the rim, take an umbrella." It meant, if it wasn't raining, it would be hailing, snowing or sleeting. But that day there was no rain, nor hail nor snow. It was a beautiful winter's morning, with a low sun that sent rays skipping across the land.

The black windows of Dawnstar were far below them now. Lux could see the outline of where a meteor had crashed thousands of years before, creating the basin called Korat Crater. He looked in the direction of Daven and was happy to see the endless, fractured blue sea beyond. Turning, he spotted the fire trees of the Shengan Jungle – a thick, orange line – and, no more than a dot on the horizon, the tall glass towers of Lindhelm. An icy breeze froze his cheeks, but it wasn't enough to ruin the view.

"Wow!"

"Come and look, Brace," said Fera.

"No thanks." Brace was kneeling down, as close to the ground as possible.

Ester called the young Hunters to order. "We know our mission," she said. "Drop these in the spots Tesla's sent to me." She swept a Light-map out of her Gauntlet and sure enough there were fifteen red dots.

Ester was so business-like during missions that sometimes Lux found himself switching off when she gave them her briefing talk. So, he was very surprised when he heard what she said next.

"And that leads me to a bit of a change we're going to have today. Specifically, for you, Fera."

The younger girl's face went red.

"I was annoyed that you didn't get on the leadership track last night. I've been your squad leader now for three years and if anyone's ready for leadership, it's you. So . . . that's what we're going to do. I'm going to teach you how to lead a squad."

"Excuse me?"

"I mean it. You're ready. So, from today, I'm teaching you. Next year, there's no way they'll turn you down."

Lux, Brace and Fera exchanged a surprised glance. Fera, their leader? She'd wanted it for ages, but for Ester to start training her in secret? It was . . . exciting!

Fera frowned, nervous. Then something seemed to harden inside her. "Okay, let's do it."

Brace's mouth was wide open. "So, let me get this straight: we're going to be taking orders from *her*?"

"Yes," said Ester.

"From *her*?"

"I don't mind," said Lux brightly.

Ester swept her Light-map into her Gauntlet, preparing to leave.

"But . . . but . . ." Brace spluttered.

"Braceson James, you should be happy for your friend. She's worked hard."

"I know, but—"

"No 'buts'. Now be quiet and listen to your new leader's instructions."

Ester stood alongside Lux and Brace, so that Fera was in front of them all. It took Fera a moment to realise what she was doing.

"Uh . . ."

Lux nudged her gently. "The map."

"Oh yes," she said, going red again. "Ester, could I see the map again, please?"

Fera soon worked out how they could deliver the black disks to the fifteen locations most efficiently – starting with the wishing well and finishing with the abandoned graveyard that overlooked the old road to Lindhelm.

The weather held for most of the morning, and Lux had to admit that the mission was more pleasant than he'd anticipated. He'd always enjoyed walking with his grandpa in Daven, but all the hiking he did as a Light Hunter had become a drag. However, that day, in the sun, they didn't see any Monsters – no footprints or claw marks – and the beautiful green valleys were a big change from their day-to-day at Dawnstar.

"I could get used to this," he said as they ate the packed lunches Ester had brought along.

"Well, don't," she said. "Because I guarantee you we'll be out fighting something by the end of the week."

The first thirteen Guardian-Teslas only took six or so hours, including the half hour they spent rescuing Brace after he slipped down a well trying to fish out an old coin. But the final two locations – in the bottom of a tree-filled valley and the graveyard – were much longer walks. The sun was starting to set by the time they'd planted the second-to-last disc in a copse of trees.

"Zippy, Dippy – get out of here!" it squeaked.

"Trust me, I want to," said Brace.

Lux, who was starting to feel like he'd been walking for six months instead of six hours, agreed. "That'll do, won't it?" he said. He knew Tesla would disagree once he found out they'd skipped the last disc, but with how tired he was, he hardly cared.

Lux and Brace waited for Ester's decision. But she referred them to Fera, who was looking up the valley to the old graveyard.

"If I was Tesla, I'd want us to finish the job," she said, taking the final disc from Brace and starting up the hill. Ester followed.

"Remind me," said Brace, as he dragged himself miserably off the floor, "to join the leadership track next year instead."

· CHAPTER 8 ·

Ester had once told Lux a story, during one of their training sessions, of how her mum had seen a ghost up at the old graveyard. It had happened during a mission to battle a Minotaur in the Shengan Jungle, back before Tesla had invented the teleporter and Light Hunters had to walk and fly everywhere. Her squad were taking a shortcut through the graveyard when a long, thin creature appeared out of nowhere. At first, they'd thought it was a Monster and prepared to attack. But when it didn't move, and eventually seemed to fade to nothing, they realised it was something else. Rumours had circulated Dawnstar about the haunted graveyard ever since.

Ester's story was very much in Lux's mind as they trudged up the hill.

The sun was setting now, painting the sky red and pink and casting long shadows over the grass. Soon, stars replaced the endless blue and the moon started to rise. Fera cast a *Flame* to keep them warm.

"There's supposed to be ghosts up there, you know?" said Brace.

"We know," said Fera.

"My uncle told me before I came to Dawnstar. It was your mum who saw them, wasn't it, Ester?"

She didn't respond.

The graveyard, when they reached it, was surrounded by a broken-down wooden fence, so that the Light Hunters had to be careful not to trip over the flattened posts. Moss-covered gravestones climbed to a stone shack – no more than a single room – covered in creeping plants. Among the graves were bare trees. The wind whistled and a fog had descended, bringing with it a light rain.

"I am *so* glad we came," said Lux sarcastically, sheltering under a tree.

"Why don't you do that thing you did in Ringtown?"

Brace was referring to the time Lux had cast a *Catch* above them like an umbrella. Normally, he'd have done it. But after Fera's injury . . .

"Maybe in a bit."

"I'll use my Gauntlet," said Ester.

She pressed a few buttons and a Light blanket appeared in the air above them. Raindrops crackled where they hit the blue energy.

"Haven't you finished yet?"

Maya's voice came to them all via the Shells in their ears – tiny devices that let Light Hunters communicate with Dawnstar.

"Not yet. Last one," answered Fera.

"Hurry up. Tesla's saying I've got to stay in the lab until you're done. I'm hungry."

Fera pinpointed the location for the final Guardian-Tesla and gave the black disc to Lux. She wandered with him to a spot behind the building, beside a large gravestone, where they planted it, treading it down so any animals wandering by would be reluctant to try it for lunch.

The air was much colder now, and Lux's teeth were chattering. Fera's lips were slightly blue too, and tiny icicles had formed in her hair.

"Cast that *Flame* again," said Brace, coming up to meet them, "it's absolutely freezing—" He stopped dead, staring over their shoulders.

Lurking behind the building, lit by the full moon, was a Monster. But it was one of the strangest Lux had ever seen. Three metres tall, it stood on two legs and was formed entirely of blue-green ice crystals. An icy mist froze the very air around its body so the raindrops were locked in place, like someone had stopped time. Its eyes were red dots, and they were staring directly at Lux.

"Ester," called Fera uncertainly.

The older girl, who was further down the hill, saw instantly what had spooked them. She looked at the Monster, the frozen rain, then started to run up towards them.

"Get back!"

Lux's heart was hammering. He backed away from the Monster,

but there was a blinding flash of Light, as if a thunderbolt had just struck. When he opened his eyes again, he was somewhere else entirely, surrounded by pure white. It was completely silent, like he was in an enormous cathedral. No smells, no taste. He jerked – his grasp of reality fighting against what had just happened.

There was no sign of the other Hunters.

The only other thing in that vast, endless white was the ice-Monster, still surrounded by a bubble of frozen rain.

Lux started to panic. As a Healer, he could do little in a fight without the rest of his squad.

The Monster's eyes drilled into him. He heard a grinding, rasping sound. And a word: *Ark*.

The word repeated, communicated somehow by the creature. Then, just as quickly as he had arrived, there was another thunderclap and Lux was back in the graveyard.

The Light Hunters jumped in shock.

The Monster had gone.

The frozen bubble of rain shuddered and fell. Lux felt suddenly warmer.

"Everyone all right?" asked Ester.

"What *was* that?" said Fera.

"It definitely wasn't a ghost," said Brace. He leaned against a tree, catching his breath.

Lux tried to calm himself. The Monster, the whiteness, that word: *Ark*. He was sure he'd heard it somewhere before . . . but what did it mean?

"It took me," he said.

The other Hunters looked at him.

"Away. From here."

"Don't be silly," said Brace. "You were here the whole time."

"It took me to this . . . white place. It spoke to me."

Ester stopped working her Gauntlet and stared at Lux. Brace started to speak, but she cut him off. "What did it say, Lux?"

"Ark."

The rain was drumming on the trees, heavier than before. Down the hill, the crater ridge was a dark, curved line. Beyond it, Dawnstar shone, its orange lights warm against the black.

"Let's get home," said Ester, looking concerned. "We need to speak to my father."

· CHAPTER 9 ·

Artello Nova's quarters were right at the top of Dawnstar, away from the main building, in a tiny courtyard. Lux had visited often, as had all Light Hunters: receiving missions, discussing Monster threats and, in his case, dealing with the aftermath of the battle in Kofi. But Ester had never taken him there with more urgency than she was now.

He'd heard of odd things happening to Light Hunters. It was all part of the job. As the famous Light scholar, Professor Majeson Medela, had once written: "Light is everything. Every single thing. The very fabric of our world." Mess with that and things could go badly wrong. But a Light Hunter disappearing and returning, as if no time had passed? It was impossible.

"Something's wrong, isn't it?" he said as they arrived outside her father's quarters. "Is it Deimos?"

Lux was talking about the man who'd arrived in Daven the

previous year to kidnap him. The man had who wanted to use his powers for evil. The man who'd set the Cerberus on Kofi to draw him out. And the man, though Lux found it hard to think about, who'd killed his grandpa.

"Maybe," said Ester.

In summer, the courtyard outside Nova's rooms was beautiful, with lawns of lush green grass, fresh fountains and pink cherry blossoms. Today it was dark, barely lit by a moon smothered by a bank of clouds.

Ester opened the door to her father's rooms quietly. It was warm inside, heated by a log fire. It looked the same as ever, with Nova's mahogany desk, as well as his shelves full of old weapons and Monster statues.

"Is that you, my girl?"

Nova, his long brown hair tied in a neat ponytail, was sitting at his desk, working with a knife at one of his Monster models.

"You're back late. I was going to get you to help me with this. Such funny creatures, Hydras." He lifted the half-finished figure, twisting it in the Light. "So many necks and heads it gets hard to carve the detail without someone holding it for you. Legau once fought a Hydra, you know? Nearly took his head off. Be a darn sight quieter if it had, eh?" He laughed, waiting for her to join in. When she didn't, he turned in his chair. "I said, it'd be a darn sight quieter if—"

Nova's expression turned grave as he saw Ester's anxious face. He put down his model. "Deimos?"

Ester shrugged.

Nova indicated for Lux to sit on one of his sofas, then the Luminary moved around the room, pouring glasses of water for Lux and his daughter. He listened carefully as Ester told him about the graveyard, then he sat back, rubbing his chin.

"You're certain the word was 'Ark', Lux? Fear makes us hear things. And nobody would blame you for being afraid. Think carefully – are you certain it was Ark?"

Lux thought. The ice-Monster's speech had been odd but yes, it was definitely Ark. And now that he saw the keen look of interest in Nova's eye, he remembered where he'd heard the word before too. Deimos had mentioned it back in Kofi: "A structure used by the Ancients to contain all their knowledge on Light and Shade, believed to be buried beneath a town in this region."

Nova spoke again. "And this white place. You didn't see anything else at all?"

"No."

"Hmm. You did the right thing bringing him straight here," Nova told his daughter. He walked to his desk, thinking. Ester gave Lux a reassuring smile.

Lux watched the old man position one of Maya's Shells in his ear and talk to someone quietly. He tried to listen, but Nova's hushed voice was drowned out by the crackling fire.

Finally, Nova finished and sat next to Lux.

"It's not easy being Lux Dowd, is it?" he said. "If it's not purple energy, it's ice-Monsters." He repositioned his injured arm. "I'm going to be honest, Lux: I can't explain this now. I have my own thoughts about what might have happened. And there are other events this week of which you will have no knowledge that make me feel this way. As soon as I can tell you anything, I will. If this is Deimos, nothing has changed from what I said last year. Your grandpa charged me with keeping you safe and I will. For now, I want you to go about your duties and if anything else happens, I want you to report it to me straight away. Is that clear?"

"Yes."

"Good. Then I believe you have somewhere else to be."

In all the excitement of the day Lux had completely forgotten he'd agreed to spend the evening with Maya and Tesla investigating his new powers. They'd done it every week that year, unless a mission prevented it. But after the graveyard, he felt like he'd rather eat his own foot. Still, he didn't tell Nova this. Instead, he picked himself off the seat and walked dutifully to the door.

"If Deimos is back, it won't be like last time, Lux, I promise you that," said Nova.

Lux saw his grandpa's pale face as Deimos flicked away the *Revive* cast that would have saved his life, and he prayed that Nova was right.

· CHAPTER 10 ·

Lux had only let Dawnstar's chief Inventor, Tesla, down once. He'd promised to help him work on a healing cast called *Antidote* – a cure for any kind of poison – that hadn't been successfully cast since Ester was little. Rather than help, Lux had spent the evening with Brace in the recreation room, seeing who could get the most points on a wooden ball game. To say that Tesla had gotten mad was an understatement: his shouting nearly broke every Light-lamp in Dawnstar. But his words had had an impact on Lux, who hadn't missed a session since.

This was why, even though he needed a rest more than anything in the world, Lux made his way through Dawnstar's corridors to the training wing.

As he walked, he took a moment alone with his thoughts.

The ice-Monster . . . where had it come from? And that word, Ark. One thing he knew for certain was that Nova had heard of the word. His normally blank expression had shifted to one of keen interest at Lux's mention of it.

A skyship boomed as it landed somewhere in the hangar next door, but Lux ignored it, sliding into the training wing and putting all of his questions out of his head. The last thing he needed at that moment was Tesla getting annoyed with him for not focussing.

"There you are," said the Inventor, who was busy repairing the damaged frame of his glass Light-chamber.

"I was with Nova," explained Lux.

"I know perfectly well where you were," said Tesla. "Doesn't mean I want to sit around like a tomato waiting to be chopped. Come and get yourself into position. I still want to make my card game tonight if possible."

The training room was empty, dark and cold, aside from a Light-lamp casting a pool of white Light, and Tesla's chamber. There was also a large wooden box, out of which Maya was hanging.

"So glad I came," Lux whispered sarcastically to Maya.

She and Tesla were like two very different peas in the same pod. The grumpy Inventor rubbed like sandpaper against cheerful Maya. But nobody could deny that the technology-obsessed pair had formed a pretty spectacular team in the year since Maya had arrived at Dawnstar. Their biggest project was trying to work out more about Lux's new powers.

"Before you start telling me about what happened today and how tired you are and that you'd rather rest," Tesla told Lux, "I know." He snapped off a piece of the chamber and tossed it over his shoulder, missing Maya's head by inches. "The wind doesn't blow in Dawnstar without me feeling it. But what we're doing tonight is very important indeed."

Lux took off his jacket and reached for the chamber handle.

"A-da-da, not yet. Maya, explain."

"We're doing something different tonight," she said, guiding Lux to the box she'd been searching through, which was full of strange devices. She'd set up a table alongside it, on top of which was the bronze sphere he'd seen her working on that morning.

Lux looked at the sphere. The relief carvings of the three-peaked mountain barely showed in the training wing's Light, but the gap with the piece missing was clear.

"It's called the Key to the Ark," said Tesla, lifting the ball.

Lux felt like he'd been knocked upside down. *The Key to the Ark.* Had he heard that right?

"Tesla, I don't know what Nova told you but—"

"You thought I didn't notice when you went near this thing in my lab this morning," said Tesla. "But I saw it react to you. I was going to do some work with it anyway after that. Let's just say your run-in with the Monster at the graveyard today bumped it up my to-do list."

Lux moved closer to the sphere, but Tesla pulled it away. "Not yet."

He gave the ball to Maya and wheeled back to his Light-chamber.

"Tesla's been piecing it together for years," said Maya. "Light Hunters have been finding bits out near Monster lairs, in Ancient ruins, places like that. Ester's mum found one." She spun the sphere, showing Lux a piece with a damaged corner. "It was a man named Professor Ghast who called it the Key to the Ark. He was the Inventor here before Tesla."

Lux recalled all the times he and Maya had read his sister's old Light Hunters books. He couldn't bring a Professor Ghast to mind.

Maya went on, "The name always made us think it opens something, but we never could work out what. We've just had it sitting around. It's only a coincidence I was cleaning it this morning. But after your trip to the graveyard, well . . ."

"Well," Tesla took over, tapping the Light-chamber meaningfully, "we've got an experiment to do. Step this way."

Ancient ruins. Keys to Arks. None of it made sense to Lux. What he did know was that, after injuring Fera, he really didn't want to be playing with strange artefacts in a Light-chamber.

"I'm really not sure this is a good idea. Yesterday . . ."

"Don't concern yourself with that," said Tesla, guiding him inside.

"But—"

"Lux!" Tesla barked his name in such a way that made clear he didn't have much choice.

The glass chamber had a bit of a funny smell, and the windows were dirty. Maya approached with the bronze ball and handed it to Lux. He nearly dropped it, it was so heavy.

"You'll be fine," she reassured him. "Just do what Grumpy says."

"I heard that!"

Maya gave Lux a mischievous smile and returned to her tools.

50

There was a loud *clang* as Tesla shut the chamber door, reminding Lux of a teleporter. Tesla and Maya's voices sounded like they were underwater.

"All I want you to do," said the Inventor, drawing a Light-screen filled with letters out of a Gauntlet, "is hold your hand over it."

Lux looked unsure.

"Just do it."

He shifted the cold metal ball to his right hand and held his left above it. Nothing.

"Thought so," said Tesla, speaking loudly. "Okay, now I want you to actually put your hand on the ball."

Lux breathed and did as he was told. He'd been expecting nothing to happen. But something did happen. Instantly, he surged with energy. There was a purple tone to his skin that told him his new powers were gathering. He winced, nearly letting go.

"Hold it!" cried Tesla.

Lux felt sick, but he kept his hand on the Key, pressing it down.

The energy built, reaching the point where normally it would have leaked out. The ball, which was suddenly lighter, juddered, then all the pieces moved apart, floating as if joined by some invisible thread. In the centre was the same purple energy as Lux's.

"Whoa!" said Maya.

"How do you feel, Lux?" asked Tesla.

"Like I want this to end."

"One moment."

Lux kept his hands exactly where they were, praying the Inventor knew what he was doing. The jigsaw pieces tugged slightly on his skin as they floated. Outside the chamber, Tesla was tapping at his Gauntlet.

"You're doing great," said Maya.

The purple energy in the Key swirled like leaves in the wind: beautiful and terrifying.

"All right, you can let go."

Lux didn't quite know what Tesla meant by let go, as he wasn't really holding anything. He shook his hands, and as if someone had switched on a magnet, the jigsaw pieces snapped together again, and the ball dropped heavily into his palm. Slowly, his own energy calmed.

"That's it?"

"Far from it," said Tesla. "What's just happened is one of the most incredible things of my entire career. But in the interests of safety, we must stop there today." He let Lux out of the chamber, taking the Key.

"Did you get what you need?"

"That, I will spend the next hour working out," said Tesla, already so absorbed in his work that Lux might as well have been a tree.

"Come back tomorrow," said Maya. "I'm sure he'll tell you more then."

Lux didn't argue. Any chance to get away without throwing Light was fine by him.

"Something's happening," he told Maya as she accompanied him to the door. "I don't know what, but something is."

"Let's hope we're ready then," she said.

· CHAPTER 11 ·

One thing about Lux Dowd that nobody could understand was his ability to sleep anywhere, anytime. A busy skyship, an evening of fireworks – no problem. And incredibly, after he got back from Dawnstar's training wing that night to find the lights off in Squad Juno's room and Fera and Brace already asleep, he slipped under his covers for one of the best night's sleep he'd had in weeks. The ice-Monster, Nova, the Ark – all of it just faded into a dream.

He woke in the morning to his curtains being thrown open and bright sunshine blasting him in the face.

"Wakey, rise and shine," said Fera, smiling fondly. Her left arm seemed healed now, and she waved at Lux, who sat up, blinking in the bright light. He noticed it was cold and sank back down.

Fera and Brace hurried around the room, putting on their Light Hunter uniforms.

"Come on," said Fera.

"If it's before eight o'clock, I'm not going to be happy," moaned Lux.

"Nova wants us. Ten minutes. Go!"

Fera's words were like a rock to Lux's skull. He wiped sleep from his eye. "Why?"

"To give us a bag of sweets. I don't know! Get up. Don't make us late again."

Lux pulled on his uniform in a daze, so that by the time he'd finished, he looked like an untidy scarecrow. Shortly after, they were hurrying through Dawnstar.

Missions came to Light Hunters in all sorts of ways. From Tesla, Legau, even posted on a board in the dining hall. But the most important ones came from Nova himself.

They found Ester waiting outside his rooms, tapping her heel impatiently.

"Don't worry about punctuality, you three. It's only my dad's biggest—" She saw Lux's scruffy uniform. "Goodness, come here."

She fixed his collar and a Monster badge that had come loose.

"Do we know what this is about?" asked Fera.

"We will soon."

Ester threw open the doors and sat them on one of her father's sofas, grabbing a black remote from his desk. There was a click, and the wooden floorboards rumbled, rising as the ceiling disappeared. They came to rest under the glass dome, which snapped into place. Above was a beautiful view of the blue sky.

"One minute late," said Nova, who was leaning against the dome, checking his watch. "Early for Juno."

"Blame Lux," said Fera.

He and the others joined Nova at the glass. It was warm where the sun beat down. Thin white clouds scooted across the sky.

"I won't waste time as we have little," said Nova. "You're probably wondering why I've called for you at such short notice. And your conclusions are probably right. I have a mission for you. You'll be aware of the conversation I had with Lux last night and his session with Tesla in the training wing, is that correct?"

Brace and Fera nodded guiltily. There were few secrets in Squad Juno, and Lux had told them everything as they'd hurried along that morning.

"Good," Nova went on. "In which case, I will now reveal why yesterday's events at the graveyard carry such significance."

He opened his desk and retrieved an envelope. "I recently received a message from a man called Professor Ghast who lives in Lindhelm."

The name caught in Lux's mind. Hadn't Maya mentioned a man called Ghast?

"He's an old . . . friend of mine. I haven't heard from him in a long time." A ghost of sadness haunted Nova's face. "He was a Light Hunter. Leader of Squad Phoenix. My wife's squad.

"Professor Ghast is one of the most knowledgeable people in the world about Ancient ruins. He claims to have found something very important in our fight to put an end to Monster attacks once and for all. However, he refuses to disclose this in case his letter falls into the wrong hands. He's requested a Light Hunter squad to collect it. I have decided to send Squad Juno."

They blinked in surprise.

"Er," Brace did his best to sound polite, "we've defeated four Monsters this year. Surely you'd be better sending someone els—"

Nova indicated for quiet, although he couldn't hide an amused grin at Brace's lack of enthusiasm. He laid Ghast's letter flat on his desk and tapped another remote. The observatory's glass dome turned black, and an image of the letter appeared there.

Artello,

It is years since I have written to you, and you will perhaps find the arrival of my letter a great surprise.

I will be brief, as I am not certain there is enough trust remaining in our friendship for you to send me what I require.

In short: I have found a way to stop the Monster attacks.

The word I discussed with you all those years ago has finally borne fruit.

Ark.

I will say no more in case this letter falls into the wrong hands. But if you have any faith remaining in me, send a squad as soon as possible to collect my message.

You can find me at Lindhelm University.

Do not delay. We have disagreed on much, but I believe our goal has always remained the same. I might finally have found a way to let us realise it.

Sincerely,

Emory Ghast

Lux stared at the word "Ark".

"I received Ghast's letter at the start of the week. Blame an old man's pride, or a lack of foresight on my part. But I am now sure, Brace, to answer your question, that after the events of yesterday, you understand why I have selected your squad to be my representatives.

"You are to go today," he went on. "Tesla is already awaiting your arrival and has the teleporters prepared. I'm sure I needn't impress upon you the importance of this mission. Professor Ghast is a serious man. If he says his findings are important, they are. And if he says they must remain secret, they must. Go, find out what he's learned, and return to me as soon as possible. Is that clear?"

The mission Nova had outlined was so far from what Lux and his squad-mates had been expecting that they could hardly speak. They nodded.

"Good. Ester, kit them out and leave as soon as possible. Dismissed."

Nova returned to his desk, studying a report.

Shock was written on Lux, Fera and Brace's faces. They moved mechanically back to the sofas, ready to head down. As they sat, Nova spoke from his desk.

"Lux, I'd like a word before you go."

Lux stood, wondering if he'd done something wrong. But there was no irritation on Nova's face. He stepped off the platform and watched as the rest of his squad left the room.

· CHAPTER 12 ·

Of all the stories Lux's grandpa told him as a little boy, his favourite was of the hero Juno, and how she'd single-handedly defeated a dozen Monsters. Lux had known Juno's tale *was* just a story, but it had lit a fire in his imagination all the same. That he was now *in* Squad Juno – named for her star – was one of the proudest things in his life. And when, after the others had disappeared, Nova tapped his remote once more, turning the dome black again, Lux found Juno instantly.

"Never ceases to amaze me, Juno," said Nova. "So fragile, so beautiful. I've been thinking about your squad's star recently."

Lux stayed quiet. Nova liked to talk sometimes before reaching his point, but Lux had received enough good advice from Dawnstar's Luminary that he knew it was worth listening.

"True hero, you know, Juno? Many ways she could have been thrown from her goal in the story. But she remained true. We could all benefit from being a little more like her." Nova turned to Lux. "How have you been, anyway? It's a while since we've spoken properly."

The question took Lux by surprise. "Fine, I think."

Nova laughed. "I hear you've been having trouble with your new powers again."

Lux shifted awkwardly.

"Fera doesn't blame you for her arm, you know? None of us do."

"I know."

Nova lifted Ghast's letter. "This is a strange mission I am sending you on. Are you worried?"

About finding Ghast? Lux thought. *No.* If he truly knew how to stop the Monsters, the sooner they located him the better. But the graveyard was still playing on his mind. And his new powers . . .

"Yes. And no."

"Normally, I wouldn't dream of assigning you such a mission. Sending you and your squad-mates anywhere after yesterday is a dangerous thing. But you proved to me with Kofi last year that an old man's instincts are sometimes wrong. I'm going to trust you this time.

"I have a good feeling about Ghast, Lux. When your grandpa was Luminary, he always told me when I had a good feeling to go with it. The world will help you out," he said. He glanced at Lux's grandpa's badge on his arm. "You decided to wear it then?"

"Yes," said Lux.

Nova opened his desk and took out an object about the size of his fist. The Key to the Ark.

"I understand you and Tesla did an experiment with this." He observed the ball in the starlight, the mountain carvings running around it like silver threads. "He thinks it might be important somehow. I want you to take it with you."

Nova opened Lux's hand and placed the ball inside.

"What am I supposed to do with it?"

"I trust you'll know that when the time comes."

Nova took in the stars in the dome one final time, before tapping his remote and returning the observatory to normal. The bright blue of day made Lux squint.

"Careful out there. Your mission is to visit Ghast. But I fear Deimos may be involved somehow. Keep your wits about you."

Lux felt a little shaken on his way back through Dawnstar, placing the Key to the Ark carefully in his bag. He was worried it might react to his new powers just by being close. And the mission with Ghast . . . it was odd, but he'd never thought Deimos might be involved. After what Nova had said . . .

He shivered.

Knowing how quickly Ester worked in preparing for a mission, Lux decided to head straight for Tesla's lab rather than Squad Juno's room. It was quiet when he arrived. For a moment he thought he'd made a mistake, that he'd have to search the whole of Dawnstar to find his squad. Then he heard laughing from the lab's second room. He made his way through and found everyone standing by the teleporters.

"At last!" said Brace. "Finished hobnobbing with the boss?"

"Something like that."

"You're going to Lindhelm!" said Maya excitedly. "You'll have to say hello to my sister."

"She works at the university," Lux explained to a confused Fera.

"And your family live near Lindhelm, don't they, Fera?" said Maya. "If you get any downtime after the mission, maybe you can visit them."

Fera frowned.

Lux shook his head slightly at Maya, telling her to drop the subject.

"Stop yapping, we need to go," said Ester. "Fera, you're in charge again."

Brace leapt up. "What?"

"I'm going to be watching. And if I feel I should step in, I will. Otherwise, Fera's in charge."

The younger girl played nervously with her uniform. "Ester, this is important. Maybe we should—"

"You're in charge."

Fera knew better than to argue with Ester when her mind was made up, so she stayed quiet.

There was a loud hiss and a cloud of steam rose up behind the teleporters as Tesla opened their lids. "If you lot have finished wasting my time, we're ready," he said.

Maya handed the Light Hunters a fresh Shell each. They slotted them in their ears. "Can you hear me?"

"Loud and clear," said Brace.

He went to the first teleporter, ready to climb in, but Fera held him back. She got into the pod, looking determined.

"Well, well, has Zippy finally got over her fear of my magical transporting boxes?" said Tesla, surprised.

Fera set her jaw. "Just do it."

Tesla pressed a series of buttons on the wall as Lux watched her through the glass, her cheeks bright red. There was a *whump* sound, and just like that, she was gone.

Tesla turned to the others, rubbing his hands with glee. "Who's next?"

· CHAPTER 13 ·

Lux always liked to go last whenever Squad Juno teleported. Partly because, like Fera, he found the process uncomfortable. And partly because it meant if Tesla or Maya got their destination slightly wrong, he wouldn't end up with Brace falling right on top of him.

As Lux climbed into the glass box and Tesla pressed the combination of coloured buttons, the first thing he felt was a kind of implosion. This was replaced by a lightness, then darkness, only to explode into fierce day – sparks and stars as far as the eye could see. Lux shot through them, faster and faster, until just one remained.

Then he was back.

He was, in fact, on top of a very, *very* tall tower in the city of Lindhelm.

"And here he is," said Fera, welcoming him.

Brace and Ester had landed a little more awkwardly and were

lying on the roof with arms and legs bent.

"*Please* tell me we haven't landed where I think we have," said Brace, looking anxiously at the blue sky surrounding them.

Lux leaned over the edge of the tower. Despite having no fear of heights, even he had to hide a little panic. The building was unimaginably tall, so tall that all you could see as you looked out was blue sky and green fields. The view down, on the other hand, was like nothing he'd ever seen. A forest of stone and glass buildings poked above a blanket of white clouds. The buildings were all at different heights, shining in the cold winter sun. Lindhelm's skybus station was a perfect black cone, with skyships buzzing around it. Wind whistled through the buildings, and Lux could hear the loud, clanking sounds of a city at work.

"You've been saying you want to fly," he told Brace. "Well, here you are."

There was a hissing noise in Lux's ear and Maya's voice came on his Shell, snapping at Tesla. "I *know* they might not have landed yet. That's why I'm *asking* them. Are you there, guys?"

Lux waited for Ester to answer as usual, but she indicated for Fera to speak instead. The younger girl, still marvelling at the city, shook herself back to the present. "Yes, all here. All good."

"Definitely *not* all good," said Brace hotly. "You've landed us on the world's tallest building!"

"Well, yes . . ." said Maya awkwardly. "It wasn't on purpose."

"Don't lie," came Tesla's voice.

"Okay, it was on purpose. I just thought you'd enjoy the view. Can anyone see the university?"

Lux looked, pressing down a weird, dizzy sensation. There was nothing that particularly stood out as being a university, although in truth it could have been any of the tall spires.

"Can't see it, but we'll find it," he said.

"Maya, can I ask how you were planning on getting us down?" said Fera.

There was a long pause on the other end of the Shell. "Lux could throw a *Catch* like he did when we jumped off Deimos's skyship."

For a moment, he panicked, thinking Maya was serious. The last thing Lux wanted was to throw another *Catch* after the incident with Fera.

"No, thanks," said Ester.

"Well, I'm a tech-head," said Maya dismissively. "I don't know about all this field stuff. But you lot are clever. You'll come up with something." Before they could argue, she wished them luck and clicked off, saying something about 'fixing a scrombulator.'

"Remind me to fire a dozen Light-arrows at her when we get back," said Brace.

Suddenly, there was a loud noise and a brilliant white skyship came thundering overhead, blocking the sun. The wind whipped up, forcing Lux to grip a rail for support. The craft sank slowly, avoiding another tall glass building and turning towards the skybus station.

When it was gone, Brace climbed hesitantly to his feet. "So, how *are* we going to get down? Because, and I know I'm not ruining my macho reputation when I say this, I'm not having a great time right now."

Lux searched the roof. His grandpa had once taken him up Daven's clocktower when the mayor had asked him to repair the broken mechanism there. They'd reached the top using a ladder and wooden hatch. Sure enough, there was a hatch built into this roof too, near the edge of the tower. Together with Fera he managed to get it open. Inside, was a ladder.

"This way."

Ester headed down, but Lux and Fera had to stay to help Brace, almost carrying him as he squeezed his eyes shut.

It turned out, when they reached the bottom of the ladder, that Maya had teleported them to the top of Lindhelm's famous library, with its dozens of floors of books lit beautifully by the sun. Lux stared, amazed, as they worked their way down, wondering how long it would take to read every one. Perhaps if he did, he could find out something about his new powers.

A young, smartly dressed girl was welcoming people inside when they reached the main entrance. She almost jumped when Squad Juno passed her on their way out. Brace flashed her a smile.

"I can see you're feeling better," Ester told him.

Lindhelm was about as far from Lux's hometown, Daven, as anywhere he could imagine. There were hundreds of people hurrying about, avoiding Light-trams and carts, crossing busy streets, serving food from tiny stalls, singing for shailings. They were dressed differently too, with huge, flared trousers and collars. It was noisy, with people chattering and regular electric clashes as Light-trams pulled up to collect waiting passengers.

"This city is *bright*," said Brace, blinking at the light reflecting off the glass library.

"Wait until summer," said Fera.

Painted in black and yellow on a nearby wall was a map of the city. It was so complex that Lux was reminded of the mazes he sometimes did in Dawnstar's games room. He scanned it for the university, but no luck.

"Ester, have you got your Light-map?"

"Of course."

Lux waited for her to bring it out. She didn't.

"Can we look?"

"We don't need it."

"I want to see where—"

"We won't need the map," echoed Fera, grinning at his forgetfulness.

"But if we want—"

"We won't need it," said Fera, spinning and holding out her hands as if she owned the city, "because I used to live here."

· CHAPTER 14 ·

As a Light Hunter, Lux had visited all sorts of towns and cities. Just that year alone, Squad Juno had been to Princefoy, Port Loray and Vensca. But as exciting as any trip was, nowhere he'd visited could hold a candle to the sheer size, the sheer wonder of Lindhelm.

The City of Glass.

It had certainly earned its name. Glass was everywhere: the houses, shops, Light-tram stops, even some of the skybuses. Lux felt like he was inside a glittering diamond.

Fera led them from the library towards what he guessed was the city centre, hurrying down a street of builders constructing a new glass house, and along a wide river towards an open square. A great crowd had formed around a neat lawn, which was itself surrounded by shops, selling ice cream and packs of cards and little models of the city.

The group headed north, tracking a run of cafes along the

River Lind. Brace chatted away, pointing out anything interesting he saw.

"Do you know the last Monster to attack Lindhelm?" he said at one point, barely avoiding knocking into a waiter with a tray of drinks.

Brace had an almost encyclopaedic memory for Monster attacks. Lux had tested him and found him to be wrong only once.

"I don't, but I'm sure you're about to tell us," said Fera.

Brace grinned. "I'm glad you asked." He disappeared into his mind as they rounded a corner and walked between a boulevard of tall trees. "It was a Griffin. Massive one. It had claws the size of a fencepost and could knock down a building."

Lux stopped suddenly in the path, looking through a break in the trees. "Like that one?"

In a huge open space on the other side was an enormous white statue of a Griffin. Scattered around it, as far as the eye could see, were more huge Monsters: a Dragon, Cerberus and Behemoth.

"The memorial garden!" said Fera excitedly. "I've not been since I was little."

Lux climbed through, so that he was beside the Griffin, which was as big as a house. Each town or city had its own memorial garden – a way of remembering all the Monsters that had attacked them over the years.

"Incredible," said Brace. "Imagine having to fight them all at once."

Lux could think of nothing worse. He wandered among the beasts, amazed at their size. He ran his hands along the Griffin's cold stone legs, only slightly smaller than the Monster would have been in real life. He approached the Behemoth, feeling its stone paws. And he went to the Cerberus; it was smaller than the one Squad Juno had defeated the year before.

Thinking of his grandpa and feeling suddenly sad, Lux hurried to a trio of wooden benches in the centre of the gardens for a rest. The others joined him – Brace carrying four small bags of food he'd brought from a stall next to the Behemoth's leg.

"A Lindhelm Parsti," he said, wrapping his tongue around the word. "Something like pastry and meat. Smells amazing."

Brace handed them each one of the packages and they sat in the low sun, eating and looking at the huge glass towers.

"What's so special about this Ghast guy anyway?" said Brace between bites. "How come I've never heard of him?"

"Perhaps because you close your ears every time someone tells you anything important," said Fera.

Lux bit into his Parsti. It tasted spicy and salty.

"There isn't a huge amount to tell," said Ester, folding her paper package neatly. "He was a Light Hunter – the Inventor before Tesla. He and my dad had a bit of a falling out and he left."

"What about?" asked Lux. The last person he'd heard of falling out with Nova was Deimos.

"Oh, everything and nothing. Ghast was a weird one. You'll see when we meet him. He . . . well, he developed this love of Monsters." She looked at the huge creatures surrounding them. "He decided he didn't want to fight them anymore. So, he didn't."

Brace looked horrified. "I will *never* not want to fight Monsters."

Lux thought about his grandpa leaving the Light Hunters after the Cerberus attack that killed his parents and sister. Could it have been something like that?

"Be that as it may, Ghast did. Speaking of which," said Ester, brushing off her jacket, "if I was squad leader now, I'd be thinking we've probably had enough time here and we should be making our way to this university."

Fera almost jumped, wrapping the remains of her Parsti and putting it in her bag.

"Yeah, come on you two, we'd better go," she said, nudging Lux and Brace, who exchanged an amused glance.

Lux looked back at the Monsters – huge, imposing, dangerous – then slid through the trees and caught up.

· CHAPTER 15 ·

One of the easiest ways to get yourself lost is to think you know precisely where you're going.

Squad Juno had learned this the hard way, during missions, trying to follow Ester's Light-map over hills and under waterfalls, through woods and down ravines, all in the hope of finding a Monster hidden in the depths of some nameless forest.

The moment Lux started to think Fera might be lost was when they found themselves walking across the same wooden bridge three times in fifteen minutes.

"Hmm," she said, puzzled. "That's really odd." She glanced worriedly at Ester, who was watching her carefully. "I'm certain this is the way."

Fera guided them across the bridge a fourth time, and through a series of winding streets, before they saw the wooden arch looming out of the River Lind once more.

"Don't bite my head off, but do you think it's possible we might be lost?" said Brace tentatively.

Lux winced. The last time Brace had asked Fera if she was lost, she had burned his eyebrows with a *Flame*.

This time, her response was more measured. "Thank you for your concern, *Brace*, but I'm not lost. The university is somewhere down here."

"We can check the map, if it's easier," offered Ester.

Fera tracked a skybus flying overhead. "It's fine. I've just got to get my bearings."

"That's what they said about me, and I'm still here twenty years later."

The unfamiliar voice came from over their shoulders, near one of the cafes. It belonged to a man wearing a purple waistcoat and matching eyepatch. He was sitting next to a simple wooden table, upon which was a top-hat, a toy rabbit and a magic wand.

"Lost?" he asked Fera, his voice rough, gravelly.

"We're fine, thanks—"

"Because if you are, I can 'elp you. I know Lindhelm like the back of me 'and knows me face." He grinned a crooked smile.

"Honestly," said Fera, raising her voice over a boat powering by on the river, "thank you for the offer, but—"

"Light 'Unters." The man leaned in his chair to look at their Monster badges. "Not seen you lot 'round this part of the city for a long while. You 'ere to deal with the Monster that's been seen flyin' aroun'?"

Ester's ears pricked up. "What Monster?"

73

"The one that's been flyin'."

"We haven't had any reports of Monsters. Are you sure you're not dreaming it?"

Ester's tone was haughty, and the man's grey eyebrows knitted resentfully. "I've seen it from this very seat."

He looked up, where big grey clouds now covered the sun, and formed a Monster shape with his hand, miming it flying around. "But what do I know?" he said, showing his yellow teeth. "You lot are the experts, eh?"

Ester gave him a wary look, indicating for the others to leave.

"It's the university you're after, ain't it?" said the man, adjusting his eyepatch. "You're wonderin' 'ow I know that. Easy. No-one comes roun' 'ere who ain't searching for that place."

"We're close?" said Fera hopefully.

"Listen," said the man, indicating the items on his table, "I need someone to 'elp me with a magic trick. 'Ow's about one of you lot 'elp and I'll show you exactly 'ow to get to the university. Can't say fairer'n that."

The man's chair creaked loudly as he sat back, waiting for their answer.

The Light Hunters exchanged questioning glances. The magician seemed familiar to Lux somehow. His grandpa's reputation as a clock repairer stretched quite far and he'd had many customers come to the workshop from outside Daven. Perhaps this man was one of them.

"I'm not lost," insisted Fera, gathering the other Light Hunters around. "Just give me a minute."

"If we cross that bridge again, we might as well move in and call it home," said Brace.

Fera thought. "All right, we'll do it," she told the man. "But you must tell us precisely where the university is afterwards. And no tricking us out of any shailings. Where do you want me?"

"I'd prefer 'im." The old man looked directly at Lux. "There's somethin' about you. Somethin' interestin'. 'Ave we met?" The man studied Lux closely as if he was a display in a museum. "Never mind. Anyway, 'ere's what I want you to do."

The man set up second chair in front of the table and had Lux sit. He tidied away the hat, the rabbit and the wand and replaced them with a single, silver cup, filled with a deep red liquid, and three items: a white cloth, a thin bottle filled with a golden liquid and a wire brush.

"This is wine," he said, addressing Lux and a small crowd that had gathered. He lifted the cup, allowing members of the audience a smell. "And these," he added, "are some objects. Now, as many of you will 'ave seen from my time 'ere, I am a clumsy man." He nudged the wine, spilling it on the green tablecloth. "And I am prone to little accidents. My friend 'ere, Lux, has kindly offered to 'elp clean up my mess in exchange for a favour. 'Owever . . ." He whipped a hand, silencing the audience, "what 'e's only just findin' out right now is that two of the objects are magical. Only one is real and will clean my mess."

Lux took in the objects again: the cloth, bottle and brush. He didn't have a clue.

"As well as my favour, I am puttin' one shailin' up for grabs."

The man reached into his pocket and took out a brass coin. "All Lux must do to win it is pick the correct object to clean up my mess. Get it wrong . . . well, you'll see what 'appens when 'e gets it wrong. Lux, my dear friend, you 'ave two guesses."

The magician stared at the river, waiting for Lux's decision. The crowd went quiet.

Lux had no idea what would happen if he picked the wrong object. Would something jump out at him? Would he have to pay a shailing of his own? He appealed to his squad-mates for suggestions, but they shrugged helplessly.

If Lux had to pick any object, it would probably be the cloth. But that seemed too obvious. Though surely the bottle couldn't help? And the wire brush would just ruin the table's fabric.

Figuring he had nothing to lose, he picked up the cloth and scrubbed at the wine. Instantly, he felt an odd sensation at the back of his head, as if somebody were touching him. He turned around. A couple of children were pointing and laughing. The adults joined in, as well as Brace, Fera and Ester.

"What?" he demanded.

Lux reached up and realised that his hair was standing on end, as if he'd been hit by one of Fera's *Bolts*.

"What our brave Lux might now 'ave worked out is that the cloth was one of the magical items. 'E now 'as 'air like a 'edgehog's, but we shall avoid mentionin' that, eh?" The magician winked at the two children, raising his eyepatch jokingly.

Lux set his jaw, annoyed.

There were two items left: the bottle of yellow liquid and the wire brush. He now knew whichever was wrong would perform its action on him, so he had to get it right, unless he wanted his hair to be brushed with wire, or his head to get wet.

"No rush," said the magician.

Deciding he'd rather have his hair brushed than get wet, Lux squeezed his eyes shut and brushed the green fabric.

Almost instantly, he felt the wire dragging red hot lines into his neck.

"Alas," said the magician, dropping his shailing back in his pocket, "another one loses." He took the bottle and poured the golden liquid over the wine. There was a loud hiss and a misty cloud formed. When it was gone, the table was like new.

"Arrowort," explained the magician. "Best cleanin' fluid in town. Anyone who'd like to purchase some, please come up. I have a special deal on. But first," he said, guiding Lux to his squad-mates, "a round of applause for my young assistant, Lux! Sometimes when we think we're makin' the right choice, we're actually makin' the wrong one."

The man gave Lux a crooked grin. "University's down that alley." He pointed at a dark passage cutting away from the river. "Left at the end."

He turned to the people crowding his table, disappearing among them, their shiny shailings out, ready to buy.

"He had you *right* stitched up there," said Brace. "I knew which it was straight away."

Fera rolled her eyes despairingly.

The four walked along the river towards the alley. As they

turned the corner, Lux looked back at the magician, who was handing out yellow bottles to eager customers. How, he wondered, without anyone telling him, had the magician known his name?

· CHAPTER 16 ·

Lindhelm University had stood in place for nearly two thousand years, its foundations digging into the city like the roots of some great tree. It stretched across town – a building here, another there – all constructed of stone and looking like a king or queen's castle, especially next to all the glass towers that surrounded it.

The first Lux saw of the university was when they emerged from the magician's alley to find an enormous building. Formed of a sandy stone, it was decorated with stained glass windows and pointed spires. Below were neat lawns, with handsome trees. People carrying books wandered by, dressed in grey gowns that dragged behind them, picking up mud from the paths. To Lux's right, a group of students were practising a play, laughing and singing.

"Our uniform's bad, but at least we don't look like ghosts," said Brace, as a young man in a pale grey robe drifted past.

Lux knew little about the university, other than that they employed a lot of Light scholars, including Majeson Medela, to whom he'd written the previous year asking if he was aware of a healing cast that might save his grandpa. Lux knew one thing though: like Brace, he'd rather lose his ability to throw Light than wear a uniform like that.

A path led to the university's main entrance, preceded by a shallow run of steps. The Light Hunters took it, admiring the delicately carved statues and colourful windows. Off in the distance, Lux spied a flash of red fabric on the roof. If the notion hadn't been so crazy, he'd have sworn it was a hot air balloon.

"I really hope he's here," said Brace, gazing concernedly at the dozen other buildings marching away from the main one.

At the top of the stairs, just before the entrance, was a black sign on the wall with gold writing.

THE GRAND UNIVERSITY OF LINDHELM. EST. 1201.
*Not by the might of our limbs was this establishment built,
but by the Light of our minds.*

"That rules you out, Brace," joked Fera.

If the university gardens were like something from a fairy tale, the inside was like a royal castle. Lux had never seen anywhere so grand, not even the luxurious skybuses that flew between Daven and Lindhelm. Everything was made from mahogany, polished to such a degree that it reflected the hanging Light-lamps. The carpets were thick and red, and the walls were painted a soft burgundy.

Hanging on them were dozens of paintings – old professors, Lux guessed, as well as one or two cats and dogs looking annoyed at having to sit for so long. Doors led off in every direction, and in the centre of the space was a wooden counter, behind which was a man so straight and tall that Lux wondered whether he was, in fact, a tree.

"Morning," said Fera, "we're looking for—"

The man lifted a bony index finger and pointed to their left, indicating for them to move. Lux and the others looked where he was pointing, then back at him.

"We're looking for—"

"I'm afraid, I'm going to have to ask you to stand on that mat," the man cut in nasally. He pointed at a rug to their left. "We *do* work ever so hard to keep the university clean."

Lux checked his boots, which were dirty from their long walk. He jumped across, embarrassed. The others joined him, Brace somewhat more reluctantly.

"Most grateful. Now, what were you saying Miss . . .?"

"Lanceheart."

The man's eyebrow raised. He cast his eyes up and down Fera's muddy uniform. "Lanceheart. Indeed."

"We're looking for a Professor Ghast."

The man behind the desk straightened his tie. "And do you have an appointment with the professor?"

Fera shrugged. "Sort of."

"Who is this jerk?" whispered Brace to Lux.

"Well, normally we ask everybody to book an appointment if

they wish to talk to one of our professors," said the man tiredly. A clock ticked somewhere in the atrium. "However, seeing as you *are* Light Hunters, I suppose I can make an exception. The name again?"

Fera told him. Without another word, the man wandered into the back room, away from the Hunters. He returned, shaking his head.

"I'm afraid you must be mistaken. We have no Professor Ghast on roll."

The Hunters looked surprised. "Ghast," said Ester. "G-H-A-S-T."

"I am aware of how to spell the name," the man replied testily. "We have no Professor Ghast on roll."

"Could you check again?"

The man looked as if she'd just asked him to read every book in Lindhelm library.

"Please," added Ester sweetly.

The receptionist sighed deeply. "Very well."

He disappeared, leaving the Light Hunters wondering what on earth was going on. Why would Ghast tell Nova to send him a squad of Hunters if he wasn't there?

"It seems I was correct the first time," said the man, returning.

"You must be wrong," argued Ester.

"I assure you I am not. I have been working here for twenty-three years. I have checked our records and the only Ghast we have on roll is a caretaker. I presume he is not the man you have come to visit."

Ester gathered her squad under the tall grandfather clock.

"I honestly want to fire a Light-arrow into his face," Brace whispered.

"He has to be here," said Lux. "The letter can't have been fake."

Ester looked thoughtful. "My father worked with Ghast for years. He'd recognise his writing. But the Ghast I knew – he wouldn't be a caretaker either." She bit her lip. "All the same, we should talk to him, just to rule him out."

The receptionist hadn't moved an inch. His moustache twitched when he saw them returning.

"We'd like to meet Ghast. Where can we find him?" said Ester.

"Wonderful." The man's tone suggested he thought it was anything but. "Ghast's office is on the sixth floor, past the Light-experiment labs, by a window that overlooks the university lawns. There are two ways up." He came out from behind his counter, stopping by the stairs. "Up these, and the Light-lift over there." He frowned at their dirty shoes, then the red carpet. "I think the best route for you would be the lift. Number six."

Lux had to hold Brace to stop him from snapping. Instead, Fera thanked the man.

"I assure you it is the very apex of my career."

As he returned to his desk, Fera threw a tiny *Bolt* cast his way. Lux looked back just as it zapped the man's backside, making him jump.

"I am *so* sorry," said Fera. "Must have slipped in my muddy shoes."

The man scowled as the Hunters climbed into the lift and rode it to the sixth floor.

· CHAPTER 17 ·

At the end of every mission, a Light Hunter squad must write a short report for their Luminary. Sometimes, such odd things happened on Squad Juno's missions that Ester didn't know whether or not to even include them, like the time Fera accidentally froze Brace's big toe, or the time Lux healed the very Monster they were trying to defeat.

When they eventually found Ghast, their meeting was so strange that Ester couldn't have included it in her report even if she'd wanted to. Her father would have thought she'd lost her marbles.

The lift spilled the Hunters into a dark, silent corridor lined with polished suits of armour.

"This place is *old*," said Brace, instantly jumping behind one of the suits and putting on a deep voice to scare Fera.

They made their way down the corridor, looking through every window to see if it gave a view of the university lawns. They passed dozens of closed doors, through which they heard loud *zwangs* of Light being thrown. At one point Lux smelled the burning stench of a *Flame* gone wrong.

"At least it wasn't me this time," said Fera.

The corridor rolled on, accompanied by dull landscape paintings. Lux was almost hypnotised by the four walls stretching into the distance, and nearly jumped out of his skin when Maya spoke in his ear.

"All right Lux, you there yet?"

He checked whether the others could hear, but she'd switched to a private Shell line.

"Yeah, we're here."

"Any signs of my sister? She's tall and beautiful, like me."

"Afraid not. We met a lovely receptionist though."

"Hmm, probably not her," said Maya. "Keep me posted." She clicked off.

The end of the corridor appeared at last, and a grimy window let in rays of weak sunlight, highlighting decades of dust. Lux looked outside. The university lawns. The nearest door had a wooden board, written on which were the words: 'Caretaker's Office.'

Ester gathered them around. "Now, this probably won't be him, but just in case, remember that Ghast hasn't been a Light Hunter for years. And he wasn't an easy man to get along with then. Be polite. Brace, that means let Fera do the talking."

Fera knocked – three sharp raps. From inside, Lux heard a *thud,* then slow, heavy footsteps. The door swung open.

"What?"

The woman that had opened it was a few years older than Ester. Small, with soot all over her cheeks.

"Oh," said Fera, taken aback.

Lux looked into the office. There was Light everywhere – the usual blue, but also green, yellow, orange – all highlighting devices that puffed and bumped. Odd chemical contraptions belched different liquids, and on the walls hung all sorts of gold trinkets – stars and squares and circles – reflecting the Light. Lux tried not to sniff in, but all the same he caught the smell of something unpleasantly eggy.

"'Oh,'" said the young woman, scowling. "You got me up on my break to say, 'Oh?'"

Fera was so flustered she couldn't talk. Lux nudged her. "I mean, erm, we were looking for the caretaker. Ghast. Are you her?"

The woman sized her up. "Who's askin'? You're not goin' to ask us to clean out them toilets again, are you? Because if you are, I ain't Ghast and neither's anyone else who works here."

"It's nothing to do with toilets," said Fera. "We just need to talk to Ghast."

The woman pursed her lips, measuring whether they were telling the truth. She seemed to relax.

"He ain't here."

"You're not him? I mean her."

"Of course I ain't 'im. Do I look like 'im? He's at 'is balloon. Don't tell 'im I told you though, else he'll have my guts."

Lux thought suddenly of the flash of red fabric he'd seen on the university roof. "You mean a hot air balloon?"

The woman looked at him like he was simple. "I don't mean a party balloon, do I? Yes, 'is 'ot air balloon. Now, unless there's anythin' else, I'm goin' back to my book."

She slammed the door.

"Balloon?" said Brace.

"I saw it on the roof."

"Wonderful." The colour drained from Brace's cheeks. "More rooftops."

"We don't actually think this could be him, do we?" said Lux after they'd wandered back down the corridor and into the lift, heading for the top floor.

"I honestly don't know," said Ester.

They emerged into a dark space with a ladder and a wooden hatch similar to the one in Lindhelm library. Heading up, they blinked in the sudden light.

It was midday now and the air was chilly, so that Lux had to button his jacket. He spotted the hot air balloon a couple of buildings along – a giant, red, fabric sausage. Beneath it was a basket, inside which he could see a man with white hair and grey overalls hurrying about.

"Over there!"

The buildings had narrow walkways linking them. Lux and Ester took them first, leaving Fera behind to gently coax Brace across. Once they were closer, it was clear that the man in the balloon was in some kind of panic. His hands were trembling as he loaded leather bags into the basket.

There was already a flame in the burner and the balloon was filling, looking like a great sleeping animal waking up. They made it across just as the fabric snapped open. The man climbed into the basket and set his sights on the horizon, away from Lindhelm.

"Wait!" Lux shouted. He wasn't sure the man had heard him over the wind.

Slowly, the balloon rose, getting higher and higher. Fera and Brace caught up with them. Seeing their man disappearing, Fera sent a *Flame* past the balloon. At first, the man was confused, searching the sky in case somebody was attacking him. Then she sent up another and he tracked it to the roof. His response to seeing the four Light Hunters was nothing short of astonishment.

"Wait!" shouted Fera.

The man cupped his ear, struggling to hear. She shouted again. On her third attempt, he waved a dismissive hand and turned back to the horizon.

Lux looked around for some way they could catch him. Suddenly, he had an idea.

"Your zip-wire," he yelled at Ester.

She understood instantly and prepared her Gauntlet. Gesturing for the others to hold on, she fired. The thread of Light shot out and embedded in the basket with a satisfying *thud*. Then they were shooting through the air.

"I hate this mission," yelled Brace, his eyes clamped shut.

Once the caretaker saw that they'd speared his cabin, his expression changed from confusion to anger. He pulled at Ester's thread, sparks flying from his skin.

"What are you doing?" he shouted frantically.

The Light Hunters closed in, until Ester was able to touch the basket. Lux joined her, dragging himself inside.

Then they were in the balloon, with the burner heating the air above their heads and the caretaker staring at them in shock. Diving down to his bags, he came up with an iron bar, teeth bared, ready for a fight. Fera conjured a *Bolt* as Brace lifted his Light-bow. But there was no need. Recognition flickered in the man's eyes, and he dragged a memory out of some long-forgotten corner of his mind.

"Little Ester Nova," he said in wonderment.

"Professor Emory Ghast," said Ester.

· CHAPTER 18 ·

Light Hunters come in all shapes and sizes.

The youngest at Dawnstar was just ten, while the oldest was sixty-three and still the fastest Conjuror around. There were women, men, and if you counted Bella, Nova's cherished pet, dogs too.

Professor Ghast, although no longer a Light Hunter, had been one of the oddest in his time. He was about the same age as Nova, but looked ten years younger, with big muscles that were heavily tattooed. All Monsters, from what Lux could make out in the balloon's shadow. He wore gold and silver rings on his fingers and his white hair was cut very short. In his nose he wore a single gold ring.

"My granddaughter's in danger," he said, before Ester could talk.

"What?"

Ghast turned to the horizon, which was a black line cut across the sky.

"Where?"

"Nearby. It's a Monster. You're here on behalf of your father, right?"

"Wait?" Ester was trying to understand what she was hearing. "Did you say Monster?"

"What you're here for will have to wait," said Ghast.

Ester waved her hands for him to slow down. "Tell us what's happening."

"I got a message," he said breathlessly, hurrying about the basket, his arms bulging as he shifted leather bags around for better balance. "The village where we live is under attack."

"What kind of Monster?"

"I don't know." Ghast's face was long, drawn. He studied the dark clouds that were gathering against the weak sun.

"We'll help," said Ester.

They had to, of course. It was their duty. But still . . . Lux felt shocked. He hadn't wanted to throw any Light on this trip. They were just supposed to be collecting information.

"Thank you," said Ghast, turning from the burner. He nodded warmly at Ester. "Help me and I'll give your father the information he needs."

"What's the village's name?" Ester slid her Light-map out, focussing on Lindhelm. The city was in the middle, while little dots represented the villages nearby.

"Ravenholm."

There was a sudden silence.

Brace and Ester exchanged a nervous glance. Fera, beside them, seemed to stiffen.

"Say that again," she said sharply.

"Ravenholm."

Her eyes widened. "We've got to get there now." She approached the burner with a *Flame* cast, throwing it and growing the fire. There was a great *whoosh* of heat, and the balloon lurched upwards.

"It's her family's village," Brace whispered to Lux.

Something stabbed Lux's heart. He hadn't spoken to Fera much about her family. But now that he thought about it, she had mentioned that the village was named Ravenholm. If it was under attack . . .

"They'll be all right," said Brace brightly, but Fera shrugged him off.

"Tell me all you know," she instructed Ghast.

The professor grimaced. "Less than I'd like and more at the same time. I received a message at the university telling me the village was under attack. I jumped straight in my balloon. I don't know what to do. I haven't fought a Monster in years." He glanced at Ester. "I *don't* fight them anymore. But Sally . . ." He wrung his hands nervously.

"Your granddaughter," prompted Ester.

Ghast pulled a leather wallet from his pocket and showed them a picture of a girl about five or six years old, with blonde hair and a bright smile. One of her teeth was missing.

"Sharp as a pin," he said admiringly.

"Do you know where the Monster is?" demanded Fera. "Is it on the farm? Near the house? What about the Lancehearts? Have you heard anything about them?"

"I don't . . ." Ghast watched Fera carefully, as if he might recognise her. "I don't know. I've told you all I know. Oh, won't this darned thing go faster?" He thumped the basket, hard.

They were leaving Lindhelm now – the glass towers of the city shrinking in the distance. Beneath them were flat green fields, broken by little woods.

"How long will it take us to get there?" asked Fera.

"Half an hour," said Ghast. "Maybe more. We must be careful when we arrive though. I won't have you hurting the Monster."

Brace and Fera nearly choked. "What?"

"Precisely what I say."

The kids appealed to Ester.

"I didn't leave the Light Hunters just to fight Monsters again now," Ghast went on. "We'll find some other way to resolve the situation."

"But . . . your granddaughter?" Fera spluttered.

A large skyship passed them in the sky, leaving a trail of Light behind. People on deck leaned over and waved at the balloon.

Fera turned to Ester, serious. "If he thinks I'm not fighting it . . ."

"Yeah!" agreed Brace.

They looked to Lux for support, but he didn't know what to say. How could he pretend to want to fight when really he was terrified of what might happen if his new powers leaked out again?

"This is *my* balloon," said Ghast. "If you won't do as I ask, I'll dump you over—"

"Enough!" Ester breathed, regaining her composure. "Enough. Let's just scout out the situation. When we know more, we'll decide what to do."

"I won't have them—" Ghast began.

"Enough!"

The professor turned away, annoyed. He helped Fera's *Flame* in the burner with one of his own.

The balloon floated on, heading towards the dark clouds. Lux couldn't believe how quickly things had changed. One minute they'd been exploring Lindhelm, the next they were in a hot air balloon, floating to Fera's family's village with a Monster on the loose.

The very idea of *not* fighting it was crazy. How would they stop it?

And yet . . .

Lux would have liked nothing more than to keep his hands firmly in his pockets.

"That got tense quickly, didn't it?" Brace whispered, coming up behind him. "Who does he think he is, anyway? Telling us we can't fight. Was he one of us or not?"

Lux shrugged.

"Are you all right?"

"I'm fine," he lied. Suddenly, he realised Brace was hundreds of metres high. "What about you?"

Brace leaned over the basket as if he were peering into a pond full of fish. "Ah, this is fine," he said. "I told you, flying's all good." He looked over his shoulder sneakily at Ghast. "What he's found about stopping Monster attacks better be worth it, because I am *not* liking him so far."

"Nova thinks it is."

"Nova thought we couldn't beat the Cerberus. He isn't always right. Are you sure you're okay, Lux?"

"I'm fine." The last thing Lux wanted was for anyone to think he was losing it.

Brace slapped him on the back in a friendly way, then wandered to Ester and Ghast. Lux looked anxiously out at the gathering clouds as a drop of rain thudded into the balloon, then another.

It started to pour.

· CHAPTER 19 ·

Ever since Lux had joined Dawnstar, he'd promised himself that whenever he saw anybody upset, he would go and talk to them, check they were okay. So, when he saw Fera leaning out of the hot air balloon, her eyes fixed on the horizon where her home would soon appear, holding the letter from her family tightly, Lux felt that usual wave of sympathy.

"Hey," he said.

Fera turned slowly, her eyes close to tears. "Oh, hey."

"I won't tell you not to worry," he said, settling next to her. He wasn't very good at this. "Because I know you will. I did last year."

"Thanks."

"Have you been reading it?" He nodded at the envelope.

"This?" said Fera, lifting it up. "Yes."

"We'll do what we can," he said encouragingly, "and we can normally do quite a lot." His confidence sounded hollow, but Fera didn't seem to notice.

"Last time it was a Cerberus," she said, tracking a formation of birds soaring beneath the hot air balloon. "Not as big as yours in Daven, but still nasty. I was seven. Something like that. I remember the old man who looked after my horses running up and shouting that it had attacked someone. The look on my mum's face . . ." Fera shook her head sadly.

"He died, the old man. Roald, his name was. Big smile." She tried to emulate it and failed. "Went with my dad to try and hold it off before the Light Hunters arrived. Apparently, it attacked the horses and Roald . . ." She trailed off. "Well, you know."

Lux thought about what his grandpa had told him about the brave villagers in Daven who'd tried to fight the Cerberus alongside the Light Hunters. Most of them had lost their lives too, including his parents.

"It's why I joined, you know? The Light Hunters, I mean. After that . . . seeing all the damage. Even though I was only little, I really wanted to help people." Fera put her family's letter in her pocket. "But you can't always. We don't save everyone." She looked worried.

There was a sudden gust of wind and the hot air balloon shot right, dropping several metres in an instant. The Light Hunters and Ghast fell, landing in the straw. They grabbed anything they could as the balloon approached the tip of a hill, topped with blackened, bare trees.

Ghast sent another *Flame* at the balloon's burner. Fera looked annoyed.

"I know he might have a way to stop Monsters. I didn't think it would be just letting them attack."

"His family's in trouble too," said Lux, sounding like his grandpa reasoning with him whenever he'd got annoyed at Maya cheating in one of their board games. "And we know he doesn't like fighting Monsters. He must be struggling with what to do himself."

Fera looked at the professor. The worry was carved into every line of his face.

"I don't care what he says, if that thing's attacking my home, I'm fighting it," she said determinedly. "You will too, won't you?"

Lux hesitated, then nodded.

The fabric of the hot air balloon flapped loudly as the grey landscape flashed by. Slowly, they climbed the low hill, sheep scattering at their appearance. Then they came down the other side, tracking a narrow, twisting stream.

Ten minutes later, Lux spotted Light on the horizon, past a series of yellow fields.

"There!" yelled Brace, seeing the same.

Ravenholm was almost the exact opposite of the glass city they'd left behind. It consisted of more yellow fields and low stone walls, as well as a handful of greenhouses, their glass roofs projecting soft blue Light. A collection of smaller wooden and stone buildings tracked a wide road. At the end, a much larger house with grand, intricate architecture sat on top of a low hill.

"Get ready," said Ester, approaching the younger Hunters. "We don't know what's going to be there, but you can bet it won't be good."

Ghast killed the burner with a *Snow* and soon they were floating in silence, with only the sharp *crack* of whipping fabric for company. The birds had gone now, and the balloon sank slowly towards Fera's family farm. The professor hadn't spoken since their argument, his mouth a tightly drawn line.

"What's that?"

Lux hurried to where Fera was pointing at a rough track near the fields, about fifteen metres below. A group of farmhands looked like they were racing back to the village.

But they weren't moving.

Lux felt suddenly cold. Freezing. He heard tiny cracking sounds, like icicles being snapped on a winter's day. He wondered if the sounds were what was left of the burner's fire. Then he noticed it was coming from *outside* the basket. The rain. He reached out with his fingers. It was frozen in place. Lux looked again at the farmhands below. They were frozen too, mid-run, their faces masks of pure fear.

"Ester . . ." he said anxiously.

"I know. It doesn't change anything. It could be the same as the Monster at the graveyard. It could not. We go in and we do what we always do."

Ghast, who'd been staring wonderingly at the frozen people, said, "You've seen this before?" He looked horrified. "Did you . . . did you bring it here?"

"Of course not," said Ester. But Lux could hear uncertainty in her voice.

The frozen villagers faded behind them in the dull light. On the dirt path between the fields were two long, blue-white lines. An icy mist rose off them, leading straight into the village.

· CHAPTER 20 ·

As Ghast brought the hot air balloon down, the Light Hunters were surprised to see a large crowd gathered in the village square, under umbrellas. They all looked up in astonishment.

"Stay," Ester told Ghast as the basket touched down. "We'll deal with this."

"I have lost one daughter to a Monster attack already, I won't lose Sally too." Ghast's tone was so final there was no arguing. Ester helped him out of the basket.

The professor had brought the balloon down some way from the crowd. They hurried over, past bakeries and bookshops, and a tavern called the Grumpy Farmer, whose wooden doors were firmly shut.

The crowd appeared to be centred around three people on wooden crates who were shouting out orders. In a pile next to them were a dozen or so black metal devices Lux had never seen, with pedals and some kind of rotor-blade at the top.

"Mum and Dad!" said Fera excitedly. "They're okay! And Barny!"

Lux looked. The trio did indeed resemble the people in her picture.

"We won't stand a chance!" shouted one man from the crowd, his fist raised angrily, his voice trembling. "This ain't a job for us."

"It's a job for the Light Hunters!" agreed another.

"We don't have time," Fera's brother argued. He was about Ester's age, with dark eyes and black hair flopping over his pale face. "There are children in that school. If we just fly over and distract it. Keep our distance . . ."

Barny trailed off, noticing the Light Hunters running towards him. The rest of the crowd saw them too. Huge grins lit their faces as they recognised their mauve uniforms. One or two even cheered.

"That was quick!" shouted Fera's dad, greeting them. "I only put in the call half an hour ago—" He was stopped by Fera's mum.

"Fera? Is that you?"

She ran into her mum and dad's arms, swinging them around. She was always the most sensible member of Squad Juno – almost a grown-up, really. Lux had never seen her look so like a child. Barny stood awkwardly nearby, not quite sure how to react.

"Look at *you*," said Fera's mum, holding her daughter at arm's length. "You've grown so *much*. And Braceson James, is that you?"

Brace smiled sheepishly. "Hi, Mrs Lanceheart."

"What are you all doing here?" Fera's dad shook Lux and Ester's hands, giving Brace a bear-hug. "Of everyone they could send . . .

Squad Juno. It's so nice to see you. And such a relief."

Fera was wriggling to get out of her mum's embrace. She exchanged a frosty glance with her brother Barny.

"Listen, Mum," she said. "We'll do all of this later. There's a Monster."

"We know. We called you."

"Not us." Then, seeing her mum and dad's confusion, Fera added, "It's a long story. Where is it?"

Fera's mum left Barny with an instruction to organise the villagers, then guided the Light Hunters under the eaves of the Grumpy Farmer. There, rain beat at the wood, but they remained mostly dry.

"It's outside the schoolhouse," said her dad, tugging anxiously at his beard. "All the little'uns are inside. We were about to fly over in the Dusters, see if we can distract it."

"Do you know if Sally is safe?" said the professor. "Sally Ghast." His eyes were wide, wild.

"Professor!" exclaimed Fera's dad, recognising Ghast for the first time. "I didn't see you. I don't know about little Sally. We think they're safe, but . . ." He trailed off.

"What kind of Monster is it?" said Ester. "Where did it come from?"

Fera's dad shrugged. "One minute everything was normal, then a boy came running from the fields saying there was a Monster freezing people. I thought he was joking at first, but—"

"Have you seen it?" asked Brace.

"Martha did."

"Big thing," said Fera's mum, taking over. "Tall. Blue. Made of ice crystals or something. Very cold."

It was clear the Light Hunters recognised her description.

"Has it attacked anyone else?" asked Lux.

"No, thank the Light," said Fera's mum. "That's the thing. It seems to be just sitting there."

"Thanks Mum, Dad," said Fera. "Go back to Barny, get everyone inside. We'll handle it."

"Are you sure you'll be safe?"

Fera gave her mum a look. The older lady zipped her mouth. "I know, I know."

Her parents gave her a kiss, then returned to the crowd. The Light Hunters and Ghast came together.

"A Monster's a Monster," said Ester. "Forget the graveyard. We go over and do what we always do. Fera, you're still in charge. You call our next move. Clear?"

They nodded, even though Lux's stomach was twisting at the very *thought* of throwing Light. What if his new powers leaked out? What if he hurt someone?

"Hang on!" shouted the professor. "We said we weren't going to harm the Monster."

"No, *you* said that," snapped Brace.

"You can't!" said Ghast, blocking their path, his eyes lit with passion. "Please, trust me. You can't."

"What do you want us to do, Emory?" said Ester. "Those children are in danger. Your *granddaughter.*"

"You don't understand. You must trust me."

Ester looked wearily at her squad-mates. Brace looked furious.
"Please. I cannot explain yet, but you will understand later."

Lux could see that Ester was in an impossible position. They had sworn as Light Hunters to defeat Monsters. But they were in Lindhelm to learn what Ghast knew. If he was telling them not to fight . . .

"We could try to scare it off," said Fera, uncertain even as she spoke. "But if it puts *anybody* in danger, we attack properly. No waiting."

"I think that's the best you'll get," Ester told Ghast.

A symphony of emotions played on the professor's face: worry, frustration, sadness. "All right," he agreed. "But I'm coming to make sure we don't mess it up."

The rain was pouring now, soaking the crowd who'd barely moved. A few were dragging the Dusters – the black metal devices Lux had seen earlier – under the shelter of a nearby bookshop, while Fera's mum, dad and brother issued orders for the rest to return to their homes.

They saw the Light Hunters and broke off. "You have a plan?"

"We're going now," said Fera.

Her mum rushed up and hugged her again. "Be careful. All of you."

Barny's face was as dark as the sky. "Do we really think this is right? I mean, they aren't even the Light Hunters who are supposed to be here. They normally send two squads—"

Fera's dad threw him a sharp look.

Fera was about to explain to her brother that they knew what they were doing but he stalked off to help with the Dusters. She slumped. Then she steeled herself.

"Ready?" she asked the others.

"Always," said Brace.

"Let's go stop a Monster."

· CHAPTER 21 ·

There was one type of weather Lux didn't like to fight in: rain. So much of throwing Light and working as part of a squad depended on the little sounds they made – the electric *clash* of Brace's Light-bow, the little *clink* as Fera prepared a *Snow*. When it rained, all the sounds were muted, so it was that much harder to tell what was going on.

The four Light Hunters and Ghast lay in the rain outside Fera's mum and dad's house, watching the village school – a neat little building with a small playground. A painted blue sign read *Ravenholm School*.

Nearby, completely and utterly still, was the Monster.

It was instantly obvious that it was the same one from the graveyard. There was something about the arrangement of blue-green ice crystals. Around its body, the rain was frozen in place. The cold had stretched to the school building, which glittered like starlight. The whole area was eerily quiet, like

Dawnstar's training wing at night.

They'd been watching the Monster closely for five minutes, trying to learn its movements. It hadn't moved an inch.

"There's no point waiting," whispered Brace.

Normally, Fera and Ester would have told him to be patient. But this new ice-Monster wasn't like others they'd fought. There was nothing to see, nothing to observe. Only stillness.

Fera seemed to decide. "Okay, Ester, you fire a Light-thread. We'll zip down and try and force it into that pass." She pointed at a narrow passage between two hills, leading out of the village. "Funnel it that way with casts. Brace, start with some arrows at its feet. I'll add *Flames.* Ester, be ready with your Gauntlet just in case. And Lux, *Protect* and *Heal.* We might need them."

Lux's insides rolled. He had to fight not to show it, ignoring Ester's inquisitive eyes.

"What about me?" said Ghast.

"You stay here," said Fera. "The last thing we need is someone in our way."

Ghast was about to argue, but Fera's sharp look made him stay quiet.

"Get Sally out safely," he said. "All of them. And don't hurt that Monster!"

Fera crawled out of the bush with Brace, so that they could see directly down onto the creature. A cold mist rose from its crystal skin. Brace shivered.

Ester held Lux back from following. "If you don't feel ready after the other day . . ."

Lux's nerves flickered.

"You must tell us now, Lux."

"I'm fine."

The Light-thread fired from Ester's Gauntlet flashed to the ground a few metres behind the Monster. Holding her arm firm, she indicated for Lux and the others to go. They slid down the wire, the frozen rain stinging their faces.

The ice-Monster heard them and turned slowly, its eyes like fire.

"I can do that too!" Brace opened his eyes wide. Then he jumped back, firing a dozen arrows from his bow, each narrowly avoiding the Monster's crystal skin and hissing in the bubble of icy air.

Normally, a Monster would have been charging by now. Not this one. It merely looked at Brace's arrows, then the Hunters, in particular Lux. A shiver climbed his neck. He tried to shake it, focussing on his Light.

"Well, that didn't work," said Brace, looking disappointedly at his arrows.

Ester had landed behind them. She whipped the Light-thread into her Gauntlet. "Fera, *Flame!*"

The younger girl's Light burned orange and red, and she threw it close to the Monster, guiding it towards the path. She threw more, forming them as fast as her fingers would allow. The Monster didn't flinch.

"Okay, this is getting weird," said Brace.

Every Monster was different. Some attacked straight away, some stalked their prey. But one thing was certain: they all responded once they were attacked. The ice-Monster wasn't doing anything.

"Try getting between it and the school," Fera yelled at Brace. "Fire more arrows."

Brace stepped around the smoky remains of Fera's *Flames*. The Monster paid no attention to him at all, its eyes locked on Lux.

Brace fired arrow after arrow, each landing with an electric *crack*. Still no reaction.

"That is *it*!" he shouted, annoyed.

Before anyone could stop him, he'd dismissed his bow and a Light-dagger appeared in his hand. In a flash, he disappeared. *Blink*. He reappeared by the ice-Monster's left leg, aiming the knife at the crystal, but it disintegrated in his hands.

Finally, the Monster turned.

It picked up Brace like he was a child's toy, throwing him into the school building, where he crashed into the wood. There was a terrified screech from inside – school children, Lux realised. The building's outer wall crumbled; wood and stone raining down. At the bottom of it all was Brace.

"No!" cried Fera.

Lux didn't wait. Steadying his shaking hands, he grew a *Heal*. The ball of Light expanded, until it was the size of his fist. He prepared to throw.

Then he paused.

Something was stirring inside of him. Purple energy crawled along his arm – thin tendrils that fizzled in the air. They grew and grew. All the blood rushed to his head.

No, no, no!

Ester gripped his shoulders, but it was no use. The energy enveloped Lux, vibrating. That horrible, horrible overwhelming sensation from Kofi . . .

He blinked.

Silence.

Lux was in the Monster's white space again. Endless white in every direction. The purple energy, the fear in his stomach – they were gone. The ice-Monster was standing before him, red eyes like beacons.

Lux wanted to move, run, anything. But when he tried, his legs were locked. He heard the Monster's voice. The same single word again: *Ark.*

Ark.

· CHAPTER 22 ·

Sometimes, before early morning missions, Lux could be so deeply asleep that Brace and Fera could hardly wake him, even if they dropped cold water directly on his face. But the darkness he felt on his way back from the Monster's white place was something else. He could hear his friends calling him, but they seemed a million miles away.

He woke on the ground, looking up at a thousand tiny pinpricks.

At first, he thought it was the night sky. Then he realised it was the Monster's frozen rain. A tiny shudder and the drops cracked and fell on his face.

"That's one way of waking him," said Fera.

Lux's squad-mates (Brace covered head-to-toe in dust) were standing in the street, looking down at him. Ghast was there too, peering into the hole Brace's body had gouged into the school. The ice-Monster was nowhere to be seen.

"It's gone," said Lux.

"Like my eyesight," said Brace, flicking dust disgustedly from his eyes to the floor.

Lux breathed in the cool air. How long the Monster would be gone, he had no idea, but at least the villagers had a bit of time.

"Is everyone all right? The schoolkids?"

"They're safe," said Ester.

"H-How long was I out for?" The world was still spinning around Lux. Fera rushed forward as he tried to stand, helping him against a nearby tree.

"Only a few seconds," said Brace. "It did it again, didn't it?"

Seconds? It had felt like hours. "The white place. It said that word again. 'Ark.'"

Ghast, still searching the school for his granddaughter, snapped his head around. "Ark?"

A guarded look from Ester told Lux to say no more for now. He shifted position, testing his legs. Ghast huffed frustratedly and returned to the school. Dozens of frightened eyes looked out, checking for the Monster.

"You can come out," said Ester.

Brace and Fera helped Lux properly to his feet, where he wiped the mud off his uniform. His heart was still pounding. The white place. The Monster . . . it had taken him. But this time, his energy . . . purple . . .

"You did your thing," said Fera carefully.

"I know."

"At least you didn't break any arms this time," said Brace. He'd managed to remove most of the dust from his face now, but a fine layer remained. He looked like a clown.

"I'll have to update my records," he said. "The last Monster to attack Ravenholm is no longer a Cerberus, it's a . . ." He hesitated. "I'm not sure *what* I'd call that."

Once Lux had fully recovered, Fera instructed Brace to wait by the school with Ester, keeping an eye out in case the Monster returned. Meanwhile, she dragged Lux through the village, informing her mum that they'd scared the creature off for now. They continued to the fields, where Fera unfroze the villagers. A few careful *Flame* casts and they slowly thawed, blinking in the winter sun, only half aware of what had happened.

Lux was thankful for the downtime. He'd been right in what he'd said to Maya at Dawnstar – something *was* happening. He didn't know what, but it was. Was the ice-Monster following them? The thought was absurd. Monsters didn't think, they didn't scheme. And yet. . .

One thing he knew was Ghast certainly seemed to have some idea as to what Ark meant.

"I made a mistake there." Fera's comment came out of the blue on their way back to the village.

"There was nothing we could do," said Lux.

"Maybe, but a leader should be able to control her squad."

"Nobody can control Brace."

Fera bit her bottom lip in thought. "I'm going to talk to Ester about her taking over again."

Most of the children and teachers had left the school and were filtering in a shocked line through the village square, meeting their parents who were still gathered there despite Fera's warnings. But Ghast wasn't having as much luck. Lux and Fera found him arguing with a young teacher in the street.

"You tell that little madam that if she doesn't get out here right now, there'll be no pudding for the rest of the week!"

"I'm truly sorry, Professor, but she really won't come out until she's finished her poem."

"Well, I'll go in and get her myself—"

Before Ghast could finish there was a sharp, shouted "No!" though the school window.

Lux and Fera gave Brace a questioning look.

"His granddaughter," he whispered. "Apparently, she won't come out until she's finished a piece of work."

Fera looked at Brace like he was mad. "Does she not realise there's a Monster around?"

He shrugged.

"I swear to the Light, that girl will be the death of me," said Professor Ghast, coming over, throwing up his arms in defeat. "Next time I'll leave her to the Monster." He sighed. "It's these poems. She writes little rhymes. About things that happen to her. Used to do it with her mum. But sometimes she gets a little ... how can I say? *Precious* about finishing them."

Ester glanced at her watch.

"Just give me a minute," said Ghast.

They waited as the last of the children came out, meeting worried parents, who'd rushed up from the square. Then, finally, a shock of blonde hair appeared in the doorway. The girl to whom it belonged crept out as if she knew she was in trouble. Then she saw her grandad and ran up, slamming excitedly into his midriff.

"Grandad! We were in our Art lesson and this *Monster* turned up. I nearly wet myself!" Sally pulled away suddenly, sizing up the Light Hunters.

"Some friends of mine," said Ghast, all of his grumpiness washed away in a moment. "They're going to come to the cottage for a bit."

"Are they here to meet Rory?"

Ghast coughed nervously, firing Sally a warning look. She zipped her mouth shut.

"Friends . . ." she said, impressed, her face like a sunbeam. Her gaze settled on Brace and her eyes flashed. She ran up and held his hand, making him jump in surprise.

"It's very nice to have you here. My grandad doesn't have many friends." She thought again. "Actually, he doesn't have any friends. Would you like to hear my poem?"

She looked up expectantly. Brace was so taken aback that he couldn't answer. Instead, Ester bent down, reminding Lux of her kinder days as Miss Hart. "We'd love to."

Sally let go of Brace and stood in the centre of them all, her chest puffed out proudly as if she was on stage at the Lindhelm Grand Theatre. She took a piece of paper from her pocket and cleared her throat.

"One day I was drawing a picture,
When through the window I spied,
A creature so big and scary,
I almost collapsed and died.
But along came some very brave people,
One so handsome and smart,
They managed to get rid of the Monster,
And now I can finish my Art."

She waited for their round of applause. The Light Hunters clapped bemusedly.

"Of course, I could have done better if *Grandad* hadn't rushed me. But it's good enough to go on my wall." Sally wormed her hand into Brace's. "I'll show you my wall of poems at the cottage. You'll really like it."

Suddenly, there was a loud, cracking noise about fifty metres behind them in the direction of the village square. A person appeared in mid-air, falling to the ground with a painful *thud*. Seven more arrived, the last landing face first in a puddle. Lux recognised them as Squads Izas and Maven – the groups Dawnstar had sent to deal with Ravenholm's Monster.

They dragged themselves up, looking thoroughly confused at the sight of Squad Juno further down the street.

"Come on," said Ester, gathering her things. "We've got a bit of explaining to do."

· CHAPTER 23 ·

In Dawnstar's library, there was a special book called *The Book of Monsters*, which contained detailed sketches and information about every Monster the Light Hunters had ever encountered. As big as five normal books, it was kept in a glass case and handled only by those responsible for its upkeep. The members of Squad Juno had asked to see it so many times that they knew most Monsters off by heart. Only one was known to be immune to Light-casts: a rare and especially dangerous beast called a Skald. The ice-Monster was something new entirely, and Squads Izas and Maven were shocked as Ester explained how their Light hadn't seemed to touch it.

"Be careful," she warned them seriously. "Stay for a while. It might return."

The clouds had gone now, and the sun beat down on wet ground as Lux and the others made their way to the village square. They were headed for Ghast's hot air balloon, which lay on the ground like a sleeping giant. Sally talked every step, about her school and poems, her teachers and her life in Ravenholm. Her eyes were stuck to Brace like he was made of chocolate.

"I live in a cottage a few miles outside the village, past Fenrir Mountain," said Ghast. "Near the Shengan River, by the jungle. Gets smoky sometimes, but it's nice."

Fera's mum and dad were in the square, helping children find their families. Barny was there too, handing out bowls of hot soup. He walked off as soon as he saw the Light Hunters.

"Don't you mind him," said Fera's mum, seeing her daughter's disappointment. "It's the one who's sulky pays the biggest price in the end. Barny'll come around."

Fera didn't look convinced.

Her dad poured a big bowl of soup each for the Light Hunters, and Ghast and Sally too. The broth steamed, but they didn't wait to eat it. They'd not had anything since the Parstis Brace had bought in Lindhelm.

"Thank you so much for everything," said Fera's mum. "You've made us safe again. When that little boy came running up shouting 'Monster,' I nearly had a heart attack. The Cerberus . . ." A tear appeared in her eye. "It brings back bad memories."

Fera squeezed her mum reassuringly.

"Don't you worry about me, you silly goose. You lot have enough on your plate. You must come to the house. We'll have a grand old meal. It's so lovely to see you Fera. All of you!"

"I'm sorry, Mrs Lanceheart, but we've got to move on,"

said Ester. "We're out here on a mission."

"Nonsense!" said Fera's mum. "You've got time for one of Albert's pies, surely?"

Fera's dad nodded enthusiastically, while Brace leaned into Ester: "Yeah, we do."

Sally, so close to Brace that she was nearly knocking him into the soup table, said:

"*I think my friend Brace is right,*

A meal would be perfect tonight."

Fera's mum and dad laughed, appealing to Ester. But she shook her head.

"We really have to go. You might be able to help us with something though. We've got to get the professor's balloon back in the air. Is there anywhere high we can launch?"

There was a delighted squeal as three young girls shot past, waving at Sally. She turned her back, rolling her eyes at Brace in embarrassment.

"I don't know about that," said Fera's dad, "but you don't need that nonsense anyway. You still out near the river, Professor?"

"By the Shengan, yes."

"No problem. We'll lend you one of our carts. You take that now, and we'll get your balloon back to you later. That sound all right?"

"Fine by me," said Ghast. "Very kind, thank you."

Fera's dad hurried to the village storage sheds, while the Light Hunters, Ghast and Sally helped her mum dish out soup. He returned in a rumbling wooden Light-cart – a machine about the size of Squad Juno's dorm room – with a large cabin, an open-air driver's platform and so much Light leaking out of the engine that it looked like Tesla's lab after an experiment gone wrong.

"Should get you there easily. Who's driving?"

Brace dived forwards, excited to try. But it was Ghast who took the job, climbing into the driver's seat and poking around.

"I'm going to sit with Brace," said Sally, hurrying into the cabin before anyone else could. Ghast was out of the driver's seat in a moment.

"No, you're not," he said, guiding her to the front. "I think our friends would benefit from a little while to talk in private."

Ester nodded appreciatively.

Sally very nearly stamped her foot in anger. But instead, she stuck out her tongue at her grandad, then smiled broadly at Brace. "I'm sorry about him. He's a real pain. I'll tell you more of my poems at the cottage."

Lux couldn't be sure, but he thought he saw Brace breathe a sigh of relief.

"You take care of yourself," said Fera's mum. "Look after each other. And once you're done, make sure you come and visit."

Fera hugged her mum through the window.

And then they were on the muddy road, rolling past the Grumpy Farmer and out of the village, the Light-motor hissing as it forced the little vehicle along.

The landscape changed from the green and yellow fields of Ravenholm to a small wood. Apple trees crowded their cart, with bright red fruits that had fallen to the floor, making a satisfying *squelch* as the cart's wheels ran over them. It smelled fresh and fragrant.

"We all okay?" asked Fera.

The Hunters, apart from Lux, nodded.

"Lux?"

They all looked at him.

"I'm getting there."

"Don't worry about your purple stuff," said Brace. "As long as we all keep an eye on it, we'll be fine."

The Light-cart rumbled on over rocks and roots.

"What do we think of him?" said Brace, lowering his voice. He pointed to where Professor Ghast was sitting with Sally, humming tunelessly. "I think he's crazy for not wanting to fight that Monster. But he seems all right otherwise. You never know Lux, he might be able to tell you a bit about your grandpa. He's old enough."

Lux touched the Luminary badge on his arm. It was dirty from their fight with the Monster.

"This Ark stuff," said Fera, "and that ice-Monster. We're going to have to come up with some way to deal with it. Because my casts did nothing."

"Let's get to Ghast's cottage and hear what he has to say," said Ester. "This whole thing might end up being a wild-goose chase for all we know."

Her comment ended their conversation. The Light-cart emerged from the woods and started down a track, tracing a bubbling stream that Lux guessed had to be the beginnings of the Shengan River. He spied a cloud of smoke in the distance. Beneath, a dull red line marked the flaming Shengan Jungle.

As they passed the foot of a low mountain, Lux felt the Key to the Ark in his bag: heavy, hefty. He wondered what on earth would be coming next.

· CHAPTER 24 ·

There was a black rock, at the foot of Fenrir Mountain – the modest peak down which they were travelling – that cast a long shadow over the land at sunset. The Light-cart drove through this now, Lux and the others shivering in the evening cold. They'd been travelling for well over an hour, and Ghast had informed them they were nearly there.

The first they saw of his cottage was a tiny hut, on top of two wooden legs, poking high above the trees. It was attached, they realised, as they followed the road around one final bend, to more elevated huts, all kept aloft by the cottage below. The whole thing looked like a house of cards, ready to fall.

A large wooden barn, covered in burn marks, stood to the right. In the mud outside were all sorts of machines, many old and rusting. It was quiet in the clearing, with only the gentle rush of the Shengan River behind the house. There was a ripe smell, Lux was surprised to notice as he poked his head through the Light-cart window, like a farm.

Ghast pulled up and switched off the cart's engine. "Welcome to my humble home," he said, opening the cabin.

Handing one of the bags he'd transferred from the hot air balloon in Ravenholm to each of the Hunters, he opened the cottage's front door. From somewhere in the clearing there came a rustling sound. Lux looked behind him, afraid the ice-Monster had followed them somehow.

"An experiment," Ghast explained. "Brewing some of my own beer in the barn." His eyes flashed excitedly, then he stepped into the cottage. Sally followed, but Lux couldn't help but notice a guilty look on her face.

Ghast's front door opened into a busy kitchen and living space, with books and beer bottles and plants and empty paper bags of food and astronomical charts and all sorts of things scattered everywhere. There was a large kitchen counter, an oven, a table and two huge sofas onto which Ghast dumped his bags. It was freezing, and he hurried to start a fire, using a small *Flame* cast. The warmth made Lux feel better straight away.

"Make yourselves at home," he said, shifting newspapers off the table.

Lux picked his way through the room, glancing at the seat Ghast had offered him. On the back was a gob of some kind of red-green substance. He decided to stand.

"Now, I don't know about you, but that bowl of soup didn't do much to tackle my hunger," said Ghast, taking a few pots and pans from the walls. "How's about I cook us something while Sally shows you around? Then we'll chat."

Lux was so hungry that the thought of eating before having any sort of serious conversation was an instant 'Yes' from him.

"Splendid." Ghast's tattoos glistened as he washed his hands. "You can show them everywhere, Sally, although perhaps not the barn. If someone were to ruin my beer, I think I'd become that ice-Monster myself."

Their tour began in the main living space, with Sally pointing out interesting pictures and experiments and charts. The walls were hidden by books, piled up high. They were all well-thumbed, with creased, cracked spines.

"*My grandad's a bit of a reader,*
As I'm sure you can probably see.
He's passing his love of books down,
All of these ones belong to me."

Sally led them to the far wall, beneath a window, where there was a pile of leather-backed adventure books.

"Do you like reading?" she asked Brace hopefully.

"Not particularly."

She frowned. "We'll change that."

They followed her down a short, cobwebbed flight of stairs into a basement area, filled with blue and yellow Light. Wooden benches lined the walls, covered with bubbling flasks and clanking Light-gadgets. It reminded Lux of the caretaker's office at the University of Lindhelm.

"Grandad spends a lot of time here," she said, picking up a

mechanical helmet and juggling it. "It's kind of his place. I don't come here often. He always tells me off for breaking things." As she spoke, the helmet got away from her and landed with a *thud* on the floor. Her face went white, and she hurried to pick it up.

"What was that?" the professor shouted down the stairs.

"Nothing," sang Sally sweetly.

They returned to the kitchen, then climbed two flights of stairs that wound around the house, before heading up a ladder and into a tight glass bubble that turned out to be a lot higher than Brace was comfortable with.

"Grandad's observatory," said Sally, tapping a bright red telescope. "He spends a lot of time here too, taking measurements and stuff."

She tidied her blonde hair, ready for a poem.

"*I like looking at the Moon,*
And the stars and galaxies too.
But more than anything else,
I like looking at you."

She fluttered her eyelashes at Brace, who froze, looking to the other Hunters for help. Fera laughed.

"You're certainly not afraid to say what you think, are you?"

"Grandad says there are too many people who don't say what they think."

Sally descended the ladder, indicating for the Hunters to follow.

She carried on showing them around, taking them to the roof where she and her grandad liked to read on summer evenings,

Ghast's own bedroom ("I won't even bother going in," she said dismissively. "Just imagine the most boring place ever,") and a bathroom with so much Light that it looked like Dawnstar.

Sally's own bedroom was different again. Rather than books and Light, which seemed to be the pattern for the rest of the house, it was mostly plain – almost like Lux's room in Daven. Except for two differences: in one corner was a tall figure formed of straw and covering the walls were what had to be over a hundred poems.

Impressed, the Light Hunters circled the room, reading as many as they could.

"These are amazing," said Ester.

"I know."

"How did you learn?"

Sally went to her windowsill, where there was a picture of a young woman with brown hair. "My mum was a poet. I'm going to be one too."

"Is this her?" said Lux gently, studying the straw figure in the corner.

"Oh no, don't be silly. He's my friend. He listens to my poems."

The Light Hunters continued to read, all the while smelling Ghast's cooking downstairs. Then he shouted that it was ready.

"Don't worry," Sally told Brace, who was idly tossing a Light-dagger, obviously bored. "You can finish reading the poems later."

Ghast's food was incredible. Even if – apart from another Parsti – Lux had no idea what half of the dishes were. Clearly Lindhelmers ate differently to the usual food served at Dawnstar.

But Lux ate it all, as did the others, helping themselves to seconds, and in Brace's case, thirds.

Moonlight was falling through the cottage windows by the time they finished, merging with the light of the fire. Ester and Brace washed the dishes while Ghast explained some of the charts on the wall to Lux and Fera. Then they joined the others on the sofas.

"Now you've helped me as promised, and I thank you for that," said Ghast. "We both do, don't we, Sally?" He squeezed her gently and she nodded.

"*The Light Hunters saved my school,*

I have to say they're quite cool."

Ghast played with his nose ring. "But now it is time for you to hear why I asked Nova to send you. Settle in," he said, moving to a wooden chest buried beneath a pile of books. "This is quite a tale."

· CHAPTER 25 ·

Back in Daven, Lux's favourite night of the week was Friday, because that was the night his grandpa closed the workshop early and they sat on the living room floor with freshly baked cookies, reading each other adventure stories.

Ghast's story, however, told of something much more important. And by the end of it, Lux's entire world had changed.

Ghast returned from the wooden chest with a Light Hunter squad leader badge, which he dropped on the table between them. It was faded, but otherwise identical to Ester's. The only distinguishing mark was a neat inscription around the edge that read, '*Squad Celan*'.

"Ester knows this, even if she was younger than Sally when I was there, but I'm not sure the rest of you do. I used to be a Light Hunter.

"I did a lot there," Ghast went on, holding the badge proudly to his arm. "I led a squad, Celan. A great little group, that included a *certain* someone's mother before she led a squad of her own."

Ghast squeezed Ester's arm fondly.

"In time, I specialised in the Inventor track, until I was lucky enough to be made Dawnstar's chief Inventor by the then Luminary, Ben Dowd."

The others looked at Lux. Ghast must have noticed because his eyes narrowed questioningly.

"Lux is Ben's grandson. *Was* Ben's grandson," Ester corrected.

"He's dead?"

Lux nodded.

"I am very sorry to hear that." Sadness marked Ghast's features. "He was a good man, your grandfather. One of the wisest I've known."

Lux managed a smile.

"He set me up with a young apprentice who'd just injured himself trying to rescue a little girl from a Behemoth. Tesla?"

Brace and Fera grinned slyly.

"I see you've met him. Tesla and I spent years researching Light, turning what we found in the ruins beneath Korat Crater into things that helped us fight Monsters. But studying something in that much detail changes a person. It changed me. I learned more about our land, the Ancients, their technology. Ester's father noticed this change in me. This was only a year or two after Deimos and his . . . well, I'm sure you've heard about that."

Silence. Lux saw Deimos's sneering face in his mind's eye.

"I started to believe we were wrong in attacking Monsters.

We were like hamsters on a wheel. As soon as we dealt with one, another popped up. There had to be a better way. I set out to find it.

"I asked Hunters to try devices I made. Your father," he told Ester, "considered this a step too far. He gave me a choice: stop or leave. I was so far in I had to go."

Ghast drank his tea, wiping droplets from his beard as he thought about what to tell them next.

"Lindhelm, that's where I came. I knew I wanted to carry on my research. What better place than the University of Lindhelm?

"And for a couple of years, things went well. I taught, I researched. Life was good. Then one of my students got injured in an experiment. The higher-ups got wind and fired me. By this point, my wonderful daughter had died, and Sally was under my care." He flashed her a warm grin. "And I needed work. Not only to pay my way, but because I was close to discovering something very important indeed.

"I pleaded with the university. Let me keep my role. They refused. But they offered me the next best thing: a job as caretaker. The work was dull, but I was near the library. And my experiments. After work, I'd continue my research."

Ester fidgeted impatiently as Ghast added a couple of logs to the fire. It flared and settled.

"Tell me, what do you know of the Ancients?"

Lux's heart lurched. Ancients. He knew little other than what Deimos had told him. He knew they'd lived in the world before, and that their ruins were all over the land. He knew they created the Monsters, and that their knowledge of Light and Shade far exceeded today's.

Ghast nodded as Lux told him, listening carefully.

"Good," he said. "Dawnstar teaches you better than I thought.

"It's no boast to say that I am the most knowledgeable person in the entire world on the Ancients. I've studied their history, their lives, their successes and mistakes. Common understanding has the Ancients as more technologically advanced than us but let me tell you that is a gross understatement. Their knowledge of Light and Shade was a burning star to our tiny flame. I've travelled the world in my pursuit of Ancient knowledge and have discovered evidence of cities that make Lindhelm look like an anthill."

Ghast pointed to maps illustrating what he was saying. Lux saw patches of grey that indicated cities. One was bigger than Daven, Kofi and the countryside between them combined.

"It's understood that Light was widely used by the Ancients. It powered their cities. It's much easier than Shade to manipulate. To them, as to us, Shade was merely an idea. Light's opposite. Something to be studied."

Ghast drank his tea.

"As always happens when knowledge goes too far, the Ancients began fighting. Over what, I've never been able to work out. I suspect they themselves didn't know.

"These battles continued, each city using more and more dangerous Light-weapons, while secretly researching Shade in the hope it might give them an edge. It appears to have done so. Soon, they could throw Shade like they threw Light."

Ghast's eyes glittered darkly. The room was utterly silent, the Light Hunters hardly breathing.

"The problem, of course, is that Shade corrupts. The battles between the Ancients became so fierce that the cities searched for something to end them once and for all. Shade was their tool of choice. A particularly brilliant woman used it to create a Monster. Then more. The rest . . . I'm sure you can imagine."

Lux thought of the shattered cities he'd visited.

Ghast walked to the fire, so that his face was buried in shadow. "All of this, we know. What I'm about to tell you, nobody outside of this room knows.

"The city to whom this woman belonged, Celena, wasn't happy with its position in the world. They encouraged the great lady to experiment with Light and Shade in ways I can only dream of. She managed to fuse them – the Light we know and the Shade we shy from – to create another power the Ancients called *Slazan*. In our language it would be *Twilight*."

For some reason, Lux shivered. He sat forward, listening closely.

"Twilight still exists, although I suspect only I, and the tiny handful of those capable of manipulating it, know of it."

The room tightened around Lux.

"What is it?" said Ester.

"I've never seen it." Ghast pulled a leather notebook out of a pile and turned to a page filled with tiny writing. "But I have a description. I found it in a cave in Fenrir Mountain. I've translated it."

He cleared his throat. "*It starts with a hot feeling, like you are next to a fire. Then fullness, that spreads to your limbs. Tingling. Threads appear at the ends of your fingers, spreading and forming a bubble of something that is not Light and not Shade. A mix. If left to build, this can race out of control and explode.*"

Ghast noticed the Hunters were staring at him.

"What colour is it?" said Lux.

The professor closed his notebook. "Purple. Blue-white and red mixed."

The ground opened up beneath Lux. "I have it," he said. "I have it."

· CHAPTER 26 ·

Twilight.

A single word to explain everything. The explosion in Kofi, the little leaks of purple energy, Fera's injured arm, the feeling back in Ravenholm.

Ghast stared hard at Lux, seeing if he was lying. "Don't be silly," he said, pacing to the kitchen counter and back. "Don't be silly. Show me."

"I can't. I can't control it. It comes when it comes."

"Pah!" Ghast turned away, dismissing him. He appealed to the others, searching for someone who would make sense.

"It's true," said Ester. "Or, at least, it sounds like it is. You remember the explosion in Kofi last year?"

"A Monster. Yes?"

"No. Lux."

Ghast shook his head. "No. I simply won't accept this."

"It's true," said Brace.

"I asked your father to send someone to carry a message. I didn't think he'd send me exactly what I was looking for. How does it ... how do you ... tell me everything!"

Lux did. He told him all about the previous year: about Deimos, Squad Juno's battle with the Cerberus, his grandpa dying, his sudden explosion afterwards, his new powers, everything. Ghast listened carefully, shaking his head in wonder.

"That is ... you do realise that you are perhaps one of only a tiny handful with this power. You understand that?"

Lux was still coming to terms with what he'd learned. Twilight ... he finally had a name for what was happening, why Deimos was so bent on capturing him. "But why me?"

"That's a question I can't answer." Ghast opened a bottle of beer from the kitchen and poured it into his empty tea cup, taking a large swig. "I simply cannot believe what I'm hearing."

"We can tell." Sally rolled her eyes wearily at the Light Hunters.

Ester took a deep breath. "I feel like there's a lot we can tell each other. But first I want to ask you a question, Professor. You said a moment ago that my father had sent you exactly what you were looking for. But we still don't know what you've found out about stopping the Monsters."

Ghast sank his beer, wiping his lips.

"Yes, yes, I suppose that's true." He crossed to another pile of books and searched through them. Then he seemed to change his mind. "No, no. I think it's time, Sally."

The impact of the professor's five words on his granddaughter was immense. Her face lit up and she leapt out of her seat. "Really?"

"Get him ready."

Sally raced out of the room, knocking her grandad's empty beer bottle onto the carpet.

"I could tell you what I have found – about the years of travelling and research it's taken to find it. But it will perhaps be better if I show you. Please put on your shoes and follow me."

The Light Hunters exchanged puzzled glances but put on their jackets and shoes all the same. The moon was high in the sky when they got outside, making the leaves of the surrounding trees look soft and ghostly.

"This is exciting," said Brace, rubbing his hands against the cold.

Lux was a million miles away, still stunned by what he'd learned. Twilight. It was incredible. He finally had a name. But hadn't Ghast said it was a mixture of Light and Shade? Did that mean Lux had Shade inside of him?

The professor led them to the large barn they'd seen when they arrived. Inside, they could hear Sally singing a pleasant tune. Then came a loud snort. Fera jumped.

"What I'm about to show you has never been seen by anybody other than me and Sally. It will likely be a bit of a shock, so I want you to prepare yourselves."

Ghast unlocked the door.

At first, Lux couldn't make out what was inside. Then he spotted Sally's blonde hair picked out by a shaft of moonlight. Next to her were ... two eyes?

Two red, glowering eyes.

And now that Lux looked closely, he could see a snout too, covered with hard, spiked armour that ran down a long, curved back. A thick tail met four great limbs and steam hissed loudly from a pair of nostrils. There was a smell too. The same one Lux had smelled when he'd first arrived. Not pleasant, but not unpleasant either. Like a farm.

But those red eyes.

It had to be a Monster.

The other members of Squad Juno must have come to the same conclusion, because they all stepped back, conjuring their Light-bows and blades.

"Hey!" shouted Sally, upset.

Ghast joined her, racing in front of the Light Hunters. "Stop!"

"Professor," said Ester slowly, "there is a Monster right next to your granddaughter."

"He's called Rory," said Sally, stroking the creature's flank to calm it down.

"But . . . but . . ." spluttered Brace.

"Please, lower your attacks and I'll explain," said Ghast, dancing anxiously in front of them.

Ester kept her Light-blade out for a few seconds, then slid it warily into her Gauntlet. The rest of Squad Juno followed.

"I suggest you tell us what's going on."

The professor backed into the barn towards the Monster. With a fond pat of its snout, he led it slowly into the moonlight.

Lux was even more amazed now that he could see the creature

clearly. It was a Fire-drake – about the size of the cart they'd taken back from Ravenholm. Its skin was fire red, and between its scales, molten flames licked and twisted.

"Meet Rory. Not my choice," added Ghast, shrugging, "but it's the name he's been given. And kind of apt, I suppose."

As if he'd heard the professor, the Monster roared loudly, letting out a blast of hot air.

"Why isn't it attacking?" said Fera. Her voice was a mixture of horror and amazement.

"He's tame," said Ghast. He scratched the Monster fondly. "I tamed him."

"But . . . that's not possible," said Lux.

"I assure you it is. Rory is our pet."

"Then my father . . ." prompted Ester.

"Yes, this is part of the message I want you to relay to your father," said Ghast. "Our fight is nearly over. After seven long years, I have finally done it. I've found a way to tame Monsters."

· CHAPTER 27 ·

Lux could still remember the first time he'd seen a Monster – just over a year earlier, when he'd swam across Daven harbour in the hope of stealing a book from the lighthouse library. The horrible creature he'd run into had scared him more than anything he'd ever encountered. That same fear gripped him now, as he stared at the flame-red Fire-drake called Rory.

Fera inched forwards, gently touching the Monster's scales. She pulled her hand away instantly, before putting it on again. "It's warm," she said, amazed.

Seeing that Fera hadn't had her arm ripped off, Brace and Ester approached too, looking warily at Rory's scales and spikes.

"Go on," Ghast prodded Lux. "He won't bite. Not anymore, anyway."

Lux placed his hands on the scales above Rory's nose. They felt like stone.

It was such a strange feeling. He'd spent a year fighting Monsters, learning about them, their strengths, their weak points. Monsters were his enemy. And yet here he was, petting a Firedrake like it was a cat.

"You get used to it," Ghast told him.

They ran their hands along the Monster's back, looking directly into its dark eyes, into the cloud of steam issuing from its nostrils.

"You'd probably like an explanation," said Ghast.

"Yes, please," said Ester.

"I had one plan in mind when I left Dawnstar. Killing Monsters was wrong. Despite the damage they cause, they have just as much right to live as we do. So, I knew I wouldn't be searching for how to rid the world of the beasts, but how to *tame* them."

Ghast tickled Rory, who let out a contented puff of steam.

"That's what I spent my time doing. First as professor, then as caretaker. For years, I found nothing of use. Then, during that trip up Fenrir Mountain, I came across a treasure trove of information, most of which hasn't been seen in thousands of years."

Ghast handed Rory to Sally, who led the great Monster back into the barn, whispering into his ear.

"There was a cast," Ghast went on. "One I've never seen in any of the books at Dawnstar or the university, or anywhere for that matter. *Lethia*, the Ancients called it. We'd call it *Turn*.

"I managed to capture Rory shortly after moving in here. He was injured, else I'd never have managed it. I brought him back and sheltered him."

Ghast indicated a series of chains, and scratch marks in the corner of the barn.

"I nursed him back to health, before turning my attention to the cast. It was clear from the information I'd unearthed that *Turn* was used to change things. Iron to gold. An autumn leaf to one full and green. I wondered – silly though it sounds – whether it could tame a savage Monster.

"So I tried. I cast and cast. Nothing. Rory remained as dangerous as when we brought him in. But I was onto something, I knew it. And I did something we are told as Light Hunters never to do: I tweaked the cast. A little shift of Light, a little push here.

"After weeks of trying, I threw the *Turn* in such a way that something changed. I saw it instantly. All the anger in Rory was gone, replaced by gentleness, kindness. The Monster you see before you."

Lux saw Rory playfully nudge Sally, sending her into a fit of laughter.

"I've no idea what I did. I've never been able to recreate the feeling. And besides, I have no other Monsters to try it on. But I had found something. I want to tame every Monster, stop these attacks."

The Light Hunters were absolutely silent – the only sound in the clearing the gentle ripple of the Shengan River.

A cast.

That's all it took to turn a Monster into a pet. It was almost funny. And yet, if Ghast was right . . . Lux thought of all the villages and towns they'd save, the children no longer orphaned.

"Wait," said Brace. "If this is true – and trust me, I'm not saying it is – but *if* it is, you can't remember what you did. How can we possibly do it to every Monster?"

A sly grin from Ghast. "We come at last to why I've called you here today. I suggest we go back into the house, it's cold."

The professor's cottage felt like an oven after the frigid night-time air. The Light Hunters removed their coats and settled by the fire.

"One victory does not make a successful plan," Ghast went on. "And I have not rested just because I have turned one Monster. I carried on with my research. And I read about a place, an important Ancient ruin called the Ark."

The colour drained from Lux's face.

"Yes, the very word you mentioned at Ravenholm, Lux. Inside that ruin might be the key to taming Monsters once and for all. And finally, after two years of searching, I have found this place. I have been there."

The cottage was closing around Lux. The ice-Monster, Ghast, the Ark – how was it all linked?

"It is, in fact, very close by. In the Shengan Jungle. It's a tower, built by the Ancients. I've worked my way quite far inside. But I've hit a wall. A Twilight wall.

"I need two things to get past it, hence my letter to your father, Ester. Despite our differences, some things are too important to let grudges hold us back."

Ghast leaned beneath his sofa and pulled out a pile of papers. He found a sketch of what looked like a door, surrounded by purple energy. Jutting out of it was a jigsaw-like piece of stone.

"This is the wall. Incredibly, your father's sent me Lux, with his Twilight. That's one of the things I need. But the second, I'm certain not even you will be able to provide. It's an artefact. A sphere. I'd like you to return to your father and tell him all I've told you. Tell him he'll be able to put an end to Monster attacks for good if we can just find this key. He must make it his most urgent task."

Brace, Ester and Fera all leaned in to see Ghast's drawing more clearly.

But not Lux.

He felt numb.

Rising from his seat, he walked through the cottage to the bedroom where he'd dumped his bag. Bringing it to the front room, he laid it carefully on his seat and pulled out the Key to the Ark. The bronze metal shone orange in the firelight, as the pieces pushed slightly apart, revealing the purple energy that Lux now knew to be called Twilight.

"This is the key you're looking for."

· CHAPTER 28 ·

There was a picture of Ghast above his fireplace, in his grey overalls, wisps of Light at his fingers. The Ghast in front of Lux now looked nothing like the relaxed, calm man in the painting. His mouth was open so wide in shock that Brace could have fired twelve Light-arrows into it and still had space to spare.

Lux handed the Key to the professor, who stared at it as if it was a bar of pure gold. The jigsaw pieces came slowly back together.

"This is…" Ghast was speechless. He turned the Key, examining every segment. "This is … Where did you get it?"

The rest of Squad Juno were just as shocked as the professor. They waited for Lux to answer.

"Nova. We had it at Dawnstar."

Ghast looked closely at the mountain peaks carved into the segments and laughed. "Your father," he told Ester excitedly. "Your father! This is it!"

It wasn't the first time someone had approached the Light Hunters with a plan that had ended in failure, and Ester's expression told Ghast she was sceptical.

"No promises," he told her. "I can see you're uncertain. No promises at all. But I think the Ark will give us what we need."

Ghast paced the room like a child about to open their birthday presents.

"Let's go then," said Brace.

"Ah . . ." Ghast lay the Key carefully on the table. "That wouldn't be such a good idea. The Ark is a . . . dangerous place. Dark. Far better we wait until morning when we're fed and rested."

"Dangerous, how?" said Fera.

The professor's eyes narrowed. "Best if you see that for yourselves."

A gust of wind blew into the cottage, rattling the slates on the roof.

"We'd need to wait for tomorrow anyway," said Ester. "We can't go racing off without contacting Dawnstar."

Ghast handed the Key to Lux. "Take good care of that. For now, I suggest we take a break. It's been a long day and we've all learned some things we've never known before. Let's get some sleep and we'll come together in the morning."

The very *last* thing Lux wanted to do at that moment was sleep. Ghast was right, he'd learned so much it felt like he'd been rocked by a dozen earthquakes all at once. But the others seemed to agree with the professor, and Lux's grandpa had always told him to sleep on things before acting, so he didn't argue.

Professor Ghast sat at the kitchen table with a fresh beer and a tall pile of books, going over his notes. Fera and Brace stayed up a little longer, chatting quietly about what they'd learned, and Ester went to try and get hold of Dawnstar on her Shell. Sally announced – after a short, whispered argument with her grandad that Lux couldn't quite hear – that she was going to tend to Rory. Lux, for his part, was utterly exhausted, even if he was far too amazed to go to sleep. Instead, he took the opportunity to wash, borrowing a bar of soap from Ghast's cupboard.

When he came out again, Fera and Brace had gone to bed. Feeling anxious, Lux decided to go for a walk outside.

The moon was covered by clouds now, so he could see more of the stars: white, blue and red. He found Juno, remembering what Nova had told him about the hero never giving in, never stopping fighting.

It was strange to think that one day the Light Hunters might be able to.

If Ghast was right – if there really was a way in the Ark to tame every Monster – the Light Hunters would no longer be needed.

Still, something made Lux feel uneasy. He couldn't quite put his finger on what. His Twilight? His Light? Shade? Nova had once said that Shade twists people, making them capable of horrible acts. Was that him? Was he like Deimos?

Lux's thoughts were interrupted by a sound from the barn.

Buttoning his jacket, he crept towards the door, hoping to peer through a gap at the Monster. He hadn't got far when he heard a voice.

"*Sneaking about in the courtyard,*
A little bit scary, I think.
My money's on Lux or Brace,
I'll see when they look through the chink."

Lux had already pushed his eye up against the crack as Sally sang her last line. He was surprised to see her green eyes staring back.

"You can come in, you know."

Lux opened the doors carefully, still worried that Rory might roast him with a flame. Instead, he found the Monster nuzzling Sally as she washed his scales.

"I knew it was one of you two," she said. "Although I'd have preferred Brace . . ."

Lux didn't know whether to be offended or relieved.

"At least it isn't Grandad," she went on sourly.

"Is everything all right?" Lux asked, noticing her frown.

"Fine."

Sally sunk her cloth into a bucket of water and slopped it all over Rory. He shook it out of his eyes.

"Oh, it's *him*," she said.

"Brace?"

"Grandad."

She tipped the water forcefully into the dirt, making Rory jump. "Sorry," she said, stroking him.

"What's happened?"

"*Grandad says I can't go to the Ark,*
In the morning with all of you.
How am I supposed to make friends,
If I don't get to do what you do?"

148

She sighed, picking up a dry cloth ready to polish Rory's scales.

Back in Daven, Lux and Maya had spent almost all of their time together. They didn't really have other friends. If poor Sally was the same . . .

"If it makes you feel any better, it's pretty boring, what we do," said Lux. "Being a Light Hunter sounds really cool, but most of it's just waiting around, finding out where a Monster is."

He sat on one of the wooden dividers, happy to have something on his mind other than Twilight. Sally looked out from behind her curtain of hair.

"It must be fun though."

"The fights are good. Although I don't think your grandad would like me saying that."

"My mummy died because of a Monster." Sally let the cloth hang at her side. "That's when I moved here."

"I know, your grandad said. My mum and dad died too. And my sister. They're not nice, Monsters. Well," he added, indicating Rory, "some of them are."

"I can fly him, you know?"

It took a moment for Lux to process what she'd said. "On his back?"

Sally directed his attention to a saddle hanging from a wooden roofbeam.

"I can take you," she offered mischievously. "Grandad normally doesn't let me unless I ask, but I sometimes go anyway. And tonight . . ."

She raised a tempting eyebrow.

Lux couldn't tell if she was being serious. He would have been lying if he said he didn't want to go. But a Monster? Would it even be safe?

"I'm very good," said Sally, reading his mind. "I can loop-the-loop. And I promise he won't flame you."

Lux thought for a moment. Rory *did* seem friendly.

"Oh, go on then," he said, amazing himself even as he spoke. "As long as we won't get in trouble."

"Tonight, I don't even care," said Sally resolutely.

· CHAPTER 29 ·

There were three hundred and eighty-six recorded Fire-drake attacks in *The Book of Monsters* at Dawnstar, including the one Squad Juno had dealt with in Ringtown that year. Fire-drakes weren't the *most* dangerous Monsters – that dishonour normally went to Behemoths – but they were up there. And Lux was about to fly on one . . . it was like he'd given leave of all his senses.

Sally had him lift the heavy saddle off the rusty hook and slide it over Rory, who huffed irritably, making Lux feel nervous. But he calmed once it was in place.

She used her bucket to climb on top of him. "Come on."

Lux had never ridden an animal. He'd been too scared the day they'd brought horses to his school. So, he made a bit of a mess of swinging his leg over, nearly toppling the bucket and himself with it. When he finally got up, he settled behind Sally. He could feel heat in his legs from Rory's scales. The Monster smelled earthy, and its strong muscles rippled with every movement.

"Right, boy," said Sally, rubbing Rory's ear, "I know you're not very good at being quiet, but you must try tonight, okay?"

Rory wagged his tail.

"I'll take that as a yes."

Sally guided them out of the barn into the courtyard, twisting to warn Lux to be quiet too. It was still cold, and he wished he could fetch Brace's jacket to go on top of his own.

"It's weird at first," Sally whispered. "Not like grandad's balloon or a skybus. Hold on tight or else you'll end up down here as flat as a Parsti."

Lux was just about to tell her that maybe they shouldn't fly after all, when Rory opened his wings – so wide they spanned the entire cottage – and flapped them twice. The Monster flew directly up, clearing a dozen metres before Lux could even blink. Each beat carried them higher, until very quickly Ghast's home began to look like a tiny toy.

"Wait!" he yelled, but his words were swallowed as Rory floated right, over the tall trees behind the cottage. The Shengan River sparkled in the moonlight.

"Hold tight," warned Sally.

She shook the reins and Rory dived, his massive limbs brushing the canopy, tearing off leaves, so that Lux had to hold a hand up to stop them going in his eyes.

Then the Monster climbed. And climbed. Rotating like a top. Lux became dizzy, the moon and stars blurring into long bands of white.

The air was stingingly cold. Soon the low clouds in the dark sky were rushing towards them, then Rory burst through, coating them all in a fine mist. Lux held the Monster with his knees, borrowing its warmth.

Rory climbed for a short while longer, until Sally took his reins, and he came to a neat stop. It was deathly quiet, with nothing but the moon and stars for company, like they were sailing on an ocean of clouds. Sally was right – it was different to flying in a skybus. Much . . . better! Brace would have absolutely loved it.

"Amazing, isn't it?" she said proudly.

"*It's wonderful to fly,*

So very, very high,

On Rory in the sky."

"I can't believe we're doing this." Lux really meant it.

"Neither could I the first time Grandad let me. Well, I say he let me. I actually sneaked off and did it and never told him. But you know . . ."

The clouds rolled along, Rory's steamy breath creating new ones. In a break in the white, Lux could see Lindhelm in the distance, as well as Ghast's cottage. Fenrir Mountain was visible too, guarding the area like a wolf, and the Shengan River. Even the jungle's flaming canopy was a red slash in the dark.

"Want to try a loop-the-loop?"

A twinkle in Sally's eye worried Lux. But before he could protest, she'd whipped the reins and Rory was moving.

This time they fell like a stone, the great Monster's wings at his side, accelerating so quickly that Lux had to hang on tight.

The wind whipped by terribly fast, hitting his cheeks. The ground raced towards them – Ghast's cottage getting bigger and bigger and bigger . . .

Just as Lux was starting to worry, Rory lifted his head and skidded horizontally towards the woods, then up again, his wings beating like hammers, then backwards, so that Lux could no longer tell what was up and what was down.

"Sally!"

"Hang on!"

Rory finished his loop with a flourish, turning in a lazy arc until he was hovering above Ghast's cottage, his wings almost silent.

Lux felt sick. But it was a good sick. The kind you feel after doing something amazing.

Sally tickled Rory and he shivered in pleasure.

"*There never was a Monster so fair,*

As Rory when he's flying in the air."

She turned to look at Lux, who was shaking his head in wonder. "Told you it would be good."

"It was amazing!"

Sally tied up her blonde hair. "I think I'll bring Brace one day."

"He'd love it."

"He likes flying?"

"More than anything."

"*Does* he now?" Something clicked in Sally's mind.

Lux rubbed Rory's warm scales, amazed the Monster had kept him alive. "Wouldn't it be incredible if he could talk?" he said, the idea suddenly occurring to him.

Sally avoided his eyes.

"You are joking me?" he said.

"Shh!" She turned quickly and put a finger to her lips. "Grandad . . ."

"Can he talk?" said Lux urgently.

"Yes! Well, no. I've been teaching him to listen. He can't make our sounds. But I think he understands."

She let go of the reins and whispered into Rory's ear. Without any other movement, the great Monster flapped his wings and turned on his side, so that Lux was barely hanging on.

"Okay! I get it!"

Sally whispered again and Rory righted himself.

"Good boy! You'd be amazed what you can do when you try. That's what Grandad says."

After twenty minutes, Lux was about ready to go down, but Sally insisted on one final loop. So up they went, tearing into the clouds. Then at last, slowly, the Monster floated down, landing neatly in the barn.

Sally gave Rory a kiss, then Lux helped her take off his saddle, stroking the Fire-drake as he did. A tame Monster. One that could understand their language. It was all so . . . impossible.

"See," said Sally, kicking dirt over Rory's claw marks so her grandad wouldn't find them in the morning. "Monsters aren't so bad, are they?"

Lux watched Rory, already sleeping contentedly in the corner. Incredible though it was, he was starting to agree.

· CHAPTER 30 ·

Lux almost never remembered his dreams. There was one – the night the Cerberus attacked his hometown – that stuck with him. And for some reason he always remembered his dreams about food – both the good and bad ones. But the normal dreams, the everyday kind . . . nothing.

However, the night of their stay at Ghast's cottage, he did remember his dream.

He was in Lindhelm, with the magician, sitting at the wooden table and trying to clean the wine from the cloth. But instead of brushes and bottles of yellow liquid, it was his own Twilight he was using . . . But like the brush and bottle, it didn't clear the wine, rather it hit the back of his own head, burning until Lux woke in a cold sweat.

Breakfast that morning was eggs and bacon.

Lux smelled it as soon as he entered the kitchen, sizzling with butter and salt.

Brace and Fera were already up, along with Sally and Ghast, who were preparing what looked like a feast. But it was clear there was still tension between the professor and his granddaughter. Sally was stomping around, banging knives and forks.

Lux joined his friends by the fire, rubbing sleep from his eyes.

"Sleeping Beauty arises," said Fera.

Lux didn't respond, still trying to shake the uneasy feeling from his dream.

"Crazy last night," said Brace. He whispered so Sally and Ghast wouldn't hear. "Do you reckon he's really onto something with all this Monster-taming stuff?"

Lux thought of his flight on Rory. "Maybe."

"If he is . . ." Brace whistled, impressed.

"Where'd you get to anyway?" Fera asked Lux curiously. "We didn't see you after the talk."

Sally, laying plates on the table, whipped her head around at Fera's question, looking panicked.

"Nowhere," said Lux. "Went for a walk. Trying to take it all in."

"Testing your new Twilight powers, I bet," said Brace. He shifted his voice so that he was mimicking Ghast. "'One of only a handful of people in the world capable of—'"

Lux elbowed him.

"At least it has a name now," said Fera. "Next time you break my arm, we know what to blame."

The bacon was really crackling and Ghast whipped the pan off the heat, forking three pieces haphazardly onto each plate. Sally followed, rearranging them so that they sat neatly at the edge.

"Grandad, why?" she said.

"Why what, sweetheart?"

"Why can't I go?"

Ghast sighed. It was clearly not the first time he'd answered the question that morning. He put the pan in the sink, wiping his hands on a cloth. "I've told you," he said gently. "This could be dangerous. I don't want you getting hurt. Besides, someone needs to look after Rory. You're the best at that."

Sally narrowed her eyes, not even close to being convinced by his flattery. "He could come with us."

"He can't," said Ghast.

"This is stupid."

She stormed to the cupboard, bringing out five paper bags of sandwiches, and placed them on the table. One had a red bow.

"Packed lunches," she said grumpily. "Including one for *Grandad*." She shot him a dark look. "Yours has a little extra," she told Brace. "Maybe you could bring me something back from the Ark as a present?"

"O-Okay."

Sally turned on her heels and stomped off to her room, slamming the door.

"Don't you worry about her," said Ghast. "She'll calm down."

The front door clicked open, and Ester came in, rubbing her hands. "Chilly," she said.

"Any joy?" asked Fera.

"Yes, got through." Ester took her Shell out of her ear and slipped it into her pocket. "Dad says we should go but be cautious.

158

And he has a message for you, Professor: Meddling in Ancient technology has got Light Hunters in trouble before. Remember that."

"Good, good," said Ghast, coming to the front room. "I knew your father would recognise a good idea when he heard one."

For the next half hour, the Light Hunters ate as much breakfast as they could – Ghast repeatedly warning them that the journey to the Ark would be a long one. Lux didn't need telling twice. He ate a pile of eggs and toast as big as his head.

"Now," said the professor, as they finished another helping, "it's not the smoothest sailing from here to the Ark. But it is downriver. But if we make good time, we'll be there by lunch."

He showed them on a map where they were heading. Ester copied it with her Gauntlet.

"You said yesterday this place was dangerous. Are we talking Monsters?"

"It's more the building itself. It's hard to explain. Best just to see it."

Ghast started to clear their plates before they could ask him any more questions.

His boat was locked in a shed behind the barn, out towards the woods. He got the Light Hunters to drag it out. It was Light-powered – brightly coloured with reds, blues and whites, although all the paint was chipped. A name on the side read, 'Happy Monster'.

"Sally's idea," Ghast explained.

The frozen ground made dragging the boat a little easier. It was lovely in the woods, with sunshine falling through the branches like rain.

They reached the river – a broad channel flowing fast and free. In the bank was a mooring post, to which Ghast had Lux and Ester tie the boat. It strained in the water, knocking against the rocks.

"You're also going to get very wet here," said Ghast, rolling his sleeves. "I suggest if you have any blankets, get them out now."

After a bit of effort, they managed to get under way, twisting and turning at a fair pace as the river swept them along. Soon, it levelled out, and they were floating alongside a well-trodden path.

"I must ask," Ghast spoke to Lux quietly, "before we go on, you do have the Key, don't you?"

Lux opened his bag, lifting the heavy sphere.

"Good." Ghast indicated for him to put it away with a worried glance at the water. "Keep it safe. We'll need that before the day is done."

The professor guided them with a long stick. In the distance, Lux spied what had to be the outcrops that formed the passage Ghast had mentioned back at the cottage, and beyond that, the great trees of the Shengan Jungle.

Somewhere inside was their destination.

· CHAPTER 31 ·

The cliffs rose up either side of them, topped with tall trees. The flow of the river soon eased somewhat, and then they were cutting through the crystal blue.

"How did you find this place anyway?"

The professor, still using his stick to pick out their route, turned at Brace's question and gave him a searching look. "Are you asking because you truly want to know, or because you still don't believe in my work?"

Brace went red, realising that Ghast had overheard his conversation with Lux and Fera that morning.

The professor sighed. "If you must know, with great difficulty. After Dawnstar, I learned there were a lot more Ancient ruins than I'd ever imagined. Hundreds. But it wasn't until I looked into the *Turn* cast that I first came across a place called the Ark.

"It was clear, instantly, that it was important. The Ancients talked about it with reverence. 'A tower that guarded the world.'

"Soon, I began to find links between *Turn* and the Ark, but I could never find the place. I read old books, visited old ruins. Nothing.

"Then one day, quite by chance, I met a travelling scholar at the university in Lindhelm. Odd fellow, not a hair on his body. His head looked like that Key of yours, Lux. He'd been researching something similar, and he had the entrance of the tower narrowed to the edge of the Shengan Jungle.

"As you can imagine, this renewed my determination, and I scoured the roots of the fire trees, burning myself on more than one occasion."

He showed the Light Hunters his forearm and the purple scars beneath his tattoos.

"Then I found it. The scholar was right. I purchased our cottage near Ravenholm and have been carrying on my research ever since."

The river turned around a sharp bend, before dropping down to a flat plain. Beyond that was the Shengan Jungle.

Lux had heard about the jungle his whole life: a forest whose canopy was literally on fire. But he'd never seen it up close. It was clear the fire trees were enormous – as tall as five houses. Their spade-shaped leaves were thick, creating a wall of red topped with black smoke. Below, huge trunks stabbed the dark jungle floor. The River Shengan flowed straight into them.

"Don't worry, it's not as dangerous as it looks," said Ghast. "As long as you watch out for falling leaves. It's a defence mechanism, you know?" They were so close now that Lux could feel the heat of the flames on his forehead. "Used to be flocks of Perosaurs and they'd eat the leaves. The trees evolved the fire to stop them."

Soon, the air tasted of smoke, growing so thick that they could hardly see more than a few metres. They floated on, like driftwood.

If Ghast was telling the truth, if the Ark really contained something to tame all Monsters, then they were doing something incredible. Perhaps the most incredible thing the Light Hunters had ever done, Lux thought. And without him, they couldn't do it at all. But what if he couldn't control his Twilight?

He was woken from his thoughts when the *Happy Monster* butted against a wooden jetty on the riverbank just before the jungle. Ghast tied the boat, helping out the Hunters, who came away shakily, happy to be on firm ground again. A stone path led up and down a small rise into the trees.

"We walk from here," said Ghast, swinging on his pack and setting off.

The inside of the jungle was eerily silent, with only the distant cracks and pops of burning wood to break the quiet. The trunks of the fire trees were enormous, two metres wide or more, and the ground was hard and ashy. Tiny embers fell like rain.

"It's not far," said Ghast.

Soon, they came across a very curious thing – an almost perfectly rectangular pond, behind a stone plinth about as high as Lux. The water was thick and gloopy, and next to it was an abandoned camp.

"I don't know why they needed a fire," said Brace. "It's not like it's cold."

He was right. Outside the jungle it had been winter, inside it was a summer's day. Lux took off his jacket and the other Hunters did the same.

When they finally reached the Ark, Lux could hardly believe it was there.

Their route took them into a dip, where there were dozens of holes in the ashy ground, as if somebody had spent an afternoon digging for treasure. Then into a clearing. Here, there were no fire trees, and cold air poured in from above. Grass was growing in the ash, fighting for space amongst small rocks.

In the clearing's centre was another pond, this one filled with blue fish and tiny, leaping frogs. Ghast stopped them in an open patch of grass with another rectangular podium. He turned and looked at them.

"What?" said Ester.

"We're here."

The closest thing to a tower that Lux could see was a tall boulder to his right. But compared to the Ancient ruins he'd seen near Daven, it was a matchstick. If this was their important tower, he wasn't very impressed.

"Sometimes, in life, you have to look from a different perspective," said Ghast.

He crouched beside the pond and reached into the water. There was a scraping sound, then something peeled away and the liquid disappeared, leaving a hole in the ground. Lux looked into the darkness. The water had drained and it was silent. The air coming up from below was icy cold.

"Is this *it*?" said Brace.

"Like I say, sometimes you must look at things from a different perspective," said Ghast. He indicated deeper into the jungle, where there was another podium, and another beyond that.

For a moment, Lux was confused.

Then something clicked.

The ashy floor, the holes. If this was a tower, the only way it could be was if . . .

"It's on its side," he said, suddenly understanding. "The tower's on its side."

· CHAPTER 32 ·

A horizontal tower.

An enormous one, as tall as any building in Lindhelm. Buried underground. It was incredible.

"Now do you understand why it might be dangerous?" said Ghast.

The Light Hunters stared.

"How?" Brace spluttered.

"I don't know for sure. My guess would be something to do with Monsters. There are rumours of a big fight occurring here centuries ago. Only Monsters would be big enough to knock over a tower of this size."

It would have to be massive, even for a Monster, thought Lux.

"It's a tunnel," said Brace.

Lux tried to see what was in the hole where the pond had been, but it was too dark, and all he could hear was the slow drip of water.

Ghast beckoned for him to join him at the edge. "You're a Healer, aren't you? Toss a *Catch* down."

A layer of sweat formed on Lux's neck. He still wasn't ready to throw Light. "I . . . uh . . ."

"We'll use my Gauntlet, it'll be quicker," said Ester, rescuing him.

Ghast shot Lux an inquisitive glance, then shrugged.

Ester fired a Light-thread into the gap, illuminating more strange podiums below, which were covered in dust and were wet from the pondwater. The thread pierced stone about six metres down. The back wall of the fallen tower, Lux realised dizzily.

"Remember, you're still in charge," Ester told Fera, who looked suddenly nervous at the thought.

Gripping Ester, the Light Hunters and Ghast made their way slowly into the dark, shivering in the cold. They landed on the tower's vertical wall – their floor as they stood. Fera got Ester to light up her Gauntlet, while she cast a *Flame*, wrapping them in a bubble of Light.

Other than a set of footprints in the dust which Lux took to be Ghast's from before, the building looked like it hadn't been used in centuries. The prints led deeper into the tower, avoiding rectangular holes filled with dirt that must have once been windows. On the wall to Lux's right – the tower's floor – were more stone podiums, tattooed with some kind of blue-violet energy. Light, he wondered? Or Twilight?

"We mustn't touch the Ancient artefacts," warned Ghast, slapping Brace's hand to stop him poking a nearby mural. "This place is a treasure chest of knowledge. I wouldn't want it ruined because some curious Light Hunter couldn't keep his hands to himself."

For the next few minutes, they tracked the professor's route through a series of rooms, calling on Ester's Gauntlet every time they needed to get past an awkwardly placed staircase. Lux noticed a purple thread tracing his steps, lighting up his boots. It was like the Light-decorated floors at Dawnstar.

Fera fell in alongside him. "You're not using your Light," she said bluntly.

Lux didn't know what to say.

"Don't think I haven't noticed. You haven't used it since you broke my arm."

Lux would love to have told Fera about his worries but what could he say? He was afraid? "I'm fine, honest. Just not had much need, that's all."

Fera gave him a sceptical look. "It's okay, you know. I wasn't lying before the celebration evening. We've got your back. If anything goes wrong."

"I know."

Fera shook her head, exasperated. "You're hard work, Lux Dowd, do you know that?"

As they continued through the rooms, Lux started to notice artwork in the tower's sides. There were stick figures, tall buildings, and huge creatures that had to be Monsters.

Ghast joined him as he admired one. "I can't understand all of it, but I think they depict Ancient life."

Lux picked out white and red sections of the art that had to be Light and Shade, and further off, a large section the same purple as his Twilight.

"We think of the Ancients as a force of evil, in spite of their obvious intelligence. Because of what they've left us with. But they were ordinary people like us. Again, it's all a matter of perspective. Perhaps their creation of Monsters was necessary."

The rooms dragged on. Fifty paces, staircase, fifty paces, staircase . . .

Then something new. A room much wider, or taller, as it would have been when upright, with rows and rows of shiny black squares on the walls.

Brace went to touch one.

"Do not!" said Ghast sharply. "I have yet to work out what they are. I found similar in the ruins beneath Dawnstar the day Ester's mum . . ." He trailed off.

"It's okay, you can say it. The day she died."

"Indeed."

All of a sudden, Lux felt a sense of danger he hadn't before. They were wandering though the Ark, but what did they really know about it? Deimos was searching for it, he knew that. He'd told Lux in Kofi . . . And the ice-Monster, the white place. Ark. Ghast could be right about the Monster taming, but what if he wasn't?

It was getting cold now. Lux could see his breath as they passed through more rooms full of the polished black squares. Every whisper made an echo.

Climbing past another staircase, they at last reached their destination.

The walls were humming with a dull Twilight, turning everything purple. To their right – the tower's floor when upright – was another podium like the one outside. This time, it presented a carving of the three-peaked mountain on the Key to the Ark. On top, was a jigsaw piece of stone.

"This is as far as I've come," said Ghast, speaking into the darkness. He approached the stone wall by the podium. "This barrier has blocked my every attempt to get through. Until now. Lux, the Key."

Lux looked to Ester to check he should go ahead. She referred him to Fera, who nodded.

He took out the heavy Key, which tugged gently apart at his touch. Ghast stepped back, glee evident on his face. The hairs on Lux's neck stood on end. Behind this wall, if Ghast was right, they would find what they needed to put an end to Monster attacks once and for all.

Turning the Key so that its missing jigsaw piece lined up with the one on the podium, he felt it get drawn towards it, connecting with a loud click. There was a sudden *whoosh* and Twilight lit up the space, bringing to life swirling patterns on the walls.

Ester and Fera put out their lights.

They all waited.

There was another loud click and the Key to the Ark lifted slowly. Lux drew it to his chest, its normally cold, smooth surface pleasantly warm.

"What now?" said Brace.

But nobody needed to answer. Because a second later there came a loud scraping sound, and the wall that had kept the professor at bay slid swiftly and quietly aside.

· CHAPTER 33 ·

If you'd told Lux the previous morning, as he stepped into Tesla's teleporter, that by lunch the following day he'd have learned the name of his mysterious power and would be just moments from using it to find out how to stop Monster attacks once and for all, he wouldn't have believed you. But as he climbed through the opening in the Ark, that was precisely what was about to happen.

The group emerged into a small bowl, into which they had to descend, using the Light-thread in Ester's Gauntlet. They landed on the far wall with a *thud*, staring wide-eyed at what was around them.

"Well, I guess that's the end of the line," said Fera.

In the centre of the room was another stone podium, surrounded by a thick bubble of energy. Inside, was another jigsaw piece – only rather than stone, this one was formed of Twilight.

Flanking the podium were two things Lux had never seen

before. They appeared to be statues, formed of a dark metal like the Key to the Ark. They were shaped like people, and yet not. They had to be three metres tall, and were constructed of separate panels held together by some kind of energy. Light? Shade? Lux wasn't sure. If he had to compare the statues to anything, it would be the clockwork toys from his grandpa's repair shop. But these were no toys.

"*This*," said Ghast, looking up in wonder at the two statues, "is what I have been searching for."

He got his notebook out of his bag.

"'*Where the man and sphere collide, an end to Monsters resides.*' I read this about the Ark a decade ago. I believe here is where we'll find what we need."

Ghast reached up delicately to touch the statues' metal frames, amazed.

"Professor . . ." prodded Ester.

"Sorry. I get carried away." He came back. "Lux, if you'd put your Key in, we'll surely find what we came for."

Lux approached the Twilight bubble. Gentle heat poured off it, warming the room. He trembled, as if his body was reacting.

The podium was inside the bubble. Lux figured this was why Ghast needed him. Nobody could get through it but him. He had a duty, to every child who'd lost a parent to a Monster, to every parent who'd lost a child . . .

And yet . . .

Something was wrong.

Lux didn't know how he knew, but he knew. He recalled his

words to Maya back at Dawnstar. "*Something is happening.*" It was. Even though he didn't understand what. The Key to the Ark, the ice-Monster, Ghast . . .

"I don't think we should do this," he said, stepping back.

The Hunters woke from transfixed stares.

"You must," said Ghast. "You must. The fate of so many depends on you."

The room was freezing now. Ice cold. Lux shivered. "We should wait. Speak to Dawnstar again."

"We've waited long enough. The Key, Lux."

The heat of the Twilight bubble had completely gone now, and Lux was trembling.

"I-I r-really don't—"

In an instant, the room went black, leaving the Light Hunters and Ghast in silence. A horrible chill closed in.

Then footsteps.

"I am afraid you'll do this whether you choose to or not."

Lux knew the voice as well as his own. Quiet one moment and loud the next. Always threatening, violence running beneath its surface.

A flash of red, and the Twilight returned. Standing in front of them was Deimos and the ice-Monster.

Lux sank into a pit of despair. He'd known all along that Deimos wasn't gone. They'd never found his body.

He hadn't changed at all. He was still tall and stocky, with grey hair and a thick cigar between his lips. His black coat was covered in leather straps, and his face was pock-marked. But his eyes . . .

174

his eyes *were* different. Angrier. Darker. Any remaining Light had been lost to Shade.

Somehow, beside Deimos, the ice-Monster was the lesser threat. It stood like a guard-dog, its crystal skin throwing off ice.

Stupid.

How could Lux have been so stupid?

Back at the graveyard the Monster had been a surprise. But Ravenholm? He should have known *that* was no coincidence.

Ester and the others leapt into attack-stance, ignoring the draining cold that clawed at them. But before they could throw any Light, Deimos waved a hand and four Shade bubbles swallowed them and Ghast. The Hunters beat at the red energy, fists slamming, but they stopped at Ester's command. It was no use.

"Let me out!" yelled Brace.

"Quiet!" snarled Deimos. "You have inconvenienced me enough already. My business is not with you."

Lux was the only one free of Shade. He searched desperately for some way to release his friends, but he was just a Healer. Even if he *could* control his Light, there was nothing he could do.

Deimos threw his cigar behind him and walked slowly to Ghast's Shade bubble.

"It's been fascinating watching you this last year, old friend." He poked the Shade like a cat playing with a mouse. "Fascinating."

As Deimos talked, a change seemed to come over him. Red Shade formed a cloak around him and then disappeared, revealing another Deimos, this one's black coat replaced with a smart shirt and tie. But it was the hair that interested Lux. Or the complete lack of it.

"I enjoyed our little meeting," Deimos told Ghast, his voice lighter, friendlier. "Always wonderful to discuss the finer points of the Ancients, don't you think?" He conjured a Shade book, turning the pages like a curious professor. "And always happy to aid a fellow scholar."

Ghast did a double-take. "No . . . you?"

"Yes, it was me," said Deimos, his usual clothes returning. "Of course it was. It was me who told you where to find the Ark. Me who hinted you'd need the Key."

"But—"

"You always were a fool, Emory." Deimos pushed his former friend's Shade bubble against the wall.

"And *you*," he turned to Lux like a tiger. "You . . ."

Lux's heart jumped.

"You . . ." Shade enveloped Deimos again. This time, when he returned, he was dressed as the magician they'd encountered in Lindhelm. "*Sometimes*," he said, echoing his parting words to Lux, "*when we think we're makin' the right choice, we're actually makin' the wrong one.*"

Deimos threw his head back, laughing. So full of malice that Lux shuddered.

No . . .

"You've all danced like puppets on a string. Tesla, your father, Ester, all of you. Who do you think has been feeding Tesla the pieces of the Key? Who sent the ice-Monster to set this whole thing in motion?"

176

Deimos paraded triumphantly, lighting another cigar. He blew smoke over their Shade bubbles.

"You stopped me last year, I concede. But this time my plan will come to pass. Our world will be free, at last, from its Monster plague."

"Please, Deimos, let us out," said Ghast. "We've found a way to tame them."

Deimos exploded in laughter, each burst a jagged saw-blade. "You still believe you'll find a way to *tame* the Monsters here?" He pressed his face into Ghast's Shade bubble. "Your little *Turn* is nothing more than a cheap trick." He spun, throwing out his hands to encompass the amphitheatre. "The Ark wasn't built to *tame* Monsters, Emory; it was built to destroy them."

· CHAPTER 34 ·

Hope can sometimes be a dangerous thing. It allows us to fly so high that when we come down the fall is all the harder. Lux knew Ghast's world of tamed Monsters was a long shot. But he'd hoped all the same.

A trick.

That's all it was. All it had ever been.

"H-How . . . w-what . . ." spluttered Ghast.

"Stop mumbling, Professor, you're making yourself sound foolish." Deimos approached the clockwork figures either side of the Twilight podium. "It's actually very simple. These," he tapped the metal foot of the huge creature, "are Hex. They were built by the Ancients as a sort of . . . how can I put it? As a sort of back-up.

"See, once they became proficient enough with Shade to create their Monsters, they learned something we've learned many times since: that our creations do not always act as we intend."

Deimos laughed loudly. Beside him, the ice-Monster shifted threateningly, trailing icy air. Lux stepped back.

"The Monsters ran wild, of course. The Ancients lost control. No longer were they setting Monsters on other cities; the Monsters were *choosing* where to attack. And we know how that ends."

Deimos flashed them a devilish grin. Lux felt sick.

"Ever creative, how did our Ancient forebears deal with their creations? By creating something else to deal with them."

Deimos indicated the statues, which were reflecting the purple light.

"Horrible things, Hex. Twilight automatons. No emotion, no empathy. There are thousands of them. Built to destroy Monsters. Just waiting for the signal."

Lux grimaced. The Hex's razor limbs could slice off an arm.

"But, of course, we never learn. The Ancients made another mistake. The Hex didn't just get rid of Monsters. They got rid of *everything* alive." Deimos grinned, clearly enjoying himself. "Hundreds of thousands of people gone . . . just like that." He clicked his fingers.

"There was a time when I would have been as horrified as you. No more. The Ancients set this Monster plague on us. But it is we who've allowed it to grow. It is fools like your father, Ester, who have failed to take the actions necessary to remove these creatures from our world. I will."

Deimos stalked towards Lux. Ester yelled for Lux to run, but Deimos waved a hand, and her Shade bubble shrank, until she could no longer speak. "If we lose a few people, that's a small price to pay to start again. If we lose a *lot* of people, that is still a small price to pay."

Lux flinched at Deimos's anger. His eyes flew to his squad-mates, but all he saw was panic.

"None of this would have been possible without you, Lux. Though I wish you'd listened last year when I tried to bring you to my side by choice. But you've forced me to be more creative in my methods. I suppose it only makes our eventual victory all the greater."

Lux's throat was completely dry. He needed to say something, to fight, but his thoughts scraped his mind like spikes.

"We don't need—"

Deimos scoffed. "Don't waste your breath, Lux. I have long since lost my faith in this world. Come here."

Lux shrank away.

"I said come here!"

Deimos flashed up to him at terrifying speed, dragging him to the Twilight barrier. Brace and Fera shouted out, but Deimos waved his hand and their Shade barriers tightened.

"Put the Key inside." Deimos indicated the Twilight barrier and the podium within.

"N-No," stammered Lux. His mind was spinning. But there was one thing he was sure of – whatever Deimos wanted him to do, he could still say 'No.'

"Do it!" snarled Deimos.

"No."

The big man breathed, mastering his patience. "I was afraid this might happen."

He studied Lux's friends, trapped in Shade, and pointed a finger at each in turn. He grinned wolfishly as he landed on Fera.

In a flash, the young girl's Shade bubble disappeared. She went instantly to throw a *Flame*, but before she could the ice-Monster had pinned her against the wall.

"With just one word, this Monster will snap your friend's neck." As Deimos spoke, the creature applied pressure and Fera cried out. "Now you have a choice, Lux. You can carry out my instructions, or you can watch your friend die."

Lux felt like he was about to throw up all over the Ark's walls. The skin of Fera's body where the Monster was touching her was turning blue.

"Please, let her go."

"I will, as soon as you do as I ask," said Deimos lazily. "I will let all of you go. You have my word."

Lux couldn't. If what Deimos had said was true, the Hex would attack. Monsters, animals . . . people. He swallowed hard, his panic flooding him like an overflowing river. What could he do?

"Please, Deimos. I'll do anything else. We'll find another way."

"The Key . . ."

Fera was crying out in pain now. The ice-Monster, its skin as hard as crystal, was twisting her into the wall.

Lux couldn't. He *couldn't*. If the Hex killed only Monsters, maybe. If they left people alone, maybe he'd do it in spite of what Ghast had achieved with Rory . . .

No.

Lux saw his grandpa, the orange *Revive* cast hanging over his lifeless body in Kofi. Then Deimos. Then sadness. He missed his grandpa so much. So much. He couldn't lose anyone else.

"Deimos—"

"Break her on three," Deimos instructed the ice-Monster.

No, no.

Lux wanted to strike Deimos, kill him. But there was nothing he could do. He was too big, too strong. And Lux was alone.

"One . . ."

Help me.

"Two . . ."

Help.

"Thr—"

"STOP!"

Lux yelled so loud that the word echoed around the Ark.

"I'll do it!"

"No!" shouted Fera. But her cry died in a scream as the ice-Monster twisted again.

"I'll do it," Lux told Deimos. "Let her go."

Deimos waited for him to approach the barrier around the podium.

Lux breathed, stepping forward. The second step was easier, then the third, until he reached the Twilight. "I don't know how—"

"Walk," said Deimos.

Lux hated his power, his Twilight. He'd hated it since it had first appeared. Why him?

"One step," said Deimos, his eyes gleaming.

The Twilight barrier fell like a curtain. The black stone podium glowed blue in the light of the ice-Monster, the purple jigsaw piece sticking out like a dagger.

"Put it in."

Lux was holding the Key like it was made of gold, his fingers digging into the dark metal. He looked sadly at Fera, Brace, Ester and Ghast.

"I'm sorry," he said. And he slotted the Key inside.

· CHAPTER 35 ·

Lux had never been one for revenge. Even when one of his classmates had painted over his grandpa's shop sign to wind him up, he'd not got them back. And the previous year, no part of him had wanted to hurt Deimos like Deimos had hurt his grandpa. "If we all went around poking out the eyes of people who wronged us, everybody would be blind," his grandpa always said.

But Lux swore to himself, as the Key to the Ark locked into place, that he would get Deimos back this time.

There was a loud *bang*, then shaking. Dust rained on them from above and Twilight flashed on and off, settling to a soft purple. The walls, which had been in shadow before, lit up, revealing dozens more of the polished black squares they'd seen in the other rooms.

Quickly, the black fronts slid aside, revealing hidden Hex. Big, hulking, dangerous. They had purple lights in their chests, and they moved, unbending stiff limbs and climbing out of their chambers.

"Yes!" shouted Deimos. "Yes! At last!"

He backed away, indicating for the ice-Monster to join him by the exit.

"You've done a wonderful thing today, Lux Dowd. Those who remain will sing your name."

Without realising it, Lux had taken the Key back into his shaking hands.

"And I am a man of my word." The red Shade bubbles around Ester, Brace and Ghast disappeared. Ester and Brace raced to Fera, who was lying on the floor, gasping for air. "I said that I wouldn't harm your friends and I meant it." He smiled sadistically at the Hex climbing out of the walls. "They, however . . ."

Deimos disappeared, followed closely by the ice-Monster, who faded swiftly into the darkness.

"Lux, why did you do that?" shouted Brace.

Why *had* he done it? The podium, the Key. Whatever happened next was all because of him.

"No time for that," shouted Ester, pulling Fera to her feet. "Talk later, fight now."

The Hex were herding them against the wall. There had to be twenty of them, and loud, metallic clanks floated along the corridor as more woke up. They were huge creatures, with limbs like Light-blades.

"Brace!"

Ester's shout woke the younger Hunter from a horrified stare, and he went to conjure his Light-bow instinctively. Nothing happened.

"Erm . . ."

He tried again, backing away from the Hex. "I can't!"

Brace's normally relaxed tone was panicked. He tried again, but still nothing.

"Fera?" called Ester.

Fera tried to form a *Snow*, but the white Light fizzled out.

"Ghast, tell me what's happening."

"I don't know!"

Ester cast her concerned eyes over the Hex. She settled on one quite a bit taller than the rest. A different type? Floating above its head was a symbol formed of Twilight – two vertical lines joined by a horizontal third.

"It's stopping our Light," she said, pressing a button on her Gauntlet, just in case it would work. It sat silently on her arm.

"Get us out of here, Ghast!"

The professor almost jumped. He climbed towards the exit Deimos had taken a moment before, followed by Ester, and Brace, helping Fera.

Ester noticed halfway up the stairs that Lux hadn't moved. "Lux!"

He looked around slowly. What had he done? What had he *done*?

"Lux!"

Somehow, he forced his legs to move, climbing to where the others were waiting. Behind him, the Hex had shaken off their centuries of sleep and were picking up their speed.

"Come on!"

Brace helped Lux, and then they were running, almost in total darkness, trying to make their way back through the Ark by memory alone. All around them was hot metal and smoke, and Lux saw flashes of Twilight as more Hex awoke.

"Run!" screamed Ester.

They zig-zagged through the looming figures, diving under sweeping metal limbs and using the automatons' Twilight as a guide. Their escape seemed to go on for minutes, accompanied by the *stomp-stomp* of the chasing Hex.

"Keep going!"

Lux's legs were burning, and his chest was on fire.

A blur of daylight – soft blue against the heavy darkness. Lux and the others raced towards it, slowing underneath the opening. Ester used a metal pipe to swing herself up, then put an arm down for Brace. Together, they helped Fera and Ghast out. Lux came last, still in a daze.

The wintry daylight was blinding after the darkness. Lux had to cover his eyes for a good while before he could open them properly. All around, they could feel the Ark lurching and rumbling.

Below them, a dozen Hex were already climbing out of the hole, their Twilight chests bright purple. Brace picked up a couple of stones to try and stop them, but they skipped off the automatons' metal skin like they were made of air.

"Uh, guys . . ." said Fera.

Lux turned to see twenty, thirty, forty more Hex emerging out of holes around the clearing.

Ester pushed Ghast towards the burning forest, but before he could move one of the Hex spotted them and closed in. More came from all angles.

"Oh, Light!" moaned Ghast. "Oh, Sally."

Ester tapped her Gauntlet, trying to get something out of it. Brace and Fera tried their Light too but there were at least three more of the taller Hex with Twilight symbols, blocking it.

The Hunters and Ghast grouped together. Lux's heart was pounding. What had he done?

"If anyone has any good ideas . . ." said Fera.

No answer.

Grandpa, if you can hear me . . . thought Lux.

It wasn't old Ben Dowd who came to their rescue, but a flash in the sky. It was tiny at first, just a flickering red dot. But it was dropping at a dizzying speed. Lux saw a pair of wings, and some claws. And a head of blonde hair whipping in the wind.

"Sally!"

Ghast's granddaughter, riding on the back of Rory, came tearing in like fire, bowling over the Hex. The creatures swung their razor limbs at the new threat, but it was no use. Sally carved out a wide circle around the Light Hunters and Ghast, bringing Rory down in the gap. His claws dug into the earth with a soft *thud.* She grinned, scanning the clearing in wonder.

"There was a young girl called Sally,
Who never did as she was told.
She hoped her grandad wouldn't be angry,
Or else she wouldn't live 'til she was old."

"Glad I decided to come?" she said challengingly.

"Oh, yes," said Ghast, helping them all onto Rory. The Monster stalked back and forth, glaring at the Hex.

"Wait a minute, he flies?" said Brace.

Sally flicked the Monster's reins in answer, and Rory beat his broad wings, parting the grass beneath him and shooting into the air.

The Hex shrank to the size of ants. Lux counted at least a hundred of them, maybe more. They all tracked Rory as he disappeared into the clouds, then as one they turned towards the exit of the clearing.

Slowly, inexorably, they started to march.

· CHAPTER 36 ·

Sally managed to get them up so high that the burning jungle disappeared beneath the clouds. Rory beat his massive wings, each sinew cracking loudly.

"You are one *naughty* little girl," Ghast told his granddaughter, despite his relief. "I told you to stay at home. You could have been hurt."

"Not with Rory protecting me."

"Seriously, why didn't anybody tell me we could fly Rory?" said Brace, marvelling at the Monster's smooth, fiery wings.

"Hush," said Ester. She had a finger to her Shell, trying to contact Dawnstar.

Through gaps in the clouds, Lux could see the clearing. The full impression of the Ark was clear now, pushing up trees, so that there was a thick line where the flames were taller, like a vein under the skin.

They should never have come.

It had all been too easy. Taming Monsters – as simple as visiting Ancient ruins. If it was that simple, someone would have found it centuries ago, Lux thought. Why, *why* had he been so stupid?

"Any luck?" he asked Ester numbly.

She shook her head.

The flight back to Ghast's cottage was so peaceful that it felt wrong. The quiet, the sun, the beautiful clouds . . . it would have been charming if not for the streams of Hex pouring out below.

"How could all of these have stayed hidden?" said Fera, amazed.

Nobody had an answer.

"So, did you get me a present?" Sally asked Brace as Fenrir Mountain swung into view, a grey mass covered with snow.

Ghast looked at his granddaughter fondly. "Not now, Sally."

"He promised."

"Later, sweetheart."

Not understanding why everyone was so upset, Sally brought them down in the courtyard outside Ghast's cottage, Rory flapping his wings like bellows. The Light Hunters and Ghast jumped off, while Sally led the Monster into the barn, grabbing her bucket of water.

The cottage seemed oddly silent after their time at the Ark. Strange. Something incredible had happened – the first time in thousands of years – and yet there they were, sitting around as if they were back at Dawnstar. But what else could they do?

"Do you have any way to boost a signal?" Ester took her Shell out of her ear and showed Ghast.

"My lab downstairs," he said, distracted. "There's a booster."

Ester went off without another word, her face a mask of worry.

"We've got to do something," said Brace.

"Like what? Until Ester gets hold of Dawnstar, we're stuck," said Fera.

The three Hunters sat, their legs bouncing nervously, while the professor worked at creating a fire.

"A *Flame*," he prodded.

Fera joined her fingers, and they were all relieved to see a cast appear. "Well, at least our Light's working."

"Professor, I want to take Rory up, see how many Hex are coming out," said Brace.

Ghast looked up. "He's not a young Monster. He gets tired easily."

"Some other way then," snapped Brace. "You must have *something* in this house full of gizmos?"

Fera put a calming hand on his arm.

"Sorry," he said.

"It's all right, Brace," said the professor kindly. "Come with me."

Ghast led him to the kitchen, where there was a rotor-bladed device, similar to the Dusters back in Ravenholm, leaning against the cupboard.

"Feet in there," he said, tapping the pedals, "and you steer with the handles. Be careful, I've not flown it for a while. And don't go too high."

Brace headed towards the door.

"Don't you think you'd be better waiting—" began Fera.

"I need to be doing something."

Sally came back inside as Brace left, rubbing her hands to warm them. "It's so cold! I had to put my hands on Rory!" She took in their sour faces. "Okay, enough's enough. Will someone tell me what happened?"

Her grandad sat her on the sofa and told her everything: about the Ark, Twilight, the key, Deimos, the ice-Monster, the Hex. The whole lot.

Sally looked unimpressed. "That's a bit of a stupid name. 'Hex'."

For the first time since they'd left the Ark, Lux found himself smiling. But it didn't last long. Inside, he was struggling.

All the towns and villages – what would happen? If the army of Hex truly attacked Monsters *and* people . . . what could *anyone* do? The Light Hunters wouldn't be able to help. If they couldn't use their Light when the Hex were close, they were no better than anyone else.

Lux was happy when the basement door clicked open, and Ester appeared. She took in the mood, joining them by the fire.

"Not easy, but I got through. They know about the Hex. They're everywhere. At least seven villages surrounded and three Monster attacks. Sounds pretty bad."

Lux waited for her to share Dawnstar's plan or say something positive. Nothing came.

"What are we supposed to do?" he said mechanically. She had to have something.

"Sit tight. Tesla's working on how to get us back to HQ. He says he'll be in touch."

"We can't just do nothing," said Fera. "If they get to Ravenholm . . ." She trailed off, realising for the first time that her parents' home was at risk.

"We sit tight," said Ester. "This is the last point we should be heading off on our own."

She didn't add, Lux noted: *Because that's what got us into this mess in the first place.*

There was a loud clanking sound, and the front door flew open. Brace came back in, his cheeks red from the cold afternoon air. "Not good." He leaned the flying device against the wall. "They're like a flood."

"Where are they going?" asked Fera.

Brace didn't answer. Fera understood and bit her bottom lip anxiously.

Professor Ghast wandered to the fire. "What have we done? What have *I* done? I've been such a fool. I thought we were about to rid ourselves of this fight with Monsters once and for all. Instead, I've just given us another enemy. And the Monsters. The poor Monsters . . ."

"It wasn't just your fault—" Ester began.

"It was," said Ghast. "I led you here. I promised it was safe. It's me."

Ester began to argue, but Ghast shook his head and stormed off to the door in the kitchen that led to the rest of the house, slamming it shut behind him.

· CHAPTER 37 ·

Maya had once taught Lux a way to calm down that she'd learned from Mrs Piper at the orphanage. *Imagine an autumn leaf in your mind. Breathe out and it lifts, breathe in and it drops. Out and in, out and in. Do it long enough and your heartrate will slow.*

Lux breathed now, folded into the chair before the fireplace. Out and in, seeing that leaf.

It wasn't *only* the professor's fault. It was all of theirs. They should have all known better.

Out and in, out and in.

Lux stood, pacing to the door Ghast had just slammed. "I'll be back," he said.

He found the professor in his observatory, looking up at the sky. "Ester, give me a few minutes—"

"It's me," said Lux.

He pulled himself up into the dome's warmth. Outside, the sky was still crystal blue.

"I'm sorry about back there," said Ghast.

"It's okay."

"Strange to think they could be coming from anywhere. The Hex." Ghast looked at the trees behind his house, and the Shengan River, flowing down Fenrir Mountain.

Lux sat against the glass, running his fingers over his grandpa's Luminary badge. "It wasn't only you to blame," he said. "It was me too. I had the choice. It was me who Deimos tricked."

"You're a child," said Ghast.

"Maybe, but—"

"I've been a fool. So concerned with saving Monsters I let myself get tricked by that awful man." He shook his head regretfully.

There was a long silence. Through the glass, Lux heard Rory let out a lazy roar.

"When we first got here," he said, trying to order his thoughts, "and you were telling us not to attack the ice-Monster, I thought you were crazy. We all did. But after meeting Rory . . . I'm not sure you are wrong, Professor. Maybe *we've* been wrong all along. Maybe instead of fighting them, we should have been learning how to live with them."

Ghast turned from where he was looking out at the mountain and sank down next to Lux, groaning at his aching knees.

"I fought with your grandpa once, before he became Luminary," he said. "Brave man. We held a Griffin off a town for three hours. Mostly him. Boy did they feed us that night." Ghast rubbed his stomach at the memory.

"I'll be honest, I don't know how we reverse this, Lux. I don't know anything about the Hex."

"We'll find something," said Lux, surprised that he meant it. "You found the *Turn* cast. Nobody else found that. You'll find what we need."

Ghast smiled fondly. "That's what your grandpa said before our fight with the Griffin. I told him I was afraid. He told me to look for my courage. I told him I didn't have any. 'You'll find it,' he said."

"This isn't over," said Lux, standing. "If Deimos thinks he's beaten us, he's not reckoned with Squad Juno."

"Spoken like a true Dowd," said Ghast.

There was a moment's silence in which they looked out of the dome at the vast blue sky, then Ghast said: "You go down, I won't be long."

Lux descended into the dusty, book-filled corridor. He'd made it halfway back to the front room when he saw Sally coming in the other direction.

"Honestly, if I threw my toys out of the pram like that I'd be grounded for weeks!" She rolled her eyes at the observatory.

"Your grandad's just—"

"She's right," said Ghast, coming awkwardly down the ladder, carrying a pile of old books. He ruffled Sally's hair. "And once all this is finished, I'm going to let you punish me as you see fit."

Sally's eyes twinkled in anticipation.

She and Lux followed Ghast back down to the living area, where Brace and Fera were still watching the fire. Ghast headed straight for his basement, while Sally went out to check on Rory.

"What did you say to him?" asked Fera, impressed, as Lux sat down.

"Nothing much. We talked about Grandpa."

"Didn't think we'd end up playing agony aunts to grown-ups."

"If it weren't for us, I don't think anything would get done," said Brace.

A log snapped in the fire as Lux played with a loose thread on the sofa. "Where's Ester?"

"Speaking to Tesla outside."

Lux breathed deeply, seeing Maya's leaf again. *Out and in, out and in.* He was tired now and very hungry. Spotting a sandwich on the table, he leaned forward and took a bite. "You're not going back to Dawnstar, are you?" he said to Fera.

She and Brace shared a guilty glance. It was clear they'd been talking.

"No, I'm not."

Lux recalled how much trouble they'd got in last year for not following orders.

"And if she doesn't go, neither am I," said Brace.

"Ester will be mad," warned Lux.

"I was supposed to be in charge," said Fera. "So far I've done a rubbish job. She's been correcting me every step. I don't think I'm cut out for this leadership stuff. Maybe Barny's right, maybe I'm not really cut out for the Light Hunters at all—"

"Hey!" Brace cut in.

"But," she said pointedly, "I made this mistake and it's my family that are at risk. I'm not leaving until I know they're safe."

"I put the Key in," said Lux sadly. "I could have said no. It wasn't just you."

"That was Deimos," said Fera.

Lux wasn't going back either. He knew it already. No matter what Tesla or Nova said when they found out. He was the one who set the Hex loose; he had a responsibility to put them back. Or at least to try.

"I'm staying too."

Brace and Fera grinned. "Have you got any idea of what we can do?" said Fera.

"Not yet. But we'll find something."

"It won't be easy," said Brace. "Deimos."

"We've stopped him once."

The three kids looked guiltily among each other, like they were back at Dawnstar, in the middle of the night, stuffing themselves with food Brace had stolen from the kitchen.

"Who wants to be the one to tell Ester?" said Fera.

"Tell me what?"

They turned, feeling a cold draught from the front door. Standing in the frame, an inquisitive look on her face, was their squad leader.

· CHAPTER 38 ·

Apart from being the Luminary's daughter, Ester Nova was well known at Dawnstar for two things: being the only younger Light Hunter brave enough to argue with Legau Moreiss, even if she always got her head chewed off, and expecting her squad members to follow her orders at all times (unless they wanted to be in *big* trouble.) So, when Lux saw her leaning against Ghast's front door, having heard what they'd said, his heart skipped a beat.

"What did Tesla say?" asked Fera, trying to deflect Ester's question with one of her own.

The older girl studied the three of them, then joined them on the sofa, setting her question aside for the moment. "Not good," she said. "We're up to fourteen villages surrounded now and another two Monster attacks. The Hex have attacked Sandringham too. And some Monsters have been killed out in the wild."

Brace whistled. One or two Monster attacks a day was bad; five was awful.

"My dad's sending a skyship to pick us up. Ghast and Sally too. He thinks the professor will be useful. Should be here in a day or two."

None of the kids spoke. From the basement, they heard a loud crashing sound, as if the professor had knocked something over.

"Now, which one of you is going to tell me what you have to tell me?" said Ester, taking off her Gauntlet and laying it on the table. "Although by your scared-rabbit looks, I think I can already guess."

It was Fera who was brave enough to speak. "I'm not going back," she said simply. "None of us are. We're going to sort things here."

Ester let out a weary laugh. "What is it with you three and not following orders?"

"You put me in charge, and I let Lux put that Key in," said Fera. "You always take responsibility if something goes wrong. I will too."

"I put you in charge, but you're learning. I would have intervened if I thought we could do anything. Which we couldn't," Ester added.

"It doesn't matter. And it's not just that," said Fera. "My family . . . We set the Hex loose just down the road from them. If any place is going to be in danger, it's there."

Ester thought over what Fera had said, shaking her head

dubiously. "And what's your excuse?" she said to Lux and Brace.

"I did this, Ester," said Lux. "I was the one who put the Key in. Fera thinks it's all her fault, but it isn't. It was my Twilight and I hate it. I hate that there's Shade in me. But if we go back to Dawnstar, we won't be able to do anything. We'll just be stuck. But Ghast *might* come up with something here. He knows more about the Ancients than anyone. He's already looking, I think. I can't go back in case he needs me."

Lux met Ester's hard gaze, refusing to back down.

"And you?" she said, shifting her attention to Brace. "Are you going to tell me you feel responsible too?"

"No chance! It's them two all the way. But I go where they go. They know that. It's not changing now."

Ester planted her hands on the kitchen counter. "A Luminary's daughter not even able to control her own squad," she said, half-amused, half-despairing.

"It's nothing personal," said Fera.

"You three know my dad has a plan, right? Us not following instructions might wreck that."

The younger Hunters shifted uncomfortably. "He had a plan last year too," said Lux, summoning his courage, "and if we hadn't ignored that and fought the Cerberus, a lot of people might have died."

Ester tapped the counter, thinking. Over the other side of the room, a grandfather clock chimed loudly.

"I think this is a very bad idea," she said. "We're dealing with a new threat here, as well as the old one and now Deimos. But . . ."

She let the word hang. ". . . we agreed last year that if we ever had differences of opinion again, we'd vote on it. So, are your minds made up?"

The three kids nodded.

"Very well," she said, massaging her temples. "I hope you have a plan though, because I don't."

"*I* might be able to help you with that."

Ghast was standing in the doorway to the basement, carrying an open book, his shirt sleeves rolled up as if he'd been hard at work. "In fact, I'm pretty sure I will. But I might need your help first. If you'd all like to follow me . . ."

The four Light Hunters accompanied him down the steep stairs, which smelled faintly of mould. They emerged in his underground lab.

If it had been a mess before when Sally showed them around, now it resembled a town after a Monster attack. The tables had been cleared and objects were piled on the floor. Open books were scattered all about, as well as bottles of strange liquid. A tall bookcase had been knocked over, generating a pulsing orb of Light on the floor, and all the wooden chests were open, spilling their contents like mini avalanches.

"In case you can't tell from the mess, I've been searching for something," said Ghast, kicking aside a couple of books. "You might have heard a little crash earlier." He indicated a smashed chamber, which had left a carpet of glass on the floor.

"It looks like this." He showed them the book, which was full of neat writing in a language Lux didn't understand, and a single sketch. The picture was of a chunk of stone – turquoise, laced with what looked like Twilight.

"I don't know where it is. I don't know what it might be under. But find me this piece and I might be able to give you the answers you're looking for."

· CHAPTER 39 ·

Lux had always been good at finding things. At Dawnstar, he was the one Ester sent to locate her Gauntlet whenever she lost it. Even back in Daven, if one of his grandpa's tools went missing, it was always Lux who found it. And so, when Ghast asked them to start looking for the stone, Brace and Fera turned instantly Lux's way for instructions.

"You, over there," he said, sending Brace to the collapsed shelves. "And you, there." He sent Fera to search the wooden chests.

"I'll be upstairs," said Ester, before he could give her a job, "explaining to my father why we *won't* be following his express orders."

Lux, Brace and Fera kept quiet as she thudded up the stairs.

Searching Ghast's lab for the stone was like trying to find a one particular grain of sand in a desert. Still, Lux went to Ghast's wall of plants and pulled objects out of the drawers, laying their contents in a neat pile.

"She seemed to take that well," said Brace, studying the orb of Light near the bookshelf in case there was anything hiding underneath.

"I think she wanted to stay here herself this time," said Fera, searching an old chest. "She just couldn't admit it."

Lux thought the same.

"I hope this stone is worth it, Professor," said Brace, wiping thick, yellow slime off his face that had just leaked out of what he'd thought was an empty bottle.

"If it contains what I think it does, it will be."

They carried on combing the room, examining anything that wasn't nailed down.

It was Lux who found what they were looking for.

He was momentarily distracted by a moth that swept up to the dusty lamp at the ceiling, when he saw a tiny thread of purple poking out of the joint between two wooden beams. At first, he thought he'd imagined it. But no, it was attached to something turquoise.

"Brace, give me a boost."

Lux climbed up and brought the item down. It was cold and smooth, and thankfully, he realised, precisely what they were looking for.

"Professor . . ."

Ghast took the stone from Lux, glancing at the ceiling. "Little monkey," he smiled.

"Who?"

"My granddaughter."

The three Light Hunters looked confused.

"She has this thing, when I get obsessed with something Ancient," he explained. "Says she gets lonely when she doesn't see me for weeks, so she comes down here when I'm not looking and hides stuff. She must have put this up there. Light knows how she managed it!" He wiped dust from the stone's surface.

Lux didn't know why, but the thought of Sally doing this made him sad.

Ghast had Fera fetch Ester, who came back looking frustrated. When Lux asked how the conversation with her father had gone, she ignored him and pushed for them to focus on the task at hand.

The professor had set up a little table now, onto which he'd positioned a strange golden device – three tall prisms joined at the bottom by a scratched black stand. In the centre was an orb of white Light. Ghast had cleared a wall nearby, leaving a blank space. He held up the turquoise stone.

"First principles, that's what the Inventor before me at Dawnstar always said to start with. You four are probably wondering what the Hex actually are, would that be correct? Beyond what Deimos told you?

They nodded.

"Well, the answer is I don't have a clue." Ghast slid the turquoise stone into the Light. "I wasn't lying when I said I hadn't come across them in my research. I have, however, come across things like them. But this is unimportant, because as it stands, we don't really *need* to know about the Hex or where they come from. What we need right now, as I am sure you will agree, is a way to stop them. And with that in mind: I present to you this Vision Stone." Ghast touched the turquoise rock, which wobbled in the device's field of Light.

"You probably haven't heard of these things before, as I doubt anyone who hasn't spent the last ten years exploring Ancient ruins would have. I've found dozens." He whipped aside a blanket on the floor, revealing more of the green stones.

Lux looked at the one in the device. Purple Twilight twisted and turned on its surface.

"They provide visions. Moving images of stories. Like a memory. My little device here is crude. It will only give us a shadow version of the story, but it'll allow us to see what is stored inside this Vision Stone."

"What *is* stored in it?" said Fera, sitting forward.

Ghast approached the lamp hanging at the ceiling and lowered its flame. "You've heard of Juno, yes? The hero that your squad and star is named after? Well, there are hundreds of such mythological stories. Thousands. But what people don't realise is that many of these stories originated not with us, but with the Ancients."

Ester gave Ghast a restless look.

"I am getting there, Miss Nova. You are as impatient today as you were as a little girl. Anyway, I always thought these tales were just that: tales. But after our adventure in the Ark . . ." Ghast hesitated, deciding how to carry on. "It is perhaps best if I show you."

He floated a *Flame* towards the prism device, which rode up into the Vision Stone. The turquoise started pulsing.

On the wall he'd cleared, a fuzzy shadow appeared, crystallising into the shape of something familiar, its edges sharp and defined.

It was a Hex.

· CHAPTER 40 ·

There was a fair that came to Daven once a year, run by the people who put on the plays at Kofi's theatre. Lux and Maya used to sneak into it without fail. Merry-go-rounds, giant see-saw rides, bumper carts. Lux's favourite stand by far was the shadow puppet shows, where skilled puppeteers put on performances as magical as any he'd seen on the stage. But even these were nothing compared to the shadow show projected by the Vision Stone.

It was like the Hex was in the room with them. The shape, the curve of the metal skull, the jerky movements . . .

"Wow . . ." said Brace.

Fera yelled at him as he wandered between the Vision Stone and the wall.

"The story's not long, but I believe it's very important to us," Ghast told the Light Hunters. "Watch carefully."

Up on the wall, the shadow-Hex moved, growing smaller.

A Monster joined it – an enormous wolf. More Hex marched into position alongside the first.

The attack was sudden.

The Hex surrounded the Monster, sweeping towards it, engulfing it.

When the Vision Stone changed again, the Monster was gone.

"Professor, we know they attack Monsters—"

Ghast hushed Fera, urging her to watch.

The Hex army was now surrounding a town, the houses outlined neatly in black. The Hex closed in, as tiny, stick-like figures marched out to meet them. They too, were swallowed by the Hex's tide.

"Do we really have to see this—" began Fera.

"Watch," urged Ghast.

The Vision Stone twisted again. The wall was blank now and Lux wondered if the prisms in the device had broken somehow. He was about to look, when another shadow appeared, one instantly recognisable.

Three peaks, the central one taller . . .

The same as the Key to the Ark.

"Wait," said Ghast as Lux was about to speak.

The three peaks grew smaller, their edges more defined. At their feet, an army of Hex came into focus. The mountains started to move, slowly coming together like jigsaw pieces, lining up so that they formed a single black peak.

"Now!" cried Ghast in wonder.

The shadow-mountain shuddered, then a thin black beam fired

out of the summit. As if struck by lightning, the Hex fell down, slowly fading until all that remained was the mountain and that single, brilliant beam.

Ghast turned up the basement's lamp again, bathing the space in soft Light.

"Is that showing us what I think it's showing us?" said Ester.

"I know that mountain," said Lux. He was examining the Vision Stone closely. How? How did the stone's story and the Key to the Ark fit together?

Still in shock, he hurried up to the front room, searching for his bag. When he found it, he took out the Key, which felt heavier now, as if its importance was adding to its physical weight. Lux raced back down, holding the sphere tightly.

"Thank you," said Ghast, holding it to the Light as Lux handed it over. "I recognised this mountain range as soon as Lux showed me the Key yesterday, but I couldn't work out its meaning. I knew it was nowhere near the Ark, so it couldn't have anything to do with taming Monsters. It was only now – a few minutes ago – that I recalled seeing the mountain on this Vision Stone. And the Hex themselves, of course. I believe there may be a way to stop them.

"Dusk Mountain, it's called. On the other side of Lindhelm. I've been, though I haven't climbed to the peak. But if this Vision Stone is correct . . ."

"Hang on, you told us these stones show stories. Like Juno," said Fera.

"They do. But the Hex are *in* this stone, and they are real. We've seen them with our own eyes. And if they're real . . . whatever's at that mountain might be real too."

"But . . ." Brace spluttered, "Juno's a bedtime story. You're not saying *she* was real."

"Many things are unbelievable when we first encounter them," said Ghast, shrugging. "Your Light, for instance. It would be an unwise person to declare something false without proof."

"All right, let's say it's true," said Ester. "How do we know what to do when we get there? It took you ten years to finally enter the Ark. And even that required luck. What if we get there and there's no way to reach the beam? What if there *is* no beam?"

Ghast cleared away the golden device and the Vision Stone. "I don't know what we'll find, Ester. Brace is right, it may just be a story. But this is our only lead. If Deimos is right and the Hex kill indiscriminately, we must do something. Would you rather stay here?"

Ester didn't answer.

Lux was about to tell the others that he thought it was worth trying when there was a loud bang upstairs, then thudding footsteps.

Sally's red face appeared in the basement doorway, looking half-excited and half so shocked that Lux thought she might be unable to speak.

"I—" she started breathlessly, trying to find the right words.

"What is it?" said Ghast.

Sally squirmed, frustrated. Then something clicked.

"*Something big has happened,*

You'd better come and see.
If I told you here and now,
You wouldn't believe me."

She waited for them to move but nobody did. Growing impatient, she grabbed Brace's hand, dragging him towards the stairs. With a look to Ghast to say they'd carry on the conversation later, Ester indicated for the other Hunters to follow.

· CHAPTER 41 ·

Sally led them out into the courtyard to Rory's barn, where the Monster was settled on the hay, almost asleep. His eyes lifted lazily as they entered.

"Grandad knows this," she said excitedly, "but Rory gets tired after flying and needs a rest. So, while you lot were moping about, I thought I'd feed him."

She lifted Rory's feed bag.

"I washed him and then we decided to play a bit of a game and—"

Ghast raised an eyebrow for her to get to her point.

"Well, we finished all that and I was just closing up to come back in and—"

She trailed off, her eyes bulging in frustration. She knew what she wanted to say, she just couldn't say it.

"And I spoke."

The four Light Hunters and Ghast jumped. Lux's heart was instantly beating.

The voice was deep, like it had been buried for thousands of years beneath the ground. And it came – to Lux's astonishment – directly from Rory.

"It would benefit us all if you would pick your jaws off the floor," said the Monster, his voice rumbling loudly in Lux's chest.

Lux took in the Monster's red scales, the flames. Could Rory . . . really be speaking?

Ghast looked from the Monster to Sally in amazement. "Wha…? H-How?" He flopped onto a wooden chair, flabbergasted.

Lux felt like he was seeing a ghost. Or a waterfall flowing upwards. Or a flame that was cold.

"Y-You can talk," said Fera tentatively.

"I can do more than that," said Rory, his lizard eyes flashing playfully. "But for now, I think talking will suffice."

"H-How?" said Ghast, pressing a handkerchief to his forehead.

"The manner of how I came to talk is of no importance right now. What is important is what I can tell you."

Lux's breathing was short, ragged. This couldn't be real . . .

"You have a fine granddaughter, Professor Ghast. Very fine. She has looked after me well."

Rory nuzzled Sally, who was turning red with embarrassment. She looked at Brace and quickly away.

"We have talked for hours in this barn. Or should I say, she has talked *to* me. I know everything of your lives. Your job at the university, your research, all the places she's hidden your artefacts."

Ghast shot a surprised look at Sally, who guiltily picked up a brush and started to clean Rory's scales.

"Up until now, I have felt no need to intervene in events. You are a wise man, Professor Ghast. You have seen further than many. And your mistake at the Ark is nothing more than that: a mistake. But like all errors, we must do what we can to fix it."

Rory shifted, scratching his ear. Lux watched, still too shocked to speak. A Monster . . . talking. Not fighting but talking.

"You will, by now, have come across the mountain. Is that correct?"

Ghast looked sharply at the beast.

"What do you seek there?"

There was a moment's hesitation. Ester stepped forward. "We want to stop the Hex."

"Indeed." Rory shifted again as Sally brushed his belly. Outside the barn, a bird cawed loudly.

"You humans meddle too much. It is your weakness and your strength. I am an old Monster. Very old when measured against your short lives. I have been on this planet for four thousand and sixty-three years. Many of my fellow Fire-drakes have been around longer. We have seen much.

"I know the mountain you are interested in: Dusk Mountain. It is an old place, once used by the Ancients to pray to their gods. But its purpose changed once my type were created, and the clockwork army designed to end us. A temple was built at the summit – a counterpart to the Ark. After creating the Hex, the Ancients realised the mistake they had made. They built something to stop them. Something at the temple."

Lux and Ghast stepped forward. "The Vision Stone is right?" said Ghast.

Rory looked puzzled. "I do not know such stones."

Ghast waved a tattooed arm dismissively. "It doesn't matter. What matters is this way to halt the Hex. At the temple. What is it?"

Wispy smoke came out of Rory as he sighed. "That, I do not know. Other than that it stopped the Hex once, and that it requires the use of Twilight. The kind hidden inside Lux." The ancient Fire-drake's eyes landed on him.

Twilight again, thought Lux. Why did it have to come down to him?

"Take us," said Brace excitedly. "The sooner we get there, the sooner we end this."

"That will not be possible." Rory's head inclined to the barn roof. Falling through a crack there was the first rays of a bronze sunset. "Allow me to take you up and I will show you."

The Light Hunters and Ghast did as they were told, following Rory into the cold air of the courtyard. The Monster sank slightly so that they could climb aboard. ("I will never stop loving flying him," Brace muttered.) Then he beat his wings.

Rory soared up faster than Lux had ever seen, and soon Ghast's home was just a grey dot. The wind blew into his eyes so that he had to blink to see. Then they were above the thin clouds, looking down on a carpet of green.

"This should be high enough." Rory's voice sounded primeval in the endless quiet.

Lux spotted the Shengan River, and further out the tall towers of Lindhelm, reflecting what was left of the day's sun. But it was the black stream snaking across the land towards the city that worried him: Hex.

"Whoa!" said Fera.

"Focus on your goal, not the obstacles in your path," said Rory.

The Monster banked again, and Lux spotted at last what he was *really* showing them. Off in the distance, past Lindhelm's glass towers, were three mountain peaks, glowing purple in the fading sun.

Dusk Mountain.

But it wasn't the peaks themselves that made the breath catch in Lux's throat. Rather the army of skyships guarding them, each the deep red of Shade.

"No . . ."

"I do not know who is on that mountain," said Rory, "but if you wish to stop the Hex, you must get past those ships."

· CHAPTER 42 ·

Lux had once sat on one of Fera's *Flame* casts that she'd accidentally left smoking in Dawnstar's training wing, burning his trousers. As he sat on Rory, with the clouds as his floor, he felt a similar heat beneath him.

"Erm, what's that?" he said.

"What's what?" said Sally distractedly.

"Hot. The heat."

Sally's eyes travelled to Rory's flank, where the great Monster's scales were burning and crawling with red threads of fire.

"Oh dear."

"Oh dear?" said Ester, suddenly perking up.

"We *might* have pushed Rory a little too far."

Sally tugged the Monster's reigns, so that he started to descend.

"It's when he's tired," she explained over her shoulder. "Messes with his heat regulation."

"I am fine," said Rory sleepily.

"And I'm a horse!"

Lux could tell the situation was a little more serious than Sally was letting on, so he was relieved when they made it back to the ground safely, Rory spreading his wings wide to ensure a gentle landing. Sally leapt straight off, pulling the others down too.

"I am fine," Rory insisted. But even as he spoke, the heat beneath his scales flared, almost burning Professor Ghast's eyebrows. "Although, all this flying *can* be somewhat taxing. A rest might be in order."

Sally gave the Monster a worried look, leading him into the barn.

"Those ships must belong to Deimos," said the professor, letting everyone inside the cottage. It was cold in the courtyard, and Lux was thankful the fire was still burning. "It appears he is one step ahead of us."

"We need to get there," said Brace. "But if Rory's a no-go . . ."

The professor had taken off his jacket and was scanning his bookshelves, pulling out old bits of clockwork and strange devices. Every now and then he put something in a bag he'd taken down from a hook on the wall.

"Not now, he isn't. He hides it, but Rory wasn't lying when he said he was old. There's a way to tell the age of a Fire-drake by counting the number of ridges on their claws. Rory's have grown on top of each other."

Brace growled, frustrated. He looked to Ester and Fera for an idea. "We can't just wait."

"I doubt even a fit and healthy Rory could get us onto that mountain right now anyway," said Ghast. "Those were skyships. Led by one of the best manipulators of Light and Shade I've ever known. Rory would be no match."

There was silence as they each thought the situation over. If Rory was out, where did that leave them? Lux thought of all their training at Dawnstar. There must be something they could do, something they'd learned. Every second that passed, the Hex were advancing. They just didn't have time . . .

"A distraction," said Fera suddenly, hurrying to the map of the area that Ghast had pinned to the kitchen wall. She stared at it closely.

"What are you thinking?" said Lux, joining her. Ester came too, and Brace.

"You said this mountain is on the other side of Lindhelm. That's not far from Ravenholm."

"Correct," said Ghast, stuffing another silver device in one of his bags.

"Maybe the villagers could help us."

"The Dusters!" said Lux, catching on. "Enough go and the ships will have to move. Or do *something* . . ."

"Precisely," said Ghast.

"What do you mean, 'precisely'?" asked Brace, offended on Lux's behalf.

"I mean, that's my plan. And *this*," he said, pulling a large brass key out of a basket of odds and ends, "will get us there."

"Professor, we can't travel by key," said Brace delicately.

"It's for a door," said Ghast.

Picking up the bags he'd been filling, he handed one each to Lux, Brace, Ester and Fera, then headed to his basement. "Unless I'm mistaken, the Hex stopped you using your Light back at the Ark, no? Which means if we go overground and run into them, there's absolutely nothing we can do. We can't fly on Rory either, for the reasons discussed. And my balloon's still in Ravenholm. That means we must go underground."

The professor stopped at a wooden cupboard in his basement, decorated with red and blue squares. "Help, please."

The four Light Hunters pushed their shoulders into the wood, shifting the cupboard along the floor. Ghast whipped away a rug, throwing up a cloud of thick dust. Beneath was a hatch with a keyhole just the right size for the professor's key.

"It's dark," he said, opening it and climbing down a ladder. "Watch your step."

Lux gripped the cold rungs and travelled down for a few metres until he reached a low, granite tunnel. Intricate carvings covered the walls – similar to the ones at the Ark. Ghast used a *Flame* to light a hanging lamp, providing a pool of illumination.

"Part of the reason I bought this cottage was because during my research into the Ancients I discovered a set of ruins beneath it." He lifted the lamp, indicating for the others to follow. "I believed at first this is where I'd find the Ark but when I got here, I quickly understood I was wrong."

They reached a fork in the tunnel. Ghast led them down the right-hand path, which smelled of stale water. There was a whisper of a draught coming from somewhere ahead.

"However, I did find something special. Something I've since studied at my leisure."

He turned a corner and the tunnel opened into an enormous, dizzying cavern, lit by tiny green Lights. It had to be as big as the training wing at Dawnstar, formed of dark rock that joined at odd angles. They were standing on a wooden platform that the professor had clearly put together with material left over from Rory's barn.

Ghast indicated for the Light Hunters to wait. They heard the rattle of the brass key in the dark and suddenly the entire cavern was lit in a soft yellow Light. Lux was amazed to see great pillars, with beautiful Light and Shade ornaments, marching into the distance. But even more astonishingly, there was a railway track running beside the platform, on top of which was a pair of wooden carts.

"Don't ask me why this is here," said the professor, hurrying to a bank of levers. "I've never worked out why the Ancients would want to build this. Perhaps they were mining the rock. But Sally and I have explored it and it spreads all over the region – Lindhelm, beneath the Shengan Jungle and," he smiled warmly at Fera, "right under your parents' farm."

Lux took in the great cavern, imagining how far the web of tunnels must stretch, his hungry eyes swallowing everything he could see.

It wasn't their usual mode of transport, and it certainly wasn't stylish. But they had found their ride.

· CHAPTER 43 ·

Every time there was a full Light Hunters meeting at Dawnstar, Tesla would complain about the atrium lifts. Lux had never quite understood why. They swayed a little, yes, but that was all part of the fun. And so, when they first saw the rusted cart on the Ancient railway track, Lux was a little less concerned than the others.

The cart was canoe shaped, with a long, narrow cabin, smoothed by age. Along the sides were more Light and Shade carvings like the ones on the walls.

"Please tell me we're not going in that," said Fera nervously, peering over the wooden platform into utter darkness.

The professor ignored her, opening a door in the side of the cabin. They each sat on a bench, dumping Ghast's bags and gazing in wonder, or in Fera's case dismay, at the glowing decorations.

"Wait!"

Loud footsteps thundered down the narrow tunnel behind them.

"Don't you *dare* go without me!"

Sally burst out of the tunnel, her golden hair flying wildly. She pulled up as soon as she saw they were still there and arranged her expression into one of great hurt.

"Where are you going?" she asked her grandad, who was still adjusting the bank of levers.

"We're going to Ravenholm. I was coming to tell you—"

"You were going to go without me again!" Sally snapped. "After I saved you as well." She huffed, waiting for an explanation.

"How did you know we were down here?" said Ghast.

"*When you leave a trail as easy as you, grandad,*
Anyone who didn't find it would have to be mad."

"Professor . . ." prodded Ester.

"Yes, yes," he said, waving away her impatience. "Give me a moment."

Ghast kneeled in front of his granddaughter, taking her hand. "I'm afraid you can't come with us."

"What?" Sally turned away angrily, but the professor held her until she calmed.

"You can't come," he repeated, "because I want you to stay here and look after Rory while he recovers. And then, when he's feeling better, I want you to fly him to Ravenholm. To meet up with us. Do you think you can do that?"

Sally eyed her grandad suspiciously, checking for signs of deception. She found none and lifted her head confidently. "Yes, I can do that."

She threw her arms around him, kissing his cheek. Then she wandered to the railway cabin, high-fiving all of the Light Hunters.

"Be careful," Ghast told her. "Lock all the doors, and as soon as Rory's ready, get into the sky."

She nodded emphatically.

"Thank you. Now, up you go. We'll see you in Ravenholm."

Ghast finished setting up the Ancient track, then joined the Light Hunters in the cabin. "I'll warn you, this isn't the comfiest ride."

"Is it ever?" said Ester.

As it was, Ghast's tip-off was an understatement. Once they got going, Lux felt like the ball in one of Brace's wooden games, lurching up and down, or like he'd been hit by one of Fera's *Bolts*. He had to hold on just to stay upright. The track swung left and right, climbed sharp hills, looped around massive outcrops and rolled over endless drops.

But the views were incredible.

Boundless caverns, even larger than the one they'd started in, filled with Ancient statues. Sparkling purple underground pools, fringed with Ancient spires. Waterfalls, hidden by fine, crystal spray. Fields of shimmering flowers, swaying as if in an underground breeze.

"Professor, how come I've never heard of this place?" asked Fera as they circled another pool. "I explored every inch of Ravenholm. I never found any sign of it. My parents never mentioned it either. Did they know?"

Ghast looked guilty. "Nobody knows. I was worried if more

people came down, they would disturb what was here." Soft ripples spread like Light on the lake surface. "Perhaps I should have sought help instead of trying to do all of this on my own. I've made some mistakes. I see that."

The cart delved deeper into the darkness, before climbing again, ever so slowly, up a steep track. Ester started to tap at her Gauntlet, while Ghast checked his bags, making sure he had everything. He looked as if he was planning something, Lux thought, although he had no idea what.

"Psst!"

Fera and Brace were at the edge of the cabin. Brace beckoned Lux over.

"Lux, tell her," he said. "Her family will be fine."

The worried frown on Fera's face made it clear she was thinking about them.

"It's just these Hex, you know," she said. "If it's not Ravenholm, it'll be somewhere else. And my brother, we need him if the villagers are going to help with the distraction. Mum and Dad are too old to be flying up mountains. But Barny . . . he's not exactly my biggest fan."

Lux recalled Fera's brother's sour face when they'd first arrived in Ravenholm.

"For what it's worth, it's not exactly amazing knowing I might be the only one who can stop all this," said Lux. "With my Twilight, I mean."

He thought hard about whether to say what he wanted to say next. He spotted his grandpa's Luminary badge, which he could just about make out in the Light of the underground lake, and decided to be brave.

"If the Hex only attacked Monsters and not humans, I think I'd still save them. The Monsters, I mean." He waited for his friends' reactions, but they stared back blankly. "Is that weird? Because it seems weird to say it. But after Rory, I don't think I can hurt them, you know?"

Lux felt suddenly like he was under one of Tesla's microscopes. He'd been thinking about telling them how he felt since his flight with Rory but hadn't found the right time. Were they angry? Did they think it was his Shade coming out?

"Talk, please," he said, nervous.

Brace and Fera exchanged a glance, communicating without talking.

"We feel the same," said Brace at last. "Only we didn't want to mention it after . . ." His eyes fell to Lux's grandpa's badge.

"I haven't forgiven Monsters," said Fera. "I'm not sure I ever will. But Rory . . . if they can be saved, we have to, don't we?"

A mountain of weight slid off Lux's shoulders. "Thanks, guys."

"I don't know what you're thanking us for," said Brace. "You're the one with the Twilight. It's you who's going to have to do all the work. All we can do is help."

Yes, thought Lux, *but that's what means I might be able to do it.*

· CHAPTER 44 ·

Ester had a theory, that she often shared with the rest of Squad Juno, that Maya always contacted them at the most awkward of times. Just as they were about to save a village from a Monster or as they'd boarded a busy skybus where they couldn't talk privately. But when Lux's Shell crackled as Ghast's rickety old cart made its way through the underground caverns, he realised there was no-one he'd rather talk to.

"I *know* I left the screws on top of the teleporter," came Maya's irritated voice, "I *meant* to leave them there."

"And *I* meant to send you to the cooks to have you wash dishes for a week," Lux heard Tesla reply.

"I'd quite like that," said Maya.

Lux cleared his throat.

"There you are!" she said, relieved. "We've been wondering why we've not heard from you all."

"We're good," said Lux.

"Well, I must say you've done a *right* nice job." Maya's tone was so sarcastic that Lux could have cut himself on it. "Nova sends you to find out what the professor's discovered and instead you set a clockwork army loose. I mean, even for you Lux, that's quite impressive."

"If you've only called to wind me up—"

"I mean, don't get me wrong, it's not been all fun and games here," Maya went on. "I beat Tesla at chess so he's been annoyed with me all afternoon."

"I'll have you know she didn't beat me at all—"

Tesla's voice cut off.

"Ah, peace," said Maya.

Lux heard the Inventor carrying on in the background. "What's the latest, Maya?"

"Not good, I'm afraid. Tell Ester to hold up her Gauntlet."

A map appeared there, shining pale blue in the dark. On it were dozens of red dots, and a handful of black ones.

"Red are places the Hex have surrounded. Black are places they've attacked. We're doing our best to evacuate people but . . ." Maya trailed off.

Lux found Daven on the map. He saw with a sinking feeling that it had a red dot. Dawnstar, too.

"We might have a plan," he said.

"Tesla told me."

Fera was waving her hands wildly at Lux, trying to get his attention. He switched off his shell momentarily. "What's up?"

"Ask her about Ravenholm. There's nothing on the map."

Lux turned his Shell back on. He heard Maya hesitate at his question. She never liked giving bad news. "We've not heard anything."

Fera could tell her answer from Lux's troubled expression.

"You'd better get whatever you're planning right, guys," said Maya seriously. "Because between you and me, I don't think anyone's got much of a plan around here."

"No pressure," said Lux humourlessly.

"No pressure."

Lux clicked off his Shell. The Ancient cart climbed the track, accompanied by the sound of Ghast making tiny adjustments to two small gold devices he'd taken from one of his bags.

They left the fragrant air of the underground lake behind and passed over another waterfall. The cavern seemed to narrow around them, like it was a Monster swallowing them whole. Statues appeared either side – Monsters, like a miniature memorial garden. Beautiful, really, Lux thought. Then he caught himself and shook the thought away.

"Nearly there," said Ghast, sliding the devices back in his bag.

Lux looked for what had prompted the professor to say this and spotted a tiny circle of daylight high above. It grew larger as they closed in, and the cart began to slow down.

"Off we get," said Ghast, opening the cabin door as the cart stopped at a flat, mossy ledge.

"Not quite as posh as the stop beneath your cottage," said Brace.

"I didn't make this one."

Ghast handed each of the Light Hunters a bag – Lux's was so heavy that he had to hold it with both hands – then led them up a narrow tunnel similar to the one beneath his cottage. There was no ladder this time, just fresh, clear air. Grass climbed to Lux's knees, and a leafy tree spread its welcoming arms. Just down the way was Ravenholm.

"You are *kidding* me?" said Fera. "This has been here all along?"

"We're not always as observant as we think we are," said Ghast.

Lux breathed in the cool air, moving to the edge of the rock for a better view. His breath caught in his throat.

Twilight.

Lots of tiny dots of it lined up in the farm fields, with more behind, and more behind that. There had to be thirty, at least.

Except they weren't just dots.

Each was a Hex.

A cry escaped Fera's throat when she saw the same and she dropped to her knees. "No. No, no, no, no, no."

Ester lifted her Gauntlet, revealing a solid blue magnifying screen, through which Lux could see the Hex up close. Their purple Twilight illuminated the dark. One or two of the taller creatures with the symbols above their heads were among them. None of the Hex seemed to be moving. They were waiting, watching the town.

"I suspect the same thing will be happening in many villages around here, whether your young friend on the Shell has them on her map or not," said Ghast.

"I'm going down," said Fera.

But she didn't move. Without her Light, what could she do?

Further along the path, the Ravenholm buildings looked much as they had before – run down but homely. Little lights brightened the windows, and Fera's parents' house stood on the hill like a sentry.

Lux's eyes fell to the town square, where he was just about able to make out a group of villagers, among them Fera's mum and dad.

"People," he said.

"We must remember our mission," said Ghast carefully. He looked anxiously into the distance at the familiar outline of Dusk Mountain, lit by the white moon.

"Hang on, I hope you're not suggesting we leave," said Brace. "There are people here."

"There are people everywhere."

"But these are *my* people," snapped Fera. And before Lux could stop her, blue-white Light was crackling threateningly at her fingertips.

"Fera!" snapped Ester.

The younger girl went instantly red, and she tossed the cast quickly over her shoulder.

Ester turned Ghast gently away from Dusk Mountain. "Professor, we can't *get* up there without the villagers. Unless you want to spend the next few days walking."

Ghast sighed, realising Ester was right. "I know, I'm sorry."

Fera shouldered the bag the professor had given her and made her way down the path into town.

After a few calming breaths, Lux and the others followed.

· CHAPTER 45 ·

If there was one thing Lux had learned about being a Light Hunter, it was that just when you thought you had everything under control, something would come along to knock the wheel out of your hands. Often, that something came in the shape of *someone* very close to you.

The Light Hunters found Fera's mum and dad in the main square, surrounded by villagers. They were gathered around a low table, looking at a map of the area, glancing worriedly towards the fields, where the Hex were waiting.

Fera's mum's face lit up when she saw her daughter – momentarily confused, then relieved. She gathered her up in a hug.

"I'm so glad you're safe."

The villagers were staring at them. Lux returned a greeting from Fera's father.

"Is everyone okay?" asked Fera.

"We're all fine," said her mum.

"Barny?"

"He's fine."

A wave of relief washed over Fera. She held her mum's hand, hurrying to the table.

"You lot seem to turn up just when we need you," said her dad. "There are some . . . I don't even know how to describe them . . . things outside the village."

"We know," said Brace.

"It's a long story," explained Ester.

"I don't know what they are or where they're from, but old Bill from the next village sent his daughter to tell us they're not friendly. They killed a bunch of cows over there."

"They'll do a lot worse than that soon," said Ghast.

Fera's mum and dad looked at the professor, who avoided their gaze, unwilling to say too much more in front of the villagers.

"We should get people in their houses," said Fera.

Her mum didn't wait around, launching into action and instructing the villagers to disappear.

"Hang on, you were saying we should go over and face 'em," said one of them, a tall fellow with a beard and a metal brace on his leg.

"Yeah, you can't just tell us to go 'ome," said another.

"You must listen," said Fera. "These things are very dangerous."

"We shouldn't show we're scared!"

"Barny wouldn't be sayin' this," said a young lad with a scar across his cheek.

"Please—"

"Get to your houses now!" bellowed Ester, staring down anyone who dared to meet her eye.

The villagers looked among each other, deciding whether to take orders from a stranger. Then the tall man with the brace gathered his family and walked off. The rest slowly followed.

"I hope you lot know what you're doing because we'll pay for that later," said Fera's mum. "Ravenholmers don't like being told what to do."

"They'll like being sliced up less," said Ester.

"What's your plan then?" said Fera's dad.

It was a good question. Lux certainly didn't have one, and he wasn't sure Ester did either. Without their Light, there wasn't much they *could* do.

"I've been thinking about that, and I might have a solution." Maya's voice came loud in Lux's ear, and he put his finger to the Shell. "Sorry, listening in. Habit."

Ester, Brace and Fera were looking at Lux, wondering who was on the other end of the line. "Maya," he explained.

"Tell her to send her signal to my Gauntlet," said Ester.

Lux did as she asked. Soon, Maya's voice was coming out of the device. Fera's mum and dad looked utterly confused.

"Can everyone hear me?" said Maya.

"We can hear you," answered Brace.

"I've been thinking about what Ester told me about those Hex things. And this Light problem. You said there was one in the Ark that had a symbol above his head, is that right?"

"You've seen these things before?" said Fera's dad, shocked.

Fera hushed him. "I'll explain later."

"Yes, Maya," said Ester.

"I think that's the one stopping you using your Light. There was an old myth thingy back when we were kids. Can you remember, Lux? About that witch that turned little kids to stone with that symbol she drew above her head. I reckon this is the same kind of thing."

Lux looked sceptical. Maya was liable to flights of fancy at the best of times, and this was not the best of times. Still . . . there was something odd about the symbol Hexes. They were bigger, taller. The symbols had to be for *something*.

"I reckon if there's one of those, you've got to take it out," Maya said. "Then you'll get your Light back."

A fine rain had started to fall now. The village square was empty, but Lux could see worried faces peeking out of dimly lit windows.

"Let's say you're right," said Ester, "and that's a big maybe. How would we take it out if we can't throw Light?"

"Can't you use that red Monster you've been hanging around with?"

Fera's mum and dad looked startled. Fera waved them away.

"I'll take that silence as a 'No'."

Lux tried to think of some way they could attack the Hex. But the truth was, without their powers, they were just like everyone else.

"Frequency!"

Fera shouted out the word so loudly that everyone snapped their heads in her direction, thinking she'd hurt herself.

"Frequency!" she said again.

From Ester's Gauntlet, they heard Maya's excited voice. "Yes! Ooh, I've always loved you, Fera."

"Would someone please explain why the word *'frequency'* is getting everyone excited?" said Brace. Lux stared back blankly, just as confused.

"Tesla, in one of those long lectures he gives when we're doing his experiments, always talks about the frequency of our Light," said Fera. "How Light's at a slightly different frequency to everyday, normal light. Could the symbol Hexes be blocking the *frequency* of Light?"

Ester looked thoughtful. "It's not impossible. But it doesn't really change anything. Light has a natural frequency. We can't change it any more than you can change your eye colour."

Fera raised Ester's arm, where her Gauntlet flashed silver in the moonlight. "We can't change the frequency of *our* Light, but we might be able to change this."

A sudden, crashing realisation hit Lux. "Is that possible, Maya?"

"I'll have to talk to Tesla about how to do it from here. But yes, it might be."

"Is it safe?" asked Ester.

Maya hesitated. "It'll be unstable, but it should be all right for you to take out the big Hex. Once that's done, Fera and Brace will be able to use their Light again. Kapow-pow."

Fera's mum and dad looked thoroughly confused by everything

Maya was saying, but the Light Hunters were growing more excited by the second.

"I hope all this means you can help," said Fera's mum.

"Maybe," said Ester.

"I'll start work right away," said Maya, reminding Lux of how excited she'd sound back in Daven when she had a good idea for a prank. "Stay where you are. Should only take a few minutes."

The line went dead, and the town square was silent.

"Mum, Dad, there's going to be a fight," said Fera. "Go to the house. Stay until we tell you to come out."

"But, darling, if there's anything we can—"

"Just stay safe."

Before anybody could move, there was a loud droning sound near the big house on the hill, echoing between the wooden buildings.

"Oh no," said Fera's mum, realising what had made the noise.

"What?" said Fera.

"That."

A patch of darkness was sweeping across the moon. Lux couldn't tell what it was at first. Then, the smudge got closer, and he picked out rotor-blades.

Dusters.

Heading for the Hex.

They flew overhead, clicking like insects. Lux saw their leader, standing atop his craft as if he was riding into battle, his black hair flowing in the wind, and his white shirt grey in the moonlight.

"Barny!" was Fera's single, horrified word.

· CHAPTER 46 ·

Lux didn't remember his older sister. He was a baby when the Cerberus ended the lives of both her and his parents. All he knew of her was what his grandpa had told him, and the little red box of her things he'd given Lux on his fifth birthday. But Lux still felt a dull pain somewhere deep inside whenever he thought of her. So, he understood perfectly the terrified sound that escaped Fera's throat as she watched her brother fly in the direction of danger.

"Barny!" she yelled.

Fera turned, her face like thunder. "Mum, Dad, get inside now."

"But—"

"Now!"

Fera's mum and dad did as they were told, hurrying up the hill.

Without another word, she raced after the black cloud, chasing her brother.

"Stay here," Ester told Ghast.

"Not on your nelly!"

Shaking her head in frustration, Ester gripped the professor's arm and dragged him after Lux and Brace, who were already chasing Fera. They caught up with her down a narrow path between two wooden storage buildings.

"He'll be fine," said Brace.

"He won't," shouted Fera.

"He will."

"No, he *won't*." She jumped over a metal gate into the road. "He *won't*. You don't know what he's like. After the Monster attack here . . . he never forgave himself for everyone who died. He's had a death-wish with Monsters himself ever since. But he doesn't know what the Hex are. None of them do!"

Fera surged on as Ester and Ghast reached the gate behind them.

"They're not Light Hunters, Brace. We've got to get there."

Fera skidded around a tractor that someone had left in the road, pushing herself off the metal and racing towards the fields. Lux saw rows of purple dots ahead of him – the burning Twilight in the Hexs' chests – and the silver flash of their metal armour.

"Maya, how are you coming along with that frequency stuff?" he called into his Shell.

"Putting the finishing touches to it now. Wasn't expecting you to fight *quite* so quickly."

Lux felt his stomach churn as he carried on putting one foot in front of the other. It had been days since he'd thrown Light, or even tried to.

Twilight.

He shook the thought from his head.

They were fifteen metres or so from the Hex now, who were still lined up in long arcs. Their attention had been stolen by the Dusters overhead. Barny was leading, pumping a fist for his companions to dive. They aimed directly for the Hex, brandishing spades and rakes and kitchen knives. But they were no match. The Hex waited, silent and still, until the Dusters were right on them, then lifted their arms and tossed them aside as if they were leaves in the wind. Lux heard horrible scraping sounds as the rotor-blades bit into the ground. Then loud *thuds* as their pilots crashed down.

"No!"

Fera picked up her pace as Ester caught up with them. "Stay calm," she told Fera. "They'll be fine. It's just a fall. Stay calm."

Fera scoffed.

"I mean it," said Ester.

"Is your Gauntlet ready?" asked Lux.

Ester pressed a few buttons. From the end of the device extended the usual Light-blade. Except, this one was a deeper shade of blue than normal. Green almost, like an ocean. A different frequency of Light.

"You three distract the rest," said Ester, sweeping the blade, which spat green sparks. "Ghast, you do the same but be careful. I'm going for the big one."

Lux's heart was thudding. They launched straight into Ester's plan, turning in different directions, dragging the Hex off Barny and his friends, who were lying on the floor, tangled with their

Dusters. Ester raced through the gap, slamming into the taller Hex. She swung her blade, crashing it into the creature's metal skull, sending them both tumbling into the low stone wall.

Lux's spirits lifted when he saw the symbol above the Hex's head wink out.

"Now!" he yelled.

Brace, Fera and Ghast instantly conjured their Light – Fera and Ghast *Bolts* and Brace his usual Light-bow. Their attacks hit with a terrifying force, one that always made Lux flinch even though he'd seen it hundreds of times.

The Hex were shoved back.

"It's working!" he shouted.

Lux knew he should cast a *Protect* in front of his friends, or ready a *Heal* in case one of them got injured. But in the back of his mind . . . all he could see was Twilight.

Brace and Fera continued to slam the Hex, trying to guide them away from Barny and his friends, who were still on the floor, writhing in pain. Ghast, leaning against the wall, was already slowing down – his age catching up with him.

"Ester!"

Lux heard Brace's panicked shout before he saw what was happening.

Ester was climbing to her feet, while the symbol Hex was already standing, its sharp metal limbs poised. For a moment, Lux wondered what had worried Brace so. Then he saw the Hex chanting something. The purple symbol reappeared, different to the last.

Fera joined her fingers, trying to prepare a new cast, but nothing came. Brace tried his Light-bow. Nothing.

"Ester, it's happened again."

"Help her!"

Lux raced over to Ester, who was working her Gauntlet with Maya, changing the frequency again. The Light-blade shone a purer green, like the leaves of a beautiful tree. Lux drew the symbol Hex's attention as Ester crept up behind it and leapt. She connected, bringing it to its knees with a loud crack.

"Now!" yelled Lux.

Fera formed a *Snow* between her fingers, the icy Light glittering.

The fight went on. Lux helped some of Barny's friends through the gate into another field to safety. He knew he should throw a *Protect* to shield them. And this time, he brought his fingers together to do it. But he stopped again. He couldn't. He just . . . couldn't.

"Arghhh!"

Fera was running along the stone wall to escape one of the Hex, which was whirling its razor arms like a windmill. She tried a *Snow*, a *Flame*, anything.

Nothing's working, thought Lux.

The Hex had come together now, in a line, and were closing in on Brace, Ester, Fera and Ghast. Ester was still adjusting her Gauntlet, changing the frequency again to a soft yellow this time. But Lux knew it was no use. Whatever she turned it to, the symbol Hex would have a counter.

He was just trying to think of what they could do, when he heard a loud shout. Barny leapt from behind the wooden gate and sprang at the advancing Hex, steering them away from his sister. But he didn't notice one creature, buried in shadow, that crept up behind him. The Hex's arms sliced into his side, tossing him like a doll. He slammed into the stone wall, blood seeping through his white shirt.

"No!" screamed Fera, the colour draining from her face. She went to go to him, but the Hex blocked her path. She tried to get past anyway, but Brace and Ester held her back.

"Let me go!"

The road was completely silent now, apart from the low chanting of the symbol Hex. The Light Hunters exchanged worried glances, completely lost. Their entire plan had centred around changing Ester's Gauntlet's Light frequency. Now, there was just chaos.

It was then Lux felt it.

Images in his mind: his friends at Dawnstar, Fera's mum and dad, the villagers, the Ark, Deimos, the Hex. Emotion flooded him, filling him up. A spark formed in his stomach – its warmth riding through him, to his fingers, toes, the tip of his head. A power formed, different to his Light, older, more ancient.

This time he knew its name.

Twilight.

Light and Shade.

It leaked out of him – a shining, purple bubble in the dark.

Lux saw his friends' panicked eyes – the same fear he'd seen back in Kofi.

No, he thought. *No, no, no.*

And then he blew.

· CHAPTER 47 ·

The very first time Lux had thrown Light was in his grandpa's basement at the clock repair shop, when he was six years old. The cast – a *Catch* – had shot through him like lightning, touching every atom in his body. The same sensation rocked him now, but this time it came out of silence, from somewhere far, far away.

He opened his eyes.

He was lying in a bed in an unfamiliar room, surrounded by more beds. The walls were a deep, wine-red, with long, cream hangings. A large window lay slightly open, letting in a gentle morning breeze and the dull sound of rain drumming on the roof. A grey light poured in, making everything muted and pale.

Lux went to push his hair out of his eyes, but his arm was tucked in tight.

"There you are! I told you it'd be this morning."

Brace's voice came from somewhere behind Lux. He was

sitting on a chair with a book of puzzles in his lap, smiling warmly. "That's two shailings you owe me," he told Fera.

"Let's call that even. You already owe me ten."

Lux blinked. And just like that, the memory of what happened in the fields slammed into him.

His Twilight.

It had happened again.

He sat up, fighting to get free of the blankets. Brace eased him back down. "Not yet."

"I did it again," said Lux, horror stricken. He couldn't believe it . . . he'd been so careful.

The rain pounded the window, running down in thick lines. There were five other injured people in the room with him, most sleeping. A Gauntlet hung from the neighbouring bed – Ester's. She was asleep there, her leg elevated on a pile of pillows.

"She's fine," said Fera quickly, picking up a bowl of soup from a tray and moving to another bed. "She's broken her leg, but she'll be fine."

Lux felt as heavy as lead. "Was it . . . me?"

A long silence. Brace avoided Lux's gaze, staring out of the window at the swaying trees. It was Fera who answered, coming over with a bowl of soup.

"Yes, it was you."

The room spun around Lux – the red walls and cream hangings blurring so that he could hardly tell which was which.

No, no, no. How?

He tried to sit up, but Brace jumped forward and stopped him again. "You're not in amazing shape yourself, you know? Just stay still."

Lux wracked his brain, trying to remember precisely what had happened. They'd reached the Hex, Barny and his people, the frequency, then someone had got hurt and . . .

"Tell me," he instructed Fera. "Please."

She collected a wooden chair from the corner of the room and sat by Lux, taking his hand. "It was like last year."

"How big?"

"Pretty big. You took out some of the buildings and half the woods."

Lux took a sharp breath. Half the woods . . . "These people . . ." he said tentatively of the injured villagers in the other beds, "Were they . . . ?"

Fera nodded. Lux's eyes dropped, ashamed.

"Everyone's okay," she added quickly. "We've got them all up here in the house. The village doctor came to have a look at them. They're going to be fine."

"What about the Hex?" said Lux, suddenly remembering why they were in Ravenholm in the first place.

"Gone," said Brace. "If there's one thing that Twilight stuff is good for, it's getting rid of Hex. There were none left!"

Lux looked out at the grey sky, tracing the silver edge of a dark cloud. The Hex were gone. That meant they *could* fight them. Or *he* could, with his Twilight. But all those injured people . . .

"Barny!" he said suddenly, recalling the young man's body crashing into the stone wall.

"He's fine," said Fera.

"And the professor?" Lux searched the beds around him for Ghast.

"Oh, he's better than ever," said Brace. "He's found Fera's mum's library. Been there all night. Took those bags we brought."

Despite hearing that everyone was okay, Lux still felt sick. He'd hurt people. Even though he'd tried not to use Light, his Twilight had come anyway. Artello Nova was wrong about him managing it. Lux couldn't control it. He'd never be able to.

There were footsteps on the landing, then Fera's dad appeared with a tray of tea and a dozen cups. He pulled up when he saw Lux was awake, glancing warily at Fera.

"He's fine," she said.

"In which case, tea?" he said, offering Lux a cup. "I've got some chickens roasting too, so we'll have more soup in a bit. How are you feeling?"

Lux stared out of the window at the pouring rain.

"Thanks for the tea, Dad," said Fera.

The old man eyed Lux a little while longer, then laid a big hand on his shoulder. "It's all right son, you didn't damage anything we can't fix."

Lux just kept staring. Fera's dad nodded politely at the others and let himself out.

The dark clouds floated menacingly across the sky. Lux didn't feel like talking. His Light . . . once, it had been so simple. Just a few casts. Then . . . Twilight. Was it the Shade in it? Was it making him bad somehow?

"Have some," said Fera, pushing a cup of tea over to Lux. He ignored it.

All because of him. All these villagers, hurt because of him. He glanced down at his grandpa's Luminary badge, disgusted.

"When you're more awake, a few *Heals* would be good," said Brace. "The doctor here's all right, but . . ." He trailed off at Fera's warning glare. "What?"

"The last thing Lux wants to be doing now is healing."

Lux felt a wave of relief.

"He needs to rest. We know how much it took out of him last year. It's going to be a while before he can heal again."

No, thought Lux. Even Fera didn't get it. "I'm never using Light, you realise that?"

Brace and Fera stiffened.

"You don't understand," Lux went on, struggling to get his words out. "I'm not using Light ever again. Or healing or throwing *any* casts. I'm not doing *this*," he indicated the injured villagers. "Any of it. I can't. It's too dangerous."

"It's okay," said Fera. "We all know you didn't mean to—"

"No!" Lux's shout woke the other patients. He threw his covers off, his face burning red. "No, you're not listening. I am not doing this anymore. If I can't throw Light safely, I won't throw it at all."

Fera and Brace stared at him, not knowing what to say. Lux watched them, searching for anything to help him, for one of them to say something to change his mind.

But they had nothing.

He grabbed his jacket and trudged out of the room.

251

· CHAPTER 48 ·

Some mistakes you can never make good.

Lux had thought about this a lot. At first, after his grandpa died, he'd believed it. The old man was gone and there was no way to get him back. But as the months had passed, and Lux had settled into his new home, his view had changed slightly. He started to believe things would get better, could be fixed.

But his Twilight . . .

The rain outside Fera's mum and dad's house was falling in thick sheets, blown by a strong wind. Lux heard muffled voices drifting up from the village square. He wandered down the path, hardly focussing on where he was going. All he knew was that he wanted to be as far away from Light as possible.

In the square, people were hurrying this way and that, carrying wooden stakes and fence panels, hammers and nails. Defences in case the Hex came back. He wanted to tell them that a fence wouldn't do anything against the Hex. But he put his hands in his pockets and walked on.

Just before the road that led to the farm fields, he passed a couple of men on lookout. Lux opened the gate and stepped through.

If he wanted to avoid what he'd done the night before, wandering to the farm fields was about the last way to do it. The buildings Fera had said he'd damaged – barns and storage sheds – were lying in tatters, throwing clouds of black smoke into the sky. It was like a Monster had destroyed them.

But Lux had done this.

Behind the barns were the flattened remains of the woods – jagged tree trunks stuck up at odd angles. The smell of smoke was thick and burning orange embers hissed in the rain.

Lux let his legs carry him along the road. Brace and Fera were right; there was no sign of the Hex other than the cut-up gravel where they'd fought. A few damaged Dusters were lying against the wall, which itself had collapsed, the rubble sitting in a jumbled pile.

In the field, Lux looked into the distance, away from the farm. Valleys, lifeless under the grey sky, rolled to the horizon. He wanted to walk all the way back to Daven. Back to his grandpa's clock repair shop, to his bedroom, where he'd spent so much time playing with Maya. Put everything behind him: Light, Twilight, Deimos, the Hex.

He looked at his grandpa's badge. The old man would never have allowed this to happen. But Lux had. He'd set a clockwork army loose. No matter that Deimos had made him do it, *he* was responsible. Everyone relied on him, and he let them down every time.

Digging his fingers behind the badge, Lux tore it off. It looked old, the yellow star faded in the centre, the gold piping loose. He threw it in the mud. "Sorry, Grandpa."

"Light's alive, they weren't lying when they said I should talk to you."

Maya's voice buzzed loudly in Lux's ear. He thought about taking his Shell out and tossing it in the mud too. But he didn't.

"Hi," he said dully.

"Fera said I should talk to you. I didn't realise you'd be talking to yourself."

"It's not been a good few days, Maya."

"Tell me about it. Tesla still hasn't forgiven me for that chess match."

Maya waited for Lux to laugh. He didn't. "Are you all right?"

"I'm not sure."

There was a scratching sound on the other end of the line as Maya settled into a chair. "Come on, your grandpa always said we should share our troubles."

"What's the situation with the Hex, Maya?"

There was a long silence as she decided whether to push. She sighed. "Not good. They're everywhere now. They're not *attacking* everywhere, but Nova thinks it's only a matter of time. I really don't know what we're going to do here, Lux." Maya sounded older than he'd ever heard her sound. "Not unless you guys can do something."

Lux's attention drifted to a bird flying across the field, carrying a bunch of twigs. It dropped them, plunging to collect them before carrying on.

Maya was right. There wasn't anything Dawnstar could do. The only person who could stop the Hex was there at Ravenholm. But Lux couldn't fight every one of them on his own.

Dusk Mountain. The peak appeared fully formed in Lux's mind.

If Ghast was right and there was something there to stop what they'd started . . .

"Lux?"

Maya's voice sounded quiet in the rain. He cut her off, turning to the village. Over the top of Fera's mum and dad's house, he could see the mountain's three dark peaks climbing into the clouds.

Lux would finish this Hex attack. He would go to Dusk Mountain and face Deimos.

But not with the Light Hunters. Not with his friends.

He would go there alone.

· CHAPTER 49 ·

As a Light Hunter Healer, Lux could heal injuries, create protective walls, catch falling objects. He could even bring things back to life, as he had with Artello Nova's dog Bella at Dawnstar. But he couldn't fly. And it was flying he'd need to get to Dusk Mountain.

He approached the broken Dusters by the collapsed stone wall. They were mangled, with bent handles and twisted pedals. But even if they had been intact, it was clear they'd be nowhere near powerful enough to get him up to the summit.

He wracked his brain.

There were no skyships nearby – or, at least, he didn't think so. He'd not seen any in the village, which meant the nearest would be in Lindhelm.

Lux didn't know of any Light casts that could transport him either. Brace could flash through the air with his *Blink* cast, but he knew of nothing that went further.

There had to be some other way.

The bird Lux had seen earlier flew past again with more twigs.

Rory.

The idea hit him like a stone.

He could fly on Rory.

Professor Ghast, back at his cottage, had told Sally to let the Monster get some rest then bring him to Ravenholm. That had been . . . Lux looked at his watch . . . about seventeen hours ago. Plenty of time for her to arrive. If he could find Rory and convince him to fly to Dusk Mountain . . .

Feeling a sudden surge of hope, Lux started to make his way back towards the village.

Where would Rory be on a farm that big?

He hadn't seen any sign of the Monster's red scales in the village square. And he couldn't be in any or the barns either; they were all destroyed.

It was then Lux recalled a large shed near Fera's mum and dad's house. He'd presumed it housed Fera's horses. But it would be the perfect place to keep Rory, especially if they wanted to hide him from the villagers . . .

He splashed through the puddles, sliding through the gate back to the town square.

He was surprised to find Brace and Barny arguing there.

"I don't know *who* you are coming here and telling *me* what to do," said Barny, flicking his black hair and glaring imperiously.

"I'm her best friend," said Brace.

"You have no *idea* what all of this is about."

257

"I have idea enough to know she's got a big brother who doesn't care about her."

"Don't be stupid—"

"Fera saved your village. You should be thanking her."

Lux dragged his attention away, keeping low behind the wall outside the shops until he got onto the path up to the big house. The outside of the building was busy, even in the heavy rain, and he had to stick close to the trees to avoid being seen.

The shed was a flat wooden building with a pair of sliding doors. He crept towards them like a thief, easing one open and peeking inside.

It was cold, and he could hear rain on the tin roof. The shed was made for horses, with dividers and lots of hay. There was a loud, irritated snort from the far corner. A cloud of smoke rose above the wood.

Rory.

Lux breathed a sigh of relief.

Next to the great Fire-drake, on the wall, was his leather saddle, damp from where it had been recently cleaned. Quickly, a plan formed in Lux's mind. Saddle on, out into the rain, and up to the mountain. But . . . could he really do it?

His friends. If he didn't go, he'd be putting them in danger.

Lux lifted the saddle off its hook and dragged it to Rory, who was resting comfortably in the corner. He swung it onto the great Monster's back.

"Lux?"

"Sorry, big guy," said Lux. "We need to go for a bit of a fly."

He levered himself up, shifting to get comfortable on the leather saddle. It was quiet in the barn, aside from the rain on the roof. He oriented the great creature towards the barn entrance, hoping he'd move, but Rory stayed still.

"It is unusual for me to be flown by anyone other than Sally," he rumbled, the hot words vibrating under Lux's thighs.

"It's a special flight," he said, thinking rapidly of a reason why he might need Rory. "Sally told me to take you. We have to go to . . . the next village. To warn them about the Hex."

The ancient Fire-drake seemed to think for a few seconds, his black eyes glittering, then he shrugged. "If you say that is what we are doing then it must be so. However, I would like to ask one thing."

Amazed that his ruse had worked, Lux nodded eagerly. "Anything."

"Are you not forgetting something?"

For a moment, Lux had no idea what the Monster was talking about, and he looked around the barn to see if he'd left anything on the floor. Then he spotted Rory's head angled towards the door.

Standing there, a scrubbing brush in one hand and a fresh bucket of soapy water in the other, was Sally.

"Hello," she said, surprised.

Lux couldn't speak. He met Rory's amused eyes, then the little girl's, which were already narrowed, suspicious.

"H-Hi," he managed.

Sally regarded him carefully, like a cat. "What are you doing with my Monster, Lux?"

"I'm . . ." He tried to think of an excuse. The best he could come up with was, "I wanted to see him."

"Up in the air?" said Sally, looking confusedly at the saddle.

Lux squirmed. He needed some way to get rid of her. The last thing he wanted was for her to raise the alarm. Or worse, ask to come along.

"Your grandad was just asking after you. In the house."

Sally's eyes narrowed again. "No he wasn't, I just came from him."

"Uh . . ." Lux's heart jumped as she strode inside the barn, her hair wet from the rain.

"Lux, can I ask you a question?" Her eyes met Rory's momentarily and they seemed to communicate somehow.

Lux nodded, still searching the barn for a way to distract her. There were two horses in the stalls down the way. Maybe if he . . .

"Do you think I'm stupid?"

Lux stopped, confused. "No. Of course not—"

"Because my grandad tells me I'm the best liar in the whole of Lindhelm. But I think you might be the worst. Would you agree, Rory?"

The Monster inclined his head slowly.

"So, rather than telling me grandad wants to see me, or that you're here because you want to see Rory, why don't you tell me what's really going on?"

Lux had met some clever kids. Maya was one, despite how scatterbrained she could be sometimes. And some of the younger kids at Dawnstar were real brain-boxes, knowing more about

Light than Hunters twice their age. But Sally was something else. Professor Ghast hadn't been lying when he said she was as sharp as a pin.

He'd have to trust her.

Leaping down off the Monster, he drew the wooden door across, shutting out the cold. Then he turned, ready to tell the girl and the Monster everything.

· CHAPTER 50 ·

Sally listened carefully to what Lux told her – about his grandpa, his illness, Deimos, the fight with the Cerberus, his Twilight eruption, the last year at Dawnstar, and all that had happened the previous evening, how much danger he'd put everyone in.

Her lips narrowed as she thought it all through. "Well, that *is* a pickle."

"I've got to get to Dusk Mountain," said Lux. "On my own. I don't want anyone else getting hurt."

Sally went to Rory, who'd been listening carefully. The Monster was breathing in and out, each exhale a warm puff of air.

"And you definitely can't just . . . control your Twilight?" she said.

"I've tried. It doesn't work."

Sally really was something special. At her age, Lux had been trying to see who could build the tallest sandcastle on Daven beach with Maya. Sally already knew about Monsters, all of her grandad's research into the Ancients, the Ark . . .

"Last year I dropped an artefact-thingy that my grandad had found. It was this big goblet. I was pretending to let Rory drink from it and . . ." She clapped, miming the object falling to the ground. "I was expecting grandad to be *so* mad. But he wasn't."

Sally climbed onto Rory's back, rubbing his ears gently. The Monster shook his head in pleasure.

"He asked if I meant to do it. I told him I didn't. And he said . . ." She assumed her grandad's deep voice. "'What's important is what you mean to do. Everyone makes mistakes, but if your heart's in the right place that's all that matters.' Or something like that."

Lux knew what Sally was doing. He'd heard the same thing from Nova. And Ester. And Maya and Fera. Even Brace.

"So?" she cocked her head expectantly. "Did you mean to let your Twilight get out of control?"

Lux felt like he was back at school, being told off by Mr Winter. But there was something about Sally's passion that meant he had no choice but to play along. "No."

"And did you mean to set all those Hex things free?"

"No."

Sally stood tall, getting ready for a poem.

"*It's not what we do that should make us boast,*

But our intentions that matter the most."

"You weren't the one to blame for your grandpa. Or for the Ark, is he Rory?"

The great Monster inclined his head.

"But it is up to you what happens *now*. What you do from here. So, I'm not going to let you take Rory. Because that's not the right thing to do."

Lux stood, his eyes flaring. "Sally—"

She put up a hand, silencing him. "I don't have many friends Lux. I'm not letting one of my new ones go off to face the Hex on his own."

"We won't let our old one either."

Lux turned and found Brace and Fera standing in the stable doorway. His heart swelled at the sight.

"She's right, you know," said Brace, coming further inside.

"I'm just worried," said Lux. "I don't want it to happen again."

"You can't blame yourself," said Fera. "None of us Light Hunters should really. Monsters, the Hex . . . it's hard, what we do. We're just kids. But like Sally said, if your heart's in the right place . . .?" She waited for Lux's answer.

"Yes, obviously."

"Then that's all you can do. I'll tell you one thing, if you go up that mountain alone, you won't make it back. But maybe if we do it together . . ."

Lux had been told he wasn't to blame over and over again, that he'd find a way to deal with his powers. If he still kept hurting people . . . well, he didn't mean to. He was *trying* to help. His fears of Twilight and Light . . . maybe it *was* time to get over them. *Maybe* it was his fears causing all these problems in the first place . . .

He had a duty as a Light Hunter to heal. But he hadn't healed properly for ages. And now he'd been moments from going to Dusk Mountain alone.

What was he thinking?

A Light Hunter never did anything alone. They worked in squads. And his was Squad Juno.

"You'll help, won't you?" Lux said quietly to his friends. "If things go wrong?"

"Of course," said Fera, beckoning him into a group hug. "But we can't worry about how it will go. All we need to do is the best we can together."

Lux's eyes fell to the empty space on his arm where his grandpa's Luminary badge had been. He apologised silently to his grandpa and joined his friends. They hugged for a few seconds until Brace pushed them apart, neatening his uniform.

"All right, enough soppy stuff."

Lux walked out of the stable into the courtyard. The rain had stopped, and the sun was shining through bright clouds, making the grey stones glisten. He found Dusk Mountain, its peaks purple in the sun.

"I'm sorry guys, I don't know what I was thinking. But I'm not going to let it stop me. And I'm not going to do it alone. We've got to go to Dusk Mountain and stop Deimos and the Hex."

Brace and Fera grinned. "Now you're talking my language," said Brace.

Sally was still inside the barn, watching them.

"Thanks," Lux told her.

"Ah, it's all right. That's what friends are for."

"You're right,' he said, knowing what it would mean to her. "That is what friends are for."

Sally grinned, heading back into the barn, a sudden confidence in her step.

"Come on," said Fera, linking arms with her squad-mates and walking them towards the big house. "Let's go and tell the boss our plan."

· CHAPTER 51 ·

Lux would have been lying if he'd said, as they made their way up the carpeted staircase and along the mansion's east wing to the room with the injured villagers, that he wasn't nervous.

He hadn't properly manipulated Light in days. Weeks, really. It was the longest he'd gone without throwing a cast since he was Sally's age.

Would he still manage it?

Pushing the thought from his mind, he followed Fera through the busy house.

The sun was pouring in through the sick room window, painting the walls amber and gold. Dust motes danced in the air. The beds were still filled, with people sleeping or lying on their sides, reading.

"I knew you'd come back," said Fera's dad, passing Lux on his way out with a basket of dirty clothes. He winked affectionately.

The injured villagers eyed the door as Lux, Brace and Fera entered.

"Thought you'd help me in the end then?" said Ester. There was something hurt in her tone, something that reminded Lux of her days as Miss Hart.

"Sorry."

"I should hope so." She sat up and adjusted her injured leg, so it was comfortable. "I didn't choose you as Squad Juno's Healer so you could avoid healing us when we need you. Well?" she said, nodding at her leg.

Despite his determination, Lux still felt shaky at the thought of throwing a cast. It was one thing to *believe* he could control his Twilight, another to actually do it.

"You've got this," said Fera.

"Easy," said Brace.

Lux sat next to Ester and breathed, slowing his racing heart.

Concentrate.

That's what his grandpa had told him the first time he'd thrown Light back in Daven. Concentrate. "Manipulating Light is as easy as breathing. All you have to do is focus."

Lux brought his hands together, feeling the tingle of Light along his skin. Instinctively, he almost pulled them apart again, but he held on, allowing the Light to ripple up his arms and down his chest. A power formed – the usual blue-white, growing and pulsing.

A *Heal*.

Lux explored its edges, feeling for his Twilight. And there it was . . . nudging his Light. Sweat formed on his neck. Fera laid a firm hand on his shoulder.

"You've got it."

Lux poured all of his energy into the cast, fighting to shrink the Twilight. The purple energy pushed back. Lux saw himself in Kofi, in the Cerberus's lair, then the previous night, in Ravenholm . . .

But . . .

The Twilight *wasn't* growing.

He pressed against the energy, no longer afraid, forcing it back inside him, leaving only the glowing orb of Light. His *Heal*.

"It's ready," said Brace gently.

Lux opened his eyes. The Light was shining almost pure white now. Without wasting another second, he floated it to Ester's leg, where it weaved in and out, slowly knitting her injuries.

The villagers in the room watched Ester in silence, waiting to see if the cast had worked.

Ester flexed her ankle without any pain. "Ah, nothing like a good *Heal*."

A weight the size of the world fell from Lux's shoulders. He'd done it. He'd healed someone.

"Yes!" shouted Brace.

"You did it!" said Fera. "I knew you could."

"Are you sure it's okay?" Lux asked Ester eagerly.

"Well, I couldn't do this before," she said, sweeping the pillows off her bed with her leg. "I guess you did something right."

The injured villagers were sitting up in their beds now, watching Ester's healed leg carefully. Their faces showed caution, but also interest – one or two possibly hoping Lux might heal them too.

"Give him a few minutes," said Fera.

But excitement was surging in Lux's veins. He could heal. He could *heal* again! He went to the next bed, growing another *Heal* and sending it to a young woman with a nasty bruise at her temple. She almost put out a hand to stop it, but Brace and Fera calmed her, and she allowed Lux to do his thing. Soon, the injury was gone.

Lux fixed a man's sprained wrist, and another's nasty cut. He healed an older woman who'd burned herself in the fires after his Twilight explosion, and another whose garden spade had broken her nose.

By the time he was done, they were all looking at him in awe. He couldn't hide his joy.

"I can heal again," he said.

He grew a *Catch* and dropped it to the floor, pushing Ester's cup of tea off the bedside table. It bounced off the Light, right back into his hand.

"All right, don't show off," said Brace.

"Yes," said Ester, her tone growing serious. She cast a wary glance around the room, clearly reluctant to say more in front of the villagers. "I think we should perhaps take a walk onto your parents' balcony, if that would be okay Fera?"

The younger Hunters helped Ester out of her bed. In spite of the power of Light-healing, the pain of injuries often lingered for a few days. They guided her out of the room – Lux accepting heartfelt thanks from everyone he'd healed – to a pair of double doors that opened onto the rear balcony. The sun was still shining, reflecting off the roof.

"I won't give you any pretty speeches about last night," said Ester, leaning over the rail and looking down as Lux, Brace and Fera joined her. "You saved us with your Twilight Lux. You might not feel like you did, because you weren't in control. But this village is still here because of you. And more importantly – in terms of our mission – *we're* still here because of you.

"But we can't sit around congratulating ourselves. We've got to get up that mountain as quickly as possible. And pray that Ghast is right about there being something there to stop the Hex."

"Are we still asking the villagers to distract Deimos's ships?" said Brace.

Ester faced the three younger Hunters. "You are. I'm not coming."

"But—" started Brace.

"I can't slow you down," said Ester. "Not with this." It was obvious by the way she was moving that her injury was still painful.

"But—"

She dismissed his objection. "There's no point in arguing, Brace. We have one crack at this, and it has to be perfect. You three must get up Dusk Mountain and stop Deimos. And you have to do it alone."

· CHAPTER 52 ·

If Lux could have chosen anyone at Dawnstar to be a squad leader, it would be Fera Lanceheart. He couldn't do it; he had enough on his plate with his Twilight. Brace couldn't either. He didn't take anything seriously. Fera though? She was born to take charge.

But just because she was born for the job, that didn't mean she knew it herself.

Out on the balcony, Ester pushed off the rail. "I'll be here for you, on the Shell," she said, almost laughing at the shocked faces of her squad members. "Every step of the way. But I can't come."

She tore off her squad leader badge and handed it to Fera. "You're in charge for real now."

Fera took the badge slowly, letting it hang from her hand. "Ester, I . . ."

"I know what you're going to say. You're in charge."

Fera looked to Lux and Brace to back her up. "Ester, I'm . . . not ready. Really. The stuff so far . . . it was playing around. This . . ." She glanced at Dusk Mountain. "This is serious. I can't." She tried to hand the badge back, but Ester wouldn't take it.

"You're my choice. You've shown me you have what it takes. Nothing that's happened has changed that."

Fera walked to the balcony rail, feeling the badge in her fingers. Brace joined her, nudging her affectionately.

"We'll be here for you, won't we Lux? You won't be doing it on your own."

"Definitely," agreed Lux.

Fera took in her two best friends. "Thanks, guys."

"Well, all this is lovely, but we are against the clock," said Ester, hobbling on her healed leg. "I suggest we start thinking of how we're going to convince these villagers to help us." She looked down at the town square, where the townsfolk were still busy tidying up after Lux's explosion.

"I'll speak to them," said Fera. "It's my job. I'm in charge now."

Ester gave the younger girl a proud smile.

"Get them together," Fera told Brace and Lux. "Get everyone. Mum and Dad too. And then go check on the professor and Sally. We'll need Rory to get us up to the summit."

Brace and Lux both gave her a military salute. "Yes, ma'am."

"In the meantime, I'm going to look at these Dusters, see how they work."

Before either Lux or Brace could say any more, Fera had marched back into the house. The boys were left in the sun with

Ester, shaking their heads at their friend's newfound confidence.

"I always knew she'd rule the world one day," said Brace.

The Light Hunters normally worked in small groups. Only two squads were sent to deal with most Monsters, more only if it was a particularly dangerous beast. And, so, Lux, Brace and Fera weren't used to having to convince an entire village to help them.

Two hours after their chat on the balcony, the younger members of Squad Juno were gathered beneath the Grumpy Farmer, hiding from the crowd that was starting to form in the village square. Ester was back in the sick room, resting after Lux's *Heal*.

"I really, really regret volunteering for this," said Fera, frowning at the villagers. A kindly looking elderly lady recognised her and waved. Fera ducked beneath the veranda rail.

"You'll be fine," said Brace.

Fera's cheeks were as white as snow. "It's all right for you. Some of my old teachers are here."

Lux imagined addressing Mr Winter or Mr Garside and shuddered.

"Is the professor not around?" said Fera.

Lux looked but couldn't pick out the professor's sculpted hair or Sally's blonde bob. "I bet he's still in the library."

This is where he and Brace had found Ghast earlier – a lavishly decorated space with cushioned chairs and more books than Daven's lighthouse library. The room had been topped up with the professor's artefacts, scattered all over the floor, in varying states of disrepair. The old man, they'd found tinkering with a small, golden, pyramidal object. Lux and Brace had tried to check whether Rory would be ready to fly them to Dusk Mountain, or whether the professor knew anything more about what they'd find there, but he'd shooed them away, irritated at the disruption.

"Either that or he's actually disappeared into one of his books," said Brace.

Fera's mum and dad had erected a makeshift wooden stage in the square. The crowd had gathered around it, talking nervously. It was clear that they knew something was up, but not quite what.

Her dad broke away, approaching Lux, Brace and Fera. "Ready?" he asked, pulling up short at the sight of his crouching daughter.

"Just preparing," said Fera quickly.

He gave her a sidelong glance. "I'm going to introduce you in a second. Just tell them what you told me. I'm sure they'll help."

"Have you managed to fix the broken Dusters?"

Fera's dad laid a reassuring hand on his daughter's shoulder. "You just focus on them, let me worry about the Dusters." He hurried off back to the crowd.

"Dad, is Barny here?" called Fera.

He shook his head sadly and Fera nodded mutely.

"Don't worry, you don't need Barny anyway," said Brace once he was gone.

Fera shrugged, trying to put a brave face on it. She changed the subject. "Are you two sure you don't want to come up with me?"

Lux and Brace smiled and walked off to the back of the crowd.

"I won't beat about the bush," Fera's dad told the gathered villagers when he at last climbed to the stage. "There's an emergency going on. Bigger than anything else we've ever had in Ravenholm. Fortunately, there's a way we can help. But to explain it, I'm going to hand you over to my daughter."

Fera crept out, walking timidly across the square. She tripped slightly over the ground and corrected herself. Her cheeks turned as red as an apple.

"Hi," she started when she reached the stage. Then she stopped, looking up at the blue sky, seemingly unable to talk for a moment. When she looked down again, there was fire in her eyes.

She told them everything.

About Monsters, where they came from, Deimos, what he'd done, how he was responsible for many of the Monster attacks. She told them about Rory, the Ark, and Ghast's plan to tame Monsters. She told them about the Hex, how they'd accidentally set them free. And lastly, she told them about the professor's Vision Stone, and how there might be a way to stop the Hex on Dusk Mountain.

"But to do that, we'll need your help," she finished. "We can't get through those." She pointed to the mountain, where the Shade skyships were visible, even in daylight. "There are too many. And we need Rory to get us right to the top. We'll only have one chance. So, we need you . . ." She hesitated, scanning the crowd for sympathetic faces. "We need you to distract them on Dusters."

The villagers were completely silent. Fera waited patiently for the plan to sink in. Her mum offered Lux and Brace a reassuring smile.

"It's dangerous," Fera went on. "I won't lie. I care about you all too much. So, anyone who doesn't want to go . . . nobody will be upset. But if you can," she indicated the Dusters at the side of the square, "we might be able to stop the Hex going after any other villages."

Fera breathed deeply, finished. Lux felt proud.

The crowd around them was still silent. Then they started to speak. At first to their neighbours, then all as one, discussing what she'd said. There was shock, anger, frustration, interest, fear.

The Light Hunters waited, hardly daring to speak. They needed the Ravenholmers. Their entire plan rested on them saying yes . . .

At last, a consensus seemed to form. The man with the metal brace who'd argued with Squad Juno the day before made his way to the stage. He climbed up slowly, thinking carefully about what to say.

"I – um – I think I speak for everyone when I say this has come as quite a shock." His accent was broad and thick. "And while some of us would like to help – myself included – we're scared. If Deimos is as bad as you say. . . well, what can we do against that?"

He appealed to the Light Hunters for an answer. None of them spoke. Lux's heart dropped to his feet. He knew they were asking a lot of the villagers. But without them . . .

"We can do it," tried Fera at last.

The man with the brace stepped forward, lowering his voice. "I mean this with all due respect darling . . . but, well, you're just kids."

Fera was so taken aback by this that she couldn't speak. Lux was about to say something when his attention was stolen by a movement to his right. To his astonishment, he saw Barny, his white shirt grubby and his black hair hiding his face, climbing to the stage.

"They aren't just kids," he said. "They're Light Hunters."

"Barny," said Fera, surprised. "What are you doing?"

"Fixing a mistake." He took a deep breath and closed his eyes. "For all these years, I've been angry at myself," he told the crowd. "For not protecting this place. For not looking after everyone when the Cerberus attacked. I've never forgiven myself. And all this time I've been angry at my sister too. Going off to the Light Hunters instead of staying with our family and helping clean up the mess. But the truth is, I'm actually proud of her. She was brave when I wasn't." He looked at Fera. "I'm sorry. About everything."

Fera stared at her brother, deciding whether to forgive him. She launched at him, Barny gathering her in a bear-hug and swinging her around. When he put her down again, he addressed the crowd.

"I've spent a long time thinking about the Cerberus attack on our village. We all lost someone we cared about that day. The man up that mountain – Deimos – is responsible for that. Just as he's responsible for similar attacks all over. We have an opportunity to stop him. *And* the Hex. Imagine what you'll tell your grandchildren. Not just, I was there when the Light Hunters went to Dusk Mountain, but I WENT WITH THEM."

"Do you swear, if there's something up on that mountain, they'll make it work?" the man with the brace asked Barny. "The kids? Because we'd be risking a lot."

Barny handed the question to Fera, who spoke loud and clear. "We swear."

The man with the brace shook his head ruefully, not quite able to believe what he was about to say. "Then I'll make no-one come who doesn't want to, but those who do . . ." He looked up at Dusk Mountain. "I guess we'll come and see what we can do about helping put this man, Deimos, in his place."

· CHAPTER 53 ·

Sometimes, Light Hunters had a hundred jobs to do and only one hour in which to do them.

But the list of jobs to complete before their trip to Dusk Mountain nearly made Lux want to give up on the whole idea and crawl back into bed.

There was the greasing of the Dusters, the preparing of food, the coming up with a plan of attack, the appointing of leaders, and scouts to communicate with Ravenholm, and on, and on . . .

The Light Hunters, for their part, had their own things to prepare. Packing their bags for a start. Brace often forgot his, but Fera never went on a mission without hers. And there was also the matter of what they were going to do once they arrived at the mountain.

"We can't really have a plan if we don't know what's there," argued Brace.

"We can try and anticipate," said Fera.

"Anticipate what's on an unknown mountain with our arch enemy, who's shown a dozen times you can't predict what he'll do?" Brace raised a sceptical eyebrow. "I'll just be happy if he hasn't got any Monsters with him."

Lux took a long time to pack, as he had to make sure he had all his usual things – his Shell, his jacket, some food – but also the Key to the Ark. He'd moved to a spare bedroom in Fera's mum and dad's house, and was wrapping the Key carefully, when he heard a quiet crackle on his Shell.

"Dawnstar to Lux?"

He grinned as he continued to pack. "I'm here Maya. What's going on?"

"Oh, nothing. Just more towns and villages surrounded. Thought I'd check how you guys are getting on?"

Lux finished wrapping the Key and slid it carefully into his bag. "We're about to leave."

"Ooh, the big one?"

"The big one."

Maya was quiet for a moment. "Get him this time, Lux. For everyone."

He took the route down to Rory's stable determinedly, thinking only of what he was about to do. The clouds had gathered again, burying the barn in shadow. Brace and Fera were already inside, waiting patiently, along with Fera's mum and dad and Barny, who was making last-minute adjustments to his Duster. Rory was lying lazily on the hay, his forelimbs stretched out in front. Lux breathed in the thick, animal smell and walked inside.

"Here he is," said Barny. "And there I was thinking my sister was always the late one."

Fera elbowed him fondly.

"I tell you, you Light Hunters don't half scrub up nice," said Fera's dad, admiring his daughter's immaculate uniform. "However, I can safely say I didn't ever expect to have a Monster in my stable." He shook his head in wonder at Rory for what Lux guessed was the hundredth time.

"All set?" Brace asked him.

"Think so."

"Well, that makes two of us," said Barny, throwing away the cloth he'd been using to clean his Duster and hanging the contraption from his shoulder. "I think it's about time I made tracks."

Fera hugged her brother. "Be careful. Just distract the ships. No hero stuff."

"Leave that to you, eh? Don't worry, I fully intend to come out of this alive."

After saying goodbye, Barny hurried off in the direction of the town square where the villagers were waiting for him, whistling a happy tune.

"That boy has no fear," said his mum.

"That's what worries me," said Fera.

"You focus on your own stuff." Fera's mum hugged her. "And for Light's sake, be careful. All of you," she added.

Together, she and her husband headed out of the barn. "Give him a good thrashing from me," said Fera's dad, turning on the threshold.

And then it was just Lux, Brace and Fera.

Squad Juno had been on some tough missions, but *nothing* like this one. The fate of the world rested on their shoulders. What could they possibly say?

It was Fera who broke the silence, laying a hand on Rory's flank. "Where are the professor and Sally? They should be here by now."

"All right, all right," came Ghast's breathless voice from the courtyard. "I'll have you know I've been busily working while all you lot have been resting."

The professor hurried inside with Sally, looking a little the worse for wear, with a day's stubble and dark rings under his eyes. He was carrying a leather bag, which he hung from one of the dividers.

"There's not an easy way to say this, so I'll just say it," he said, facing the Light Hunters. "Sally and I won't be coming with you." Before anyone could respond, he forged on. "Dusk Mountain is dangerous at the best of times. And this is most certainly *not* the best of times." Ghast held Sally's hand. "I can't risk her, and I can't risk myself. I'm sorry."

He waited for the Light Hunters' response.

Fera shrugged. "That's fine. We figured you wouldn't be coming."

"I just can't risk it!" blurted the professor. Then he paused,

Fera's response finally sinking in. "It's fine?"

"Yeah. We wouldn't want either of you to come. Deimos . . . well, you've met him. He's a job for Light Hunters."

"There's only one problem," said Brace. "Two, actually. You'll have to tell us a bit about what we might find up there. And if Sally isn't going, who'll fly us to the summit?"

Ghast brightened, realising he could answer at least one of Brace's questions. "The first one's easy. I truly don't know. You saw the Vision Stone. All we can guess is that there's *something* up there that might help. If I had to give you any advice, it would be to head to any Ancient ruins you see. That's what I normally do, and it's served me well so far. But after that your guess is as good as mine."

The professor hurried to the bag he'd hung on the divider and brought out an object no larger than his hand. It was formed of a gold, pyramidal shape and a loop of silver metal. Inside the loop was a tiny orb of Light, flecked with purple. The same device Lux and Brace has seen him tinkering with in the library.

"There's a chance this might come in handy before events are through," he said, closing Lux's hand carefully around it.

"What is it?"

"Let's just say it might turn the tide in any battle with Monsters you come across."

Ghast was cut off by a noise outside. Lux saw what looked like a cloud of black insects flying towards them from the village square. He realised quickly that it was Barny and the villagers on the Dusters.

The group grew larger, until Lux could make out Fera's brother at the front, standing up like he was riding a horse into battle.

Nobody in the barn spoke as the Dusters passed overhead, disappearing over the trees and fields in the direction of Dusk Mountain.

"He's a good boy, your brother," said Ghast.

"I know," said Fera. "But about who's going to fly Rory . . ."

"Perhaps it would be best if I answer that one, Professor."

Rory's deep voice boomed out in the quiet stable, carrying with it ash and fire. The Monster had woken from his snooze and had pushed himself up on his haunches, peering around sleepily.

"I have never allowed anybody to fly me other than the little girl standing there," he said, nodding his ancient head at Sally. "However, I believe there is one in your group who is a flier."

Brace was staring out of the window, daydreaming. When Rory's words registered, he almost jumped in excitement. "Me?"

"Your passion for flying is evident in your every bone, Brace. And for that, I will trust you to take me. I only ask that you are careful; I am not as young as I appear."

An enormous grin tugged at Brace's lips. All his birthday wishes had come true at once.

"Do you feel like you can handle this responsibility?" said the Monster.

"I was born for it," said Brace.

"Then it's settled," said Rory slowly. "We have a flier."

· CHAPTER 54 ·

The three Light Hunters climbed onto the Monster's back as Lux put Ghast's device – still wondering what on earth it might be – into his bag next to the Key to the Ark.

"Are we ready?" Rory called, the breath from his nostrils warming the Hunters.

"Double-ready," said Brace excitedly, giving the Monster's reins a shake.

"Double-ready... I like that." Rory chuckled, then rose onto four legs and made his way outside.

The ground quickly turned into a grey and brown blur as Brace guided the Monster up, so much gentler with the reins than Lux thought he would be, easing the creature left and right, dipping to avoid a windmill blade and pulling up again. The Monster flared his nostrils, his molten interior burning red.

"You fly well," he told Brace.

"I know." The grin on Brace's face was so large it threatened to leap right off.

Soon, they'd left the relative safety of Ravenholm, and they were above the clouds, the sun shining like a shailing. Through breaks in the mist, Lux saw the city of Lindhelm, sparkling in the distance.

"You three are brave for what you are attempting here," said Rory, as Brace steered him towards Dusk Mountain.

"I don't feel brave," said Fera.

"This mountain is a sacred place. The Ancients who built their temples here considered it the most important location in the world. Always easy to set something in motion, harder to change one's mind. The Ark a tower to set the Hex free, the mountain a place to stop them."

The Monster flew a couple of metres higher, and the view, which before had been blocked by cloud, revealed the trio of peaks that made up Dusk Mountain, so much closer now. Their ridges shone blue and orange. The middle peak – Lux, Brace and Fera's destination – leaned ever so slightly forward, like it was waiting for them. Two rockslides resembled angry, grey eyes.

Brace flew Rory until the Monster dipped his head of his own accord and sank, causing the three Light Hunters to hold on tightly to avoid being thrown off. Icy wind blasted their faces.

At last, they broke through the clouds.

The entire mountain range was visible now, running along the coast. Their foothills were covered in trees like moss on a stone, and lively rivers tumbled to the sea.

But it was the ring of black and grey skyships that caught Lux's eye. Their hulls reflected the sun, merging with the deep red of their Shade. The biggest ship, black as a starless night, had to be Deimos's personal craft.

"Oh my Light!" said Brace. "There are so many."

"That's just . . ." Fera clutched her chest in fright. "Barny!"

Lux spotted the Dusters, a buzzing cloud between Rory and the ships. They were preparing to attack.

There was a moment, whenever the Light Hunters approached a Monster's lair, when Lux felt his stomach drop out beneath him. He trembled, his heartbeat galloped, and his palms grew sweaty.

Not this time.

As Lux looked up at Dusk Mountain, he felt calm. Pushing all negative thoughts away, he concentrated on just one: if his intentions were good, the rest would take care of itself.

Rory closed in on the Dusters, until the Light Hunters could see Barny and the villagers clearly, looking nervous, serious. The great Monster stopped fifty metres off, beating his wings.

Barny heard the *whumph-whumph* of the shifting air, and looked over, sticking up his thumb. Lux, Brace and Fera returned the gesture, nodding for him to go when he was ready. Flicking his black hair out of his eyes, Barny raised a hand, holding it momentarily as Deimos's skyships towered over them like Monsters.

Then he dropped it.

In an instant, the villagers were pedalling, their Dusters droning like angry wasps. They flew in the direction of the ships –

still a good hundred metres away – adjusting their bearing left or right and forming a loose V-shape, with Barny at the tip.

Soon, the Dusters were hidden in the shadows of the dark ships. A bloom of red energy burst forth, and long arcs of Shade flashed towards the villagers, forcing Barny to lead them quickly right. The Shade sailed safely by, crashing into the forest at the foot of the mountain.

Barny pedalled on through more Shade. Most of the ships were firing now, some even turning in the sky to face the approaching Dusters. Lux could see figures crawling across the decks, pointing down, trying to work out what was happening.

"We've got to help them," said Fera.

"We can't," cried Lux, feeling awful even as he said it.

The Dusters were a blur now against the blue sky. Barny raised his hand again, and the two arms of the V-shape split apart – one going left and high, the other right and low. They moved as fast as their furiously pedalling legs would allow, looking like birds in formation. To Lux's happy astonishment, the Shade engines of some of Deimos's ships fired, sending up loud *booms*. They moved slowly towards the villagers, taking the bait, climbing in the clouds.

But Barny . . .

Barny had split from the other villagers and was flying on his own, a lone black figure against the blue.

"What's he doing?" said Brace.

At first, Lux had no answer. It certainly wasn't what they'd planned.

Then he understood.

Behind Barny now was the biggest skyship of all. Black hull, twin burning engines, dozens of tiny people ranging back and forth, their long black coats like suits of armour. Deimos's skyship, Lux realised with a sinking feeling. Barny was going straight for Deimos's skyship.

He was, in fact, heading for the Shade engines at the stern. And he had something in his hand, something that glinted in the sun.

A knife.

"We've got to stop him!" yelled Fera.

She tried to take Rory's reins from Brace, but he kept them out of reach. "We can't."

"Brace!" she snapped.

"We *can't*."

"Brace!"

He pushed the reins aside and turned to Fera. "Has Barny trusted you today?"

Fera tried to reach the reins but missed.

"Has he?"

She stopped. "Yes."

"Then you have to trust him."

Brace held her stare. Fera appealed to Lux, but he nodded his agreement.

She sighed. "We make it worth it then," she said simply.

They watched Barny reach the engines of Deimos's skyship – two fiery red Shade panels – then work at them with his knife.

Taking that as his cue, Brace grasped Rory's reigns and leaned into the Monster's ear. "Ready?"

"Double-ready," came the ancient voice.

Brace grinned. "Let's fly."

The villagers had dragged enough of Deimos's ships aside now that there was a narrow gap, leading to one of Dusk Mountain's landslides. Rory shifted so he was face-on with it, letting out a loud roar. He beat his enormous wings and shot towards the gap like an arrow.

The wind whipped at Lux, plastering his hair to his eyes. He gripped Rory, ignoring the Monster's heat, squeezing tight.

In less than a minute they'd closed in on the gap, seeing for the first time the stunned faces of the people on Deimos's ships. Dusters, a Monster – they hadn't been expecting any of it. Lux searched for Deimos's wide-brimmed hat but there was no sign.

A couple of Shade casts shot towards them. Rory avoided them as easily as if they were flies.

Realising their attacks were having no effect, the remaining skyships started to move, closing the gap. The others – those distracted by the Dusters – turned back too, leaving the villagers safe in the sky.

Lux's heart was in his throat.

The gap was closing fast. Rory cracked his wings, Brace swinging him left and right to avoid Shade. But it was clear that they wouldn't make it.

They *had* to get through. Now, or else it would be too late.

Lux wanted to scream, leap for the gap.

He was saved by a loud explosion off to his left. Flames mushroomed at the side of Deimos's skyship, mixed with Shade and some other kind of energy – Light, perhaps. Lux tasted smoke and coughed a couple of times. He squeezed his eyes shut against the thick mist.

When he opened them, his soul lifted.

Flying towards them as fast as his pedalling legs would allow, was Barny, his black hair white with ash. On his face was an enormous grin. And where the explosion had occurred was now a hole in the black ship, revealing the grassy slopes of the mountain beyond. Just about big enough, Lux realised, for Rory to squeeze through.

"Woohoo!" yelled Barny as he flashed past, reaching to brush Fera's fingertips.

"Thank you, brother!"

Brace guided Rory towards the expanded gap, ducking beneath one of the bigger skyships and narrowly avoiding a flash of Shade.

A pair of heads appeared out of the hole in the ship, their hands coming together at their chests, red orbs forming. Before Lux could say anything, a *Snow* flew from Fera's chest, as well as a series of Light-arrows from Brace's bow, smashing into what remained of the hull and sending the man and woman flying. Their Shade casts dropped harmlessly to the mountain.

And then Rory was upon the gap, thrashing his wings in one last heroic effort, slicing through like a knife. On the other side, the air was clear. The mountain lay ahead of them, peaceful, its snowy peaks looming high.

Brace let go of Rory and turned in the saddle, his face still in shock. "Next time," he said, "when Legau Moreiss tells me I can't fly . . . remind him of this."

· CHAPTER 55 ·

Partway through Lux's first year with the Light Hunters, a blizzard had swept into Korat Crater, surrounding Dawnstar and forcing everyone to stay inside for a week. Icicles had formed in the library, the training wing, and even, if Brace was to be believed, on Artello Nova's chin. But that storm was nothing compared to the one Lux saw at the top of Dusk Mountain.

From afar, the peaks had looked welcoming, like on a painting in a gallery. But now Lux could see a blanket of dark cloud, dumping thick snow all around. A white mist covered everything, out of which bare, bony trees reached like grasping hands. The wind was howling, audible even from a distance, and crystal ice coated the ground.

"Well, that'll make things harder," said Brace.

"I hope Barny's all right," said Fera worriedly, searching behind them for her brother in the sky. All she could see was the black wall of Deimos's skyships, and iron-grey smoke.

"He got away. We saw him," said Lux.

Rory was flying them up the right-most peak, sailing by a tall, pencil-shaped outcrop carved over the centuries by wind. There were no paths on the mountain. No sign, in fact, that anybody had been there for a very long time.

"You three will be fine," said Rory, sensing their trepidation.

The great Monster flew on, easing himself over the jagged landscape, until the central peak lay directly ahead. They were close now, and for the first time Lux could see Ancient stone towers on the summit, standing up out of the blizzard like soldiers. There were two smaller stones either side – Lux thought of them as small, but really they had to be as big as houses – with one taller in the middle. He glanced over his shoulder at the peak they'd just left behind and was surprised to see more ruins he'd missed before.

"Look."

Brace and Fera studied the stones carefully.

It was horribly cold now and the mist had swallowed them, making it hard to see. A wind keened in Lux's ear. He said a silent prayer, hoping Rory had some way of seeing in the gloom.

Soon, the snow was falling around them. And then they were flying through the blizzard – shailing-sized flakes of snow blasting into their cheeks. They each took their jackets out and pulled them on. Lux clutched his bag close, feeling the Key to the Ark's comforting bulk.

Suddenly, Rory dived. Brace grabbed his reins, figuring something was wrong. But in spite of his efforts, the Monster continued to sink.

"I cannot go on," he explained, his voice muffled by snow. "I have no ability to see in this weather. I will set you down and you must continue on foot."

Lux glanced quickly at the mountain peak and was relieved to see they were most of the way there.

The Monster touched down on a frozen riverbank with a soft *crunch*, flattening the grass. He shook a layer of snow off his back, the white misting where it touched his warm scales.

"I am sorry," he said, swinging his long neck to address the Light Hunters. "To carry on would be too dangerous. I will wait for you here." He said no more.

Slowly, and with sore legs, the three Hunters climbed off the Monster, landing on the slippery rock, their feet instantly numb in the snow. Lux pulled up his hood, turning from the wind.

The river next to which they'd landed was surrounded by blackened trees. Snow was everywhere, and the wind was astonishingly strong, pushing them back. Lux looked up at the Ancient ruins, peeking above the blizzard. The route there dipped, then rose again. On either side was a sheer drop.

"I hope you've got a couple of *Catches* ready for us," said Brace, looking worriedly at the chasm.

Lux felt a familiar panic at the suggestion, but pressed down on it, making it small. *I can control my powers. I can control my powers.*

"I'll be ready."

It was horribly cold as they started through the endless white. Lux's teeth chattered wildly, and his fingers were like blocks of ice. He stuffed them into his armpits, as Fera did her best to cast a *Flame* – anything to provide a little heat. But she was too cold to hold it and let go.

"I-I w-wish I-I'd kn-known a-about t-t-this c-c-cold," stammered Brace, smacking his hands, trying to work some life into them.

They'd travelled a few hundred metres from Rory now, who they could just about see as a tiny red speck against the white. To be near his molten heat, those warm scales . . . Lux shivered in desire.

With each step, it got colder and colder, until the three Light Hunters were struggling to carry on. Their pace slowed to a crawl. Ice had formed along Brace's eyebrows, and Lux's hands were turning blue.

"This isn't normal," said Fera, looking around, suddenly on her guard. She staggered to the frozen stream, where shards of water stuck out at odd angles.

She's right, Lux thought, *there is something wrong. It's too cold.*

He looked around, his attention drawn to a copse of trees on the other side of the stream, thick with mist and snow. Inside, he saw something blue. Brace and Fera called out as he navigated his way across.

"Hey!"

Lux moved into the bare trees as if he was being drawn there against his will, moving closer to the blue smudge. There was a sound – a sparkling, twinkling sound. Lux followed it into the deep, swirling white.

Then he stopped.

All around him was complete silence.

And something else. Something terrible.

Deimos's ice-Monster.

· CHAPTER 56 ·

The creature's crystal blue skin glittered dangerously. There was no expression on its face, no sense that it even knew Lux was there other than its dead eyes, which stared blankly back at him.

Brace and Fera pulled up behind Lux, staring at the Monster.

"Wonderful," said Brace sarcastically. "I was hoping he'd be here."

The wind whipped at the lifeless trees, tossing blasts of thick snow at the Hunters. The ice-Monster didn't react.

Brace urged Lux to leave. "Come on, it's not attacking . . ."

As if reacting to his words, the Monster lunged closer to the Light Hunters, before stopping again. Its expression remained the same.

Lux's stomach was rolling. He tried to swallow but his throat was dry.

"We've got to go," whispered Fera.

Why is it here? Lux wondered. *Why isn't it attacking us?*

"Lux . . ."

He allowed Fera to lead him away. But they'd hardly moved when there was a flash of white, brighter even than the blizzard around them. When Lux opened his eyes again, he was standing in the familiar white place.

Except this time, Brace and Fera were there too. They gasped, looking around with wide, frightened eyes.

Something strange was happening. Lux couldn't put his finger on what, but the ice-Monster seemed different somehow.

"We really don't have time for this," said Fera. There was a soft *whoosh* as she readied a *Flame*. Brace followed up with his Light-bow.

But something *was* different.

"We go on three," called Fera, moving into attacking position. "Lux, be ready with a *Heal*."

His hands went instinctively to his chest, but he hesitated. The Monster . . . it was looking at him. But there was no malice in its eyes. He'd never seen that in a Monster apart from Rory.

"One," called Fera.

Sally's great Fire-drake . . . the wings, the deep red scales. Lux heard Rory's rumbling voice. 'Monsters weren't bad,' the professor had said . . .

"Two . . ."

Lux knew, deep down, that they shouldn't attack. How could they ever attack a Monster again, knowing what Ghast could do? If only he had some way to turn it . . .

He gasped.

The professor's device.

"*Let's just say that it might turn the tide in any battle with Monsters you come across.*"

The device would let him cast *Turn*.

"Three."

Fera went to toss her *Flame*, but Lux knocked her aside, spinning the cast through the air so that it landed on the ground near the trees. It flared orange, fizzling to nothing. Brace, his Light-bow poised, stared at him as if he'd lost his mind.

"Don't fire!" Lux's eyes were wild, flaming.

Brace appealed to Fera, who was still trying to work out what was going on. Lux met their fierce stares with one of his own.

"Wait!"

Reluctantly, Fera indicated for Brace to stand down.

Scrambling to his feet, Lux found the professor's device inside his bag. But how to use it? A gold pyramid, a loop of silver metal. What was he supposed to do?

"Lux, I suggest you do whatever you've got planned quickly." Fera's voice trembled as she and Brace backed away from the Monster.

He fumbled with the device. Was it something to do with the loop? The pyramid? He tried poking them, copying what he'd seen Maya do with old artefacts in Tesla's lab. Nothing happened.

Come on.

Turn. Lux didn't know the cast. The professor had never explained how to throw it. But he'd given him the device for a reason. It had to do *something*.

It was then he noticed the purple in the middle of the silver loop. The professor had said that getting *Turn* to work had something to do with Twilight. Perhaps he'd designed the artefact to help.

The ice-Monster growled.

It was the first noise it had made since they'd found it, and it rumbled in the creature's throat, shaking off shards of blue ice, which thudded to the ground. It leapt forwards, faster than Brace during a *Blink*.

"Lux!"

Out of time, he lifted the artefact to his chest, shutting out all the noise. He found his Twilight, tucked away in a far-off corner and grew it, pressing down on a wave of panic, until it rolled down his arms, his hands. He was almost wincing at the loss of control. But he breathed, thinking of his friends.

The Twilight jumped into Ghast's device, turning the Light there pure purple. It vibrated, giving off a loud wailing sound. Without any movement from Lux, the orb floated away, heading straight for the Monster.

The creature snarled, backing off, but the orb broke over it like a wave. The Twilight expanded, swallowing it up.

Lux blinked.

When he opened his eyes, he was back on the riverbank, the copse of trees at his back. The snow had gone and the blizzard too, so that lush green grass led away along the bank. The air was clear – the mist replaced by a crisp blue sky, speckled with clouds.

The river flowed gently by, and birds tweeted in the trees. A smell of pine hung in the air.

Lux looked around. Brace and Fera's faces were masks of amazement. The cold was . . . gone.

There was a growl over Lux's shoulder, and he turned to see the ice-Monster, standing completely still, positioned so as to block their path, its blue skin twinkling in the sun.

Lux stepped forward, breathing slowly. There was a horrible moment where he thought Ghast's device hadn't worked, that the *Turn* had failed.

But, instead, the Monster stepped aside, letting the Light Hunters past.

As they drew level, Lux heard a small sound to his right. A voice – rough and ancient.

"Thank you."

The creature fled, bounding through the trees.

· CHAPTER 57 ·

There was something about being with Brace and Fera that made Lux feel safer, made him feel like he could do anything. He felt it now as they crossed the newly thawed ground, heading towards the peak of Dusk Mountain.

They walked in silence, taking in what had just happened.

Light Hunters trained, over and over, to fight Monsters. Many could throw Light better than they could add or read. All those Monsters they'd killed . . . could they have tamed them instead?

The ridge curved around a large boulder, and they came face-to-face with the Ancient ruins, at the top of a narrow, rocky path.

What from back in the air had looked like little sticks were in fact great formations of rock, laced with blue energy. They were surrounded by a green meadow, dotted with trees – all neat and trim, as if the ruins themselves were keeping the land tidy. A shallow pond lay at the foot of the stones. There was not a sound to be heard. Even the wind seemed to have died.

Lux saw Deimos beneath the right-most tower.

He didn't try to hide.

He tipped his wide-brimmed hat mockingly at the Light Hunters, revealing a tangle of grey-blonde hair. His face was dark, inscrutable.

He walked slowly to a podium at the foot of the central tower, formed of the same inky material as back at the Ark. "I knew it would only be a matter of time."

Brace bristled, but Lux held him back. He searched the meadow for any more of Deimos's people, but it was empty.

"I'm intrigued to know how you got past my ice-Monster," Deimos called. He leaned on the podium, at the top of which was a jigsaw-like piece of metal. "Perhaps you three are more resourceful than I give you credit for."

Back at the ridge, Lux grabbed Brace and Fera, his mind made up. "I want you to stay here."

His friends rose up, ready to protest.

"I know, we're a team," said Lux. "And I wouldn't have got up here without you. But you have to trust me. I've got to do this alone. I was the one who set the Hex free. It was me who put the Key in. I'm responsible. It's me who's got to finish it."

"But ..." Brace looked at Fera in frustration. "But ... we'll help."

"I know you would. But it's up to me from here."

"Lux . . ." Fera's tone was stern, "Ester left me in charge and I say ..."

She trailed off, seeing his determined expression.

"It's not that I don't want you guys," said Lux, glancing at Deimos, who was watching them with mild amusement. "But we all know that if the three of us go up, he'll use you against me. Like at the Ark. And in Kofi. I can't have that happen."

Brace and Fera exchanged a glance, deciding what to do. Lux could see Brace didn't want to leave him, but Fera understood.

"If we think you need us, we're coming up," she warned.

"Deal," said Lux.

He took a deep, fortifying breath, enjoying the gentle sunlight on his face.

It was up to him now. If he could control his Twilight, and the professor and Rory were right about there being something at the Ancient ruins to stop the Hex, he might be able to do it. But it was all up to him.

He thanked Brace and Fera, proud they'd been strong enough to trust him. Then he walked up the narrow path to the three towers.

"There was a Monster once who didn't put out a call to its spawn when it was in danger," said Deimos at Lux's approach. "Solas, it was called. It was a fool for thinking it could manage alone." He glanced witheringly down at Lux's friends. "You are too."

"I'm not here to talk," said Lux.

Deimos laughed. A horrible, cold laugh that would have had Lux shuddering any other time. "You are a foolish child," he spat. "You should leave now before I send you to meet your grandpa."

Lux absorbed Deimos's words and let them go, shaking away a

painful image of his grandpa with the *Revive* cast that would have saved his life. He went to his bag instead and pulled out the Key to the Ark. Deimos was still beside the podium. He would have to go through him.

Deimos tensed at the sight of the Key. "You still have it."

"Get out of my way," said Lux. He hadn't moved more than a few steps when a red Shade wall appeared in front of him, fizzing and cracking. He tried to walk around it, but it followed him, blocking his path.

"Your last warning, Lux." Deimos looked darker than ever, angrier. "You are a fool for trying to stop me. The world *needs* this. You should have joined me when you had the chance."

Lux knew Light wouldn't get him through Deimos's Shade wall. He'd seen Brace, Ester and Fera try to break Shade bubbles with their Light back in Kofi and the Ark to no effect. He was also a Healer – he had no offensive casts.

"Monsters were attacking the people of our world long before I left Dawnstar, you know?" A ribbon of Twilight shot up out of the podium and around the tower, jumping through the air to those either side.

"Hundreds. Villages, towns, cities – destroyed. They're a menace. They were created to *be* a menace."

"Professor Ghast knows how to tame them," said Lux.

"Ghast is a fool."

"We tamed your ice-Monster."

This information made Deimos pause for second. But he brushed it away.

"For thousands of years we have been at the mercy of these creatures. Thousands! What you did at the Ark finally set in motion a way of stopping them."

"People will die!" Lux shouted, rushing at the Shade barrier. He bounced off it like a rag-doll.

"And some will live. In a world without Monsters. It will be a happier place."

Lux scoffed.

Deimos adjusted his hat, taking a moment to think. His long, black coat flowed behind him.

"We could be among those people, you know, you and I? With your Twilight and my Shade, just imagine what we could do together in that new world."

Deimos's eyes blazed at the thought. Lux tried the Shade barrier again, his heart racing. He had to find a way.

"I can save your friends, too," Deimos said temptingly. "Get them away from the Hex. They will disappear again, you know? Back underground. Once they've done their work it'll be like they were never here. No Monsters, no attacks. And the price? Just a few lives."

Lux felt sick to his very core. Had Shade really twisted Deimos this much? He looked back at Brace and Fera. Brace moved as if to come and join him. Lux shook his head.

Twilight.

That was key. It had to be.

But the risk . . . Lux had managed to control it with Ghast's device, but that was only a tiny amount. To get rid of Deimos's

Shade barrier would require much more. Get it wrong and any chance they had of saving everyone would be gone.

But he had to do something.

All of a sudden, a small voice came to Lux: *"It's not what we do that should make us boast, but our intentions that matter the most."*

If his intentions were good, the world would help him. Lux had to believe that.

He found that little spark of Twilight, like he had with the ice-Monster, and let it all come to the surface – all of it – racing down his arms, his chest.

"Lux . . ." Deimos warned.

Lux carried on. Every bone in his body was telling him to stop. That horrible, booming sensation he felt just before he exploded grew inside of him, but he ignored it.

"It's not what we do that should make us boast, but our intentions that matter the most."

Believe, thought Lux.

"I am warning you." There was a note of panic in Deimos's voice now.

Lux carried on channelling his Twilight.

"Lux, stop!"

Deimos grew a Shade cast – a deep, blood-red ball of darkness – and sent it around the barrier.

Lux flicked it away as if it was made of air.

"No!"

Deimos kindled another. Lux flicked out his Twilight and it was gone.

"Lux..."

Deimos was almost pleading. He paced quickly, breathing heavily, looking at the podium, the jigsaw piece.

But it was too late.

The orb of Twilight at Lux's chest was so large now that he couldn't hold it. He pushed it at the Shade wall, where there was a flash of strange, pinkish light and the sound of metal scraping metal.

Then all was quiet. The watery sun beat on the Ancient monuments.

Lux opened his eyes and his stomach lurched. He'd done it. He'd controlled his Twilight.

And Deimos's Shade barrier...

It was gone.

· CHAPTER 58 ·

There was something beautiful about Twilight. The colours – lavender mixed with mauve and mulberry. Lux knew them all from the times his grandpa had him painting old wind-up toys in the repair shop. He looked at his Twilight now, still dancing at his fingertips, amazed at what it had done.

Deimos . . .

It had stopped him.

Lux was vaguely aware of Brace and Fera cheering behind him.

"No!" yelled Deimos, stumbling backwards. Then, pure evil warped his features. His jaw clenched and his face went red. "No!"

He grew another Shade cast and threw it at Lux. Then another, fast as lightning.

Lux merely lifted his arm, and his Twilight deflected the casts away.

"No!" yelled Deimos. "No!"

He threw more Shade, the casts forming a crimson rainbow, but Lux didn't flinch. They fell to the ground, fizzing in the grass.

"How?" Deimos gripped the podium, the veins in his neck bulging with panic. "I won't let you ruin this!"

Lux took in the man he'd been so scared of when he'd first seen him back on Daven beach, the man who'd stopped his *Revive* cast saving his grandpa in Kofi. He was beaten.

"Ghast is wrong," snarled Deimos. "All he's shown you is a trick."

"Move," commanded Lux. Deimos gripped the stone even more tightly, like a wild animal.

"You think you're going to save everyone. All you're doing is dooming them to a life of suffering."

"Get out of my way. I don't want to hurt you." Lux allowed his Twilight to flicker threateningly. With his other hand, he pulled the Key to the Ark out of his bag. The dull, heavy metal was smooth and cold.

"You mustn't," said Deimos, looking at the Key in panic. "Think of all the pain Monster attacks have caused. So many dead. Your own parents. Think of the Cerberus in Daven. I was there. I saw it. I saw people begging for it to end."

Lux stepped forward, but images of his lost family flashed through his mind. His parents, his sister.

"And your grandpa," cried Deimos. "What happened at Kofi. No Monsters, and he'd still be alive."

Lux tried to take another step but hesitated.

His grandpa. The *Revive*.

"You did that," he said angrily.

"Tell me, Lux, what if Ghast is wrong?" prodded Deimos, the ruthless cold returning to his voice. "What if he can't tame the Monsters? This is our only chance to end them. If you stop the Hex now . . ."

A wave of sickness crashed over Lux. What if Deimos was right? What if Ghast *was* wrong? What if Lux's desperate desire for Monster attacks to end was blinding him to the truth?

"We must allow the Hex to do what they were created to do," said Deimos.

"No . . ."

"Lux, we can't take the risk."

A roaring sound was building inside Lux. Screaming. He saw Monsters – all those in *The Book of Monsters* back at Dawnstar. Teeth, claws, spikes. He saw the walls of the Intelligence wing covered with details of attacks. Dozens in the past year, thousands over the centuries. He saw his own parents, his sister. He saw his grandpa, the old man's memorial in Korat Crater.

What if Deimos was right? What if Ghast was wrong?

What about Maya? Her family? All the kids at Daven orphanage? What about Tesla, and the little girl he'd lost on his Behemoth mission? What about Nova and his injured arm? What about the people who'd died at Fera's farm?

"Give me the Key," said Deimos coolly, holding out his hand. His words were soft, coaxing.

"No!" shouted Brace.

His voice was muffled in Lux's ears. Everything around him

was colourless, grey. He was alone. Could he really ignore this way of stopping Monsters? Could he really trust Ghast? Could he believe him?

Believe.

The word rose gently in Lux's mind. His heartrate slowed and his breathing calmed.

"*It's not what we do that should make us boast, but our intentions that matter the most.*"

He pulled back his shoulders and raised his right hand. A purple thread of Twilight twisted away from it, floating to Deimos.

"Lux, no . . ."

The thread wrapped around him like a spider's web, until he couldn't move. With a wave, Lux lifted him and set him down several metres away, in the pond.

"No!"

Lux turned the Key to the Ark in his hand, seeing Dusk Mountain carved into each segment. He positioned it above the podium.

"Do it!" shouted Brace.

Lux closed his eyes and slotted the Key inside.

· CHAPTER 59 ·

A flash of Twilight.

Like the one Lux had seen in the Vision Stone back in Ghast's cottage.

The beam lit the sky, shooting up in a straight line, up, up, up, before breaking just beneath the wispy clouds.

The Twilight split into three tight beams, which fell lazily to the towers, flowing down them with a keening sound that was so loud Lux and the others had to cover their ears in pain.

Then silence.

The dark towers started to glow – a Twilight purple. They pulsed and the ground shook.

Lux gripped the podium as the grass swayed back and forth like waves on the ocean. Ripples split the pond and great cracks sounded as the mountains shifted in the air.

Lux was dimly aware of Brace and Fera joining him. He looked in the distance at the two other peaks that formed Dusk Mountain, their rocky summits hazy in the morning mist.

More Twilight beams shot into the sky.

Lux realised that it wasn't just the ground *beneath* them that was moving, but the actual mountain itself. All three peaks, shifting and reforming, bringing the two smaller towers closer to the central one.

The noise was deafening. Louder than the cries of a hundred Monsters.

The peaks moved slowly into position, causing all of Deimos's skyships to scatter in the sky.

Then they were in place, right next to each other. Nine towers, all in a row, all shining with Twilight.

"What now?" asked Brace.

He didn't have to wait long to find out.

The nine towers returned to their old inky black. All apart from the central one, which absorbed the energy from the others, beating rhythmically.

The tower started to vibrate, rippling the pondwater around Deimos. The Twilight gathered near the Key to the Ark, humming, its aura so powerful that the kids stepped back a few paces, just in case.

Then, like a dam breaking, Twilight shot away from the tower, perfect spheres of energy that coloured the world purple.

They spread, rocking Lux and the others as they passed over them, then over Deimos's skyships. They carried on, away from the Mountain, towards Ravenholm and Lindhelm, glittering far off, then to Dawnstar, Daven and Kofi and finally the sea. All directions.

In time – Lux couldn't be sure how long – the final Twilight orb flew out, starting its long, meandering journey. As it disappeared, he collapsed on the ground, all his energy spent.

He'd done all he could.

He wasn't quite sure *what* he'd done, or whether it would help, but he'd done it.

They had done it.

Whatever happened now was up to the world.

He pulled Brace and Fera down so they were sitting next to him in the long grass, stretching their feet to the pond. Deimos had gone from the water – Lux's Twilight must have run out as he watched the orbs from the towers. But Lux barely had the energy to worry. Instead, he wrapped his arms around his friends – the girl with the moon-shaped face and the boy with the spiked blonde hair.

"Thanks guys," he said.

"You don't have to thank us," said Fera.

Brace shifted, getting comfortable on the grass. He squinted into the distance at the last Twilight orb, which was just passing over Lindhelm, and shook his head. In disbelief or amazement, Lux wasn't sure.

"Remind me, next time Nova says he's got a mission for us," said Brace, exhausted, "I should go and help Tesla instead."

· CHAPTER 60 ·

There was something about spring – the season of flowers, of bees and blossoms – that reminded Lux of his days playing tag and stuck-in-the-mud with Maya in the garden of Daven's orphanage.

Six months had passed since their trek up Dusk Mountain, and spring was in full bloom. Lux was standing on the dusty floor of Korat Crater, near Dawnstar, gazing into the pale blue sky, which bore an egg-yolk yellow sun and feather clouds.

Next to him were his squad-mates, Ester Nova and Fera Lanceheart. They were tracking a red smudge that was sweeping from left to right across the sky. A Monster. A Fire-drake, in fact, who went by the name of Rory. And Braceson James was flying him.

"Do you think he'll make it?" Fera asked Lux.

"I hope so."

Normally empty, the crater was thronging with people.

Hundreds of them – parents and children, grandparents, brothers and sisters, all from the surrounding towns and cities. They were carrying bags filled with packed lunches – sandwiches and cakes – as well as balls and kites to play with. And like Lux, they were all looking up in the sky, cheering as Brace guided Rory on his flight.

A lot had changed at Dawnstar in the months since their trip to Dusk Mountain. Ghast had been right with his theory. The Ancient towers at the summit had sent out wave after wave of Twilight, carrying a message to the Hex that had surrounded towns and villages.

The message was simple.

It said: 'Stop'.

The Hex had done just that, their Twilight hearts dying like candles in a breeze. And one by one they'd made their way slowly back to where they'd come from, underground, in the dark places of the world.

With that threat gone, Lux and the rest of Squad Juno had stayed for a short while at Professor Ghast's cottage, recovering from all they'd been through. Then they returned with the professor and his books and artefacts to Dawnstar, ready to convince Artello Nova of all they'd learned of taming Monsters.

Nova had taken some convincing. Older Light Hunters like Tesla and Legau, for whom it was extremely difficult to see Monsters as anything other than enemies, even more. But slowly, as Lux and Ghast demonstrated the *Turn* cast, first taming a Kraken in the ocean near Leverburgh, then a nest of Monsters in the hills of Ringtown, they started to come around.

Lux had learned to cast *Turn* for himself, so that he no longer required Ghast's artefact. So quick did he become at throwing the cast, in fact, that he could visit a town and tame a Monster in minutes.

Soon, the work of the Light Hunters had completely changed. No longer were they fielding calls from worried town mayors asking for help against a Monster, but rather receiving sightings of the beasts, hoping the Light Hunters would send one of their tamers.

For Lux, they were the busiest months of his life. He spent so much time in and out of teleporters that he started to lose track of what day it was.

But always doing good.

Always helping.

In time, Lux and Ghast had tamed the world's biggest Monsters. And in short order, a land that had been suffering Monster attacks on an almost daily basis, suffered almost none at all.

Monsters came to be appreciated.

Not by all. Older folk, the ones who'd lived through attacks, found it hard to forgive. But children began to understand that, once tamed, the Monsters they'd recently been so afraid of were no more dangerous than cows in a field. Indeed, so great was the appeal of the creatures that the youngsters soon arranged trips to their closest Monster lair to see one up close.

All of this, of course, presented a problem for the Light Hunters. What were they supposed to do when they had nothing to fight?

Artello Nova thought long and hard about how to answer this question.

It was Fera who came up with a plan in the end. The Light Hunters had spent so long battling Monsters, she said, perhaps it was time they looked after them instead.

And that was how she, Lux and Ester came to be stood in Korat Crater, beneath a gently warming spring sun, watching Brace soaring on Rory, for the opening ceremony of the Light Hunters' very first Monster Zoo.

"There's no way he'll manage a whole loop," said Ester worriedly.

"If Rory can do one with me on him, I'm sure he can with Brace," said Lux, recalling his night-time flight with Sally from a few months before.

Up in the sky, their squad-mate guided the great Monster so that he was hovering above the crowd, to their cheering delight, snorting hot flames.

The audience hushed, already anticipating what might happen next.

Standing tall in Rory's saddle so that the crowd could get a good look at him, Brace pulled on a pair of dark pilot's goggles he'd pinched from Legau Moreiss's office earlier that day and raised his arm as a signal.

The Monster beat his enormous wings, pushing a cool wind onto the crowd below, who shielded their eyes to avoid a blast. Then he was gone, shooting into the sky, growing smaller by the second, until he looked like nothing more than a bright red star.

The great beast soared upwards, allowing the cool wind to blow him back so that he was moving in a long, lazy arc, his beautiful wings catching the sun like fire.

Then . . . an error.

Not a real one, Lux knew.

Rory pretended to hit a nasty updraft and his wing shot inwards, as if injured. He started to fall, spinning in a tight, dizzying circle.

The crowd gasped, looking anxiously among each other. All the while, the Monster continued to fall, straight for the people below, who were panicking now, running from the small patch of grass on which they'd gathered.

"He *is* a little show-off," said Ester amiably of Brace.

Above, the boy was holding Rory tightly, throwing his arms and legs around to make it look like he was barely hanging on.

They continued to tumble, then just at the very last minute, as they were only metres away from barrelling into the crowd, who were now lying flat on the ground, covering their heads, he took a firm grip of Rory's reins, pulled upwards and the Monster righted himself in the air. They soared over the heads of the crowd and landed neatly on the gravel with a soft *thud*.

There was a horrible moment of silence, when Lux worried that Brace might have gone too far with his trick. Then the crowd erupted, jumping up and cheering, waving and clapping.

Brace slid off Rory, stroking the Monster appreciatively. He walked to the crowd, bowing like an actor.

"Don't worry," he said grandly, "I was in control all along."

He directed the audience's applause to Rory, who opened a dozing eye, accepting their plaudits.

"I never realised," said the Monster, his voice as deep and rumbling as ever, "when Professor Ghast collected me from that clearing in the woods, that I'd end up doing something like this."

Lux stood by the magnificent red beast – a creature who only six months earlier had been his enemy – and realised he felt exactly the same.

· CHAPTER 61 ·

Brace waited patiently for the cheering to die down, then spoke again.

"Thank you," he said. "And please remember, ladies and gentlemen, that each of the Monsters in this crater is here by choice. None have been coerced or cajoled. As if we could!" Brace called as an aside, prompting Rory to send out a lick of flame in appreciation. Brace leapt away, much to the delight of the crowd.

"Anyway, thank you for watching," he went on. "I'll be here again later this afternoon. In the meantime, if you'd like to see a Minotaur juggling boulders, make your way over there and you can watch all the fun."

One by one, the crowd disappeared – some heading to the Minotaur, others coming up to Brace and the Light Hunters to talk, others heading for a picnic area that had been set up.

At last, Squad Juno was left alone with Rory.

"I have to say to you all that was wonderful," the Monster rumbled, smiling a mouthful of sharp teeth. "We Monsters were created to fight, but it was never our choice. For the Monsters who have come here, to entertain . . . that is our choice." He looked around the crater at the dozens of bright, colourful, happy creatures performing tricks or enjoying the attention.

"Thanks, Rory," said Fera, running an affectionate hand along the Monster's side.

"It is my pleasure."

He wandered off down the path to his stable, where Lux was sure there would be something to eat and a big pile of hay to lie on.

"Well, I don't know about you three, but I think that was amazing," said Brace.

Korat Crater was growing busier by the second, with more skybuses landing close to the passage Lux, Ester and Maya had taken to get to Dawnstar a year and a half before. Giving up their HQ's secret location had been difficult for the Hunters, who'd guarded it closely for hundreds of years. But once it was clear the Monsters were no longer a threat, there was no point in hanging on.

Lux tuned his ear to the background hum of enjoyment. His nose wrinkled at the smells of roasted meat from the stalls Dawnstar's cooks had set up near the central peak. It made him feel warm inside.

A movement caught his eye – a lady hurrying towards them, with two men. Lux realised, with a start, that it was Fera's family.

"You made it!" she said happily, as her mum gathered her up in a hug. Her dad and brother smiled a warm hello at Lux, Brace and Ester.

"We wouldn't miss this for the world," said her dad, dressed in a smart grey suit. "I just saw a Fire-drake doing a chicken dance. That's not something I thought I'd say in my lifetime."

"How did you get here?" Fera asked her mum. She was grinning, so happy to have them with her at Dawnstar for the first time.

"Light-motor. Thought we'd make a trip of it. Now that we don't have to worry about Monsters on the road. Been staying at some lovely inns."

"Come on . . ." Fera took her mum's hand and led her away, "I'll show you our dorm room. Oh, and the Guardians! You'll love them. And the training wing. You can see where Lux broke my arm."

Fera's dad shot him a questioning look, but her mum nudged him, and he wiped it away.

"Actually, we had a couple of things we wanted to say," he said. "We never did get to thank you all for what you did for Ravenholm. Without you . . ." The words stuck in his throat. "Well . . ."

"What my dear husband's trying to say is that we owe you a great debt," said Fera's mum. "Things are a lot better in our village now. We haven't got to worry about Monsters. No more drills in school. There's even a little Monster who comes to visit the village. I don't know what kind it is, but the kids seem to like it and that's what's important."

"We're glad we could help," said Ester.

"And none of this would have been possible without my little sister," said Barny, flicking his hair and gathering her up in a proud embrace. Fera could barely hide her embarrassment.

A cool breeze blew across the crater, carrying with it that incredible smell of cooked meat. Lux's stomach rumbled. He could tell Fera's dad was the same.

"Well, we can't hang around here all day when there are Monsters to meet and food to eat," he told them. "Thanks again. You're all welcome at Ravenholm whenever you want."

"I'll see you for Nova's speech," Fera told Lux and Brace. And she wandered off towards the food stalls with her family.

"I guess it's just us three," said Brace.

"Two," said Ester.

He looked confused.

"Lux and I need to do something. Why don't you go and find Legau and tell him all about your flight on Rory?"

Lux expected Brace to laugh at Ester's joke, but instead, a lantern seemed to switch on in his head. His face lit up. "You know what, that's actually a *great* idea. You two have fun!" With that, he hurried off in the direction of the food stalls.

"That was mean," said Lux.

"To Brace or Legau?" said Ester, winking.

"What's this thing we need to do then?" he asked, imagining some kind of cleaning job involving sweeping brushes and mops.

"Nothing too exciting. I have something for you." Ester started up the hill towards Dawnstar. "Give me five minutes to get it ready, then meet me at the back entrance."

"What is it?" said Lux, curious.

"Never you mind." Ester shooed him away. "Just meet me in five."

Lux shrugged, then wandered into the crowd.

· CHAPTER 62 ·

The two enormous Light-powered Guardians were standing like giants in the atrium when Lux got there, either side of the twin lifts that took Light Hunters up and down the levels of their home. He got out his star-ring, letting it catch the light, still terribly curious about what Ester was preparing.

At Dawnstar's rear entrance – a circle of thick grey stone in the wall – he used his ring to get outside, the door creaking open and letting in a cool breeze.

Ester was already there, sitting on the platform with her legs dangling over the edge. Lux found a spot next to her and sank down.

Ahead of them ran the long staircase down to the crater floor, where they could spy an ocean of people, stalls, skyships, banners and Monsters. It all looked tiny, like it was part of one of Brace's wooden games.

From behind her, Ester took a plate of cookies shaped like Monster badges and handed one to Lux. She took one herself. "I got the cook to make them," she said, admiring one and taking a bite.

"They're great," said Lux.

There was a moment of silence as they both chewed, then Ester spoke. "Well, here we are."

"Here we are," said Lux.

"We came a year and a half ago, can you remember? Well, you found me out here, anyway."

Lux had been so overwhelmed with worries about his grandpa back then, and fears of Deimos, that he'd been about to run all the way home to Daven. Now that he thought about it, it seemed silly. But then . . .

"I remember."

"You've come a long way," said Ester.

Had he? Lux thought about it. He supposed he had, although he felt like the same boy inside.

"Still can't believe what's happened," she went on. "We ended the world and saved it in two days. Not many people can say that."

Light glinted off skyships in the sky. One with a bright red and black hull caught Lux's eye, and for a moment his stomach tightened.

"Has there been any news?" he asked.

Ester knew what he was talking about. "Deimos?"

He nodded.

"Not yet. But we're still looking. If he's out there, we'll find him.

Don't worry." She hesitated, then said gently after a few seconds, "It is over Lux. He couldn't do anything even if he wanted to. The Monsters are free."

"I just shouldn't have let him get away," he said, thinking back to six months earlier, at the summit of Dusk Mountain, collapsing onto the grass. "I was so tired."

Lux and Ester ate their cookies, watching a Fire-drake flash by the opening of the canyon. A blast of warmth hit Lux's face.

"I keep wondering 'why me?'" he said. "The Ark, the mountain, all that. I think about it. Why me?"

"How do you mean?"

"I mean, why me? The Ancients . . . how did they even know I'd be here? Why my Twilight?"

"You're not the only one out there with Twilight," said Ester. "Now we know what we're looking for, we've found more."

Maya had already told Lux about the experiments Tesla had been performing with their help.

Wiping crumbs from her mouth, Ester scared away a couple of pigeons who were hanging around, interested in the remaining cookies. "By the way, I never did get to thank you for those days of rest at Ravenholm."

Lux looked confused.

"After you healed me. I had a right old time. Very pleasant. I took a lot of walks. Found this, in fact."

She reached into her pocket and pulled out a circle of black fabric with a golden star in the centre. Lux's grandpa's Luminary badge. It was a little more frayed, and there were specks of mud.

But none of that mattered. It was his grandpa's badge.

"How . . .?" he stammered.

"I noticed you weren't wearing it when you healed me. So, I went looking. Good job I managed to find it, eh?"

Lux felt tears coming. He swallowed. "This is what you wanted to give me?"

Ester nodded.

"Thank you," said Lux. He found that he was speechless.

"Just don't throw it away again. He'd have been proud of you, Lux. Your grandpa. All of us. We made a mistake and fixed it. That always meant more to him than just getting it right first time."

Lux recalled the dozens of clocks and compasses he'd dropped on the workshop floor back in Daven before fixing them. She was right.

Before he could say any more, there was a click behind them and the door into Dawnstar slid open. Silhouetted against the blue Light was Maya Murphy.

"*There* you are," she said, relieved. "I've been looking for you. I told you to wear your Shell."

"Hi Maya," said Lux, tossing her one of the Monster badge cookies. "What's up?"

"What do you mean, 'What's up?' It's almost time. Nova's speech."

Lux glanced at his watch. It was nearly two o' clock.

"We've got to go," said Maya.

Lux looked at Ester, who indicated for him to leave. "I'll see you down there," she said. "I'm going to enjoy the view a while longer."

"You sure?"

Ester breathed in the fresh air. "This is the first time in my life everything's been truly peaceful."

"Thanks, Ester," said Lux. "For everything."

"Go on."

Maya joined Lux at the edge of the platform, and together they made their way down the steep, stone staircase to the busy crater floor.

· CHAPTER 63 ·

Lux had to hurry to keep up with Maya as she slid through the crowds, gaping at the gathered Monsters dotted among them.

There were Griffins and Fire-drakes, Arachnids and Behemoths, Cerberuses and Gargoyles, Basilisks and Harpies. It was like the memorial garden in Lindhelm, only the Monsters were alive, breathing.

A large crowd had gathered in a ring around Korat Crater's central peak when they arrived, chatting away. In the middle, was the wooden stage upon which Nova would deliver his speech. The sun slanted down on it, and a single bright beam lit up where he would stand.

Maya located Tesla, hunched over a glass jar that stood on a home-made tripod, directly in front of the stage. A blue Light orb danced inside. Tesla was tinkering with a red wire that ran around the bottom of the jar.

"At last!" he said grouchily. "You were supposed to be helping me set up." He pinned Maya with an irritated stare. "Check that remote's working correctly," he instructed, before greeting Lux as an afterthought. "Hello."

Lux took in the Inventor's contraption.

"Records what it sees," explained Maya. "Like Nova's observatory. Lets us play it back."

"Nice."

There was a shuffling in the grass behind Lux and a small hand clamped down on his shoulder. He turned and felt a rush of happiness. "Sally!"

She was standing next to her grandad – out of his overalls for once and dressed somewhat smartly in his closest approximation of a suit. His hair was sculpted to a sharp point.

"Hi, Lux."

Accompanying them was Brace, along with Fera and her family.

"I found them wandering near the skyships," said Brace. "Lost."

"We weren't lost," said Ghast unconvincingly. "We were just taking in the atmosphere."

"It's great to see you."

"It is nice to see me, isn't it?" said Sally.

Ghast got out a pile of sandwiches from his bag, then unfolded a blanket, nudging members of the crowd away so that he had enough space to lay it out.

"I saw you flying Rory," Sally told Brace, bumping into him playfully. She shook her shoulders loose, pulling out one of her pieces of paper and preparing for a poem. But before she could start, Brace cut her off.

"Actually, I've written you a little something this time," he said. "If you don't mind me reading it?"

Sally looked like someone had just told her she could have three tubs of ice cream all at once. "Oh, Light yes!"

Looking slightly embarrassed at the enquiring glances of Lux and Fera, Brace forged on, taking a folded piece of paper out of his pocket.

"It's . . . uh, not as good as some of—"

"Read it," said Sally excitedly.

Brace cleared his throat.

"*I've met some brave people in my life,*
That's what being a Light Hunter's like.
But the bravest girl I've ever met,
Was Sally, the little tike."

There was a moment of silence in which Brace watched her carefully, gauging how she'd react.

"Like I say, it's not—"

"Oh, my Light!" said Sally, her mouth open in shock. "It's about me." She looked at her grandad, amazed. "He wrote a poem about me!"

Brace folded up the paper and handed it to her. "A present," he said, smiling. She took it, shaking her head in wonder.

"Oh Light! Oh Light!" She did a celebratory dance, then stopped, eyeing him shrewdly. "Aren't you embarrassed?"

Brace dropped to his knees and took her hand. "No. In fact, I'm very proud. The poem's right. I don't think I've ever met a little girl as brave as you in my life."

Sally stood, her cheeks turning red.

Brace shrugged at Lux and Fera, who were still watching him, surprised. "It's true."

It took Sally a long time to recover from Brace's poem. She flopped onto the blanket next to her grandad, holding the page delicately, promising to look after it for the rest of her life. Fera, after telling Brace how proud she was of him, took her family to meet Tesla and Maya, who were putting the finishing touches to the Inventor's device. Up on the stage, Lux could see Nova playing with Bella in his usual pale blue robes, his injured arm at his side.

"Nice, isn't it?" said the professor beside Lux. He cast a glance around Korat Crater, taking in the Monsters and delighted visitors. "I was a Light Hunter here for fifteen years. When I left, I really didn't know what I was going to do. I just knew that something was wrong with what we were doing. I don't think I ever thought I'd find a way to tame the Monsters, not deep down. But we've done it. Isn't it nice to not have any enemies for once?"

The professor took a breath of cool spring air.

"I wanted you to have this," he said, opening his bag. He brought out the Key to the Ark, which he handed to Lux. "I hope we'll never need it again, but, just in case, there's no one I'd trust with it more."

Lux marvelled at the ball's weight. All the trouble it had caused, all it had helped to achieve. He felt the age of it, a thousand years, the unbroken line back to the Ancients.

"Thanks, Professor Ghast."

"This world owes your grandad a great debt for raising you the way he did." Ghast smiled at his granddaughter. "I, for one, won't forget that."

· CHAPTER 64 ·

A hush gathered over the crowd as they saw that Dawnstar's Luminary was ready to begin. There was a click as Tesla's recording device started up, the orb of Light painting the scene around it onto the glass.

"Ladies and gentlemen," Artello Nova began, smiling warmly at the crowd and looking up at the bright sky. "What a wonderful day to be gathered here at Korat Crater. It is an honour to be on this stage today officially opening the world's very first Monster Zoo."

There was a huge round of applause. Nova waited for it to settle, throwing a bemused glance at his daughter.

"I can see you're all as happy about this as I am. I can say with true sincerity that opening a Monster Zoo in Korat Crater is not something I thought I would be doing during my time in charge of the Light Hunters.

"I don't know how many of you know this, but Dawnstar has stood, hidden in this crater, for over eight hundred years. For eight centuries, the people here battled Monsters, keeping our villages and towns safe."

"Heroes!" yelled a woman from the back of the crowd.

"Very kind," said Nova, after another round of applause. "Many of those who have worked here, giving their lives to battle Monsters, were indeed heroes. But . . ." His expression grew serious. "But . . . at no point during those eight hundred years was fighting the choice of any of those Light Hunters. Our duty has always weighed heavily on our shoulders."

The crowd went silent.

"But as you are all aware – as hopefully everybody in our world is now aware – Monsters are no longer our enemies. In a way, they never were."

Nova walked to a wooden table he had set up on the stage, where he picked up three items Lux couldn't quite make out from where he was standing.

"We must learn to live with Monsters now. Not in fear, but in a spirit of community. We can learn from each other, we *must* learn from each other, so as to undo centuries of damage.

"But you did not come here for philosophy. Rather, celebration. And it is true that today's events would not have been possible without a certain group of people. I have a little something for each of them. So, if Professor Emory Ghast, Brace James and Fera Lanceheart would come to the stage . . ."

There was murmuring in the crowd. Lux, Brace, Fera and

Ghast looked among each other – not quite sure what was about to happen. Then the three Nova had called shrugged and made their way up.

The crowd cheered at the two Light Hunters and the professor, who all smiled shyly.

"Professor Ghast, I'd like to ask you to step forward first," said Nova.

The professor made sure his nose-ring was sitting straight and his hair sculpted to a point, then made his way to the front.

"Professor Ghast was once a Light Hunter at Dawnstar," Nova told the crowd. "Without him, we wouldn't have discovered how to tame Monsters."

Ghast smiled awkwardly, glancing at Sally, who was waving at him proudly. "He's my grandad," she was telling everyone nearby.

"I fell out with the professor before he left," Nova went on, looking sadly at Ghast. "A mistake for which I will be eternally sorry." He gathered up his old friend, squeezing tight.

"I thought long and hard about what reward I should give this incredible man for what he's done. In the end, it was obvious."

Nova produced a black Light Hunter badge and attached it to Ghast's arm. A tear formed in the professor's eye.

"His Inventor badge," Nova explained to the crowd. "I had him hand it in when he left. Now I return it, with my sincerest apologies."

He held out a hand for Ghast to shake. The professor took it warmly, pulling his friend into an embrace. The crowd cheered.

"I think that means he forgives me," said Nova, when he finally broke free.

Ghast made his way back to the crowd and Sally, who ran up and hugged him tightly.

"Next up, Braceson James."

Rolling his shoulders, Brace strode confidently to the front of the stage, before cartwheeling and bowing theatrically, accepting a deafening cheer.

"For anyone in the crowd who hasn't worked it out yet, Brace is Dawnstar's joker. He is also a wonderful, loyal and brave Light Hunter that's saved more towns than Hunters twice his age. In addition, Brace is a keen flier."

The young boy's attention snapped to Nova, who produced another badge from behind his back. A Pilot badge. Brace started to hyperventilate.

"As with my old friend the professor, I thought long and hard about what to reward you with, Brace. Because your part in the taming of Monsters was much more important than many would give you credit for. In hard times, it is often the one with the brightest spirit who gives us the courage and hope to carry on. However. . ." Nova pinned the badge to Brace's uniform. "Another old friend of mine had an idea for a reward that could not be more perfect. Legau Moreiss. It turns out he has a spare spot on his Pilot training course. He wondered if you'd like the job."

At the side of the stage, Legau tipped his hat respectfully at Brace.

"So, how about it?"

Brace touched the Pilot badge in wonder. "Yes!" he blurted. "Yes!"

He bounded off the stage, running up to Legau, whose moustache twitched in shock. He shook Brace's hand.

"And now," said Nova, "to a young lady who I think many would agree is the most supportive Light Hunter we have at Dawnstar."

He indicated for Fera to join him.

"Fera's been with us for five years now, and I know her family are here to celebrate today. It was Mr and Mrs Lanceheart's village, Ravenholm, and the villagers there, who went with our Light Hunters on their great raid to Dusk Mountain that subdued the Hex threat.

"What modest, young Fera probably won't want me telling you is that she had to take over leadership of Squad Juno just before their final assault on the mountain, when my daughter Ester was injured. She did a fine job, inspiring her friends to finish their mission. And with that in mind . . ." Nova took a final badge and pinned it to Fera's arm. ". . . we are inviting her to become a squad leader. Starting next year, she will lead a small squad around the world, checking the Monsters we have tamed are safe, in their right habitat, and adjusting well to their new roles."

Fera's mouth opened in shock. Before anyone else could applaud, there was a sole cheer from the front. It was Barny, tossing up his hands and clapping loudly. The rest of the crowd joined in, *whooping* and *woohooing*.

Fera stumbled into Brace, who gathered her in a hug, lifting her arm for the crowd to cheer some more.

It was a good minute before the noise died down, as a cool breeze blew in from the crater rim. On the stage, Nova took a deep breath, ready to speak.

"There is one more Light Hunter, without whom we'd not be where we are today. Indeed, I would go as far as to say that without this young man's courage, his bravery and belief, those who wish to harm us might have won out in the end.

"But thanks to the actions of Lux Dowd, they did not. Lux, could you come to the stage please? I have something special I would like to give you."

The crowd craned their necks, trying to find him. But there was no sign of Lux.

He was gone.

· CHAPTER 65 ·

He was, in fact, sneaking around the back of a large, boat-shaped rock, near the low platform that marked Korat Crater's central peak. All along the ground were bushes with bright red berries. Lux ran his hand through them, tuning out the hum of the crowd and Nova's deep voice.

The truth was, he'd never liked being the centre of attention. The people he cared about knew what he'd done at Dusk Mountain; that was enough for him.

Almost all of them anyway.

In the six months since he'd returned from Lindhelm, Lux had been so busy with Professor Ghast, travelling the world and taming Monsters, that he hadn't had chance to visit his grandpa's memorial.

Lux started up the shallow slope now, heading for the small, grey stone, which poked out of the sandy ground, shaded from the spring sun by a pink blossom tree. A bench had been set up nearby and he sat on it, looking back down at the crowd.

"Hi Grandpa."

He told the old man about his trip to Lindhelm, about the hot air balloon ride. He told him about the ice-Monster and Ghast's cottage. He told him about the Ark, and the Hex. About the fight at Ravenholm and the dangerous flight on Rory. And at last, he told his grandpa about finding his own courage and belief at Dusk Mountain.

By the time he was done, the sun had moved around its great arc in the sky and the crowd below had dispersed. Lux could see a Fire-drake entertaining a new crowd with licks of red-orange flame.

"I think we've done the right thing," he said, hoping his grandpa would have agreed.

He pushed himself off the bench as a gust of wind shook the blossom tree, blowing a handful of pink petals down the slope. Lux watched them dance in the breeze, then spotted three figures making their way up towards him.

"I knew we'd find you here," said Maya, turning to Brace and Fera. "Told you, didn't I?"

They stopped in front of Lux. For a few moments there was silence, then Fera said, "You didn't want to go on stage?"

"Not my kind of thing."

Maya walked to Lux's grandpa's memorial and wiped a thin layer of sand from the top, polishing it with the arm of her jumper. "We made him proud."

"Yeah, we did," said Brace.

Lux felt a wave of emotion. His friends. They'd been through so much together. He knew that even if they disappeared to different corners of the planet, they'd remain fast, firm and true.

He linked arms with them and began to walk back down the slope, feeling proud.

After a few seconds, Maya stopped. "Does anyone have a spare sock?"

Lux, Brace and Fera looked at her like she'd gone mad.

"I forgot to ask earlier."

"A sock?" said Lux.

"Yeah, the older and smellier the better."

"Why?" said Fera.

Maya leaned in close, ready to reveal a secret. "Well, we've been so busy recently that we've not had any time for practical jokes or secret missions or anything. And I had this idea for how we could wind Tesla up. Nicely, of course. But I need an old sock."

"I've got loads in our room," said Brace.

"He does," confirmed Fera. "And I really shouldn't be saying this, but I know how to make old socks even smellier. Barny showed me when we were little."

"Excellent," said Maya. "Let's go now and we'll set it up before he gets back."

They walked on a few paces. Lux hung back, recalling the last time he and Maya had gone on a secret mission – their trip to try and steal the banned healing book from grumpy Mrs Henderton's lighthouse library in Daven. It seemed like an age ago.

But a practical joke would be fun . . .

"Lux, are you in?"

Maya's question hung in the air. Lux took a deep, cooling breath and a weight seemed to lift off him, joining the clouds that drifted happily in the sky.

"Lux?"

"Yeah," he said, skipping down the slope to catch up with his friends. "Let's go have some fun."

ACKNOWLEDGEMENTS

Sometimes writing a book is a doddle and sometimes it's like finding the other half of a pair of socks in an overflowing clothes basket. This year, with pandemics and new babies and lots of other changes, writing might have been a lot more difficult, but for the help of a few very important people.

Firstly, Hazel, Charlotte, Becky, Kieran, George and the rest of the guys at UCLan Publishing. The nicest thing you can say about a publisher is that you feel when you hand over your book it's in safe hands, and the eager, enthusiastic hands at UCLan are the safest.

A special thanks to Tony Higginson, book-man extraordinaire, who made a long and busy book tour back in February 2020 like an adventure. A more knowledgeable person about the world of books you're unlikely to meet.

Thanks to all the librarians and booksellers who help get our kids reading. It's not an exaggeration to say that without you this whole thing doesn't work. All us authors owe you a great debt.

Lauren, Jon and the team at Bell Lomax, and Sandra at Marjacq, I'm forever learning from your thoughts, ideas and feedback. Thanks for looking after me!

To all the teachers on Twitter out there promoting reading, eternal gratitude. Special mentions to Emily Weston and Scott Evans, who shouted so loudly about the first Light Hunters book.

To fellow children's authors Ross Montgomery and Ben Davis, thanks for the conversations. Smart advice at a time when I really needed it.

And last but not least, thanks to Team Walker – Dominika and Frankie – without whom this whole writing thing wouldn't be possible in the first place. It's hard climbing a hill, but a lot easier when there's a strong wind at your back.

Dan Walker

HAVE YOU READ LUX'S FIRST ADVENTURE?

ASK THE AUTHOR

Out of all the books you have written, which is your favourite and why?

That's a hard question. In a way, all of them are my favourites. But if I had to pick one, I would perhaps go with *The Last Monster*. As an author you're always working hard to improve your craft, and I think this is my best story yet. Hope all the readers agree!

Who is your favourite character and why?

I would say Sally. She is the character that teaches Lux the important lesson he needs to learn in the story, and she does it in an interesting way with her rhymes and poems. I also have a soft spot for Brace, because he always provides a touch of humour when things are getting too serious.

Why did you choose purple energy for Lux?
In the books, Light energy is white-blue and Shade energy is a deep red. Twilight is a mixture of the two of these powers, so it makes sense that its colour would be purple. That, and who doesn't like purple?

Which character do you relate to the most and why?
That would be Professor Ghast. Writing can be hard work sometimes – coming up with the characters, storyline, settings, making it all make sense. You're often working on your own for long stretches, solving tricky problems. This is a bit like Ghast in the book. He leaves the Light Hunters to work on something he believes in, spending years solving a problem that no-one else has.

Would you like a Monster of your very own?
As long as they're a bit calmer like the Monsters are at the end of this book! I'd especeally have one like Rory, who could fly me wherever I wanted. It would certainly save me sitting in traffic next time I'm heading into town!

If you could have any power from Lux's world, what would it be?
I think I'd go with a Conjuror's Flame. It would be nice to have a light whenever you needed it, and the heat it provided would be like having a hot water bottle at your fingertips. But I am clumsy, so I'd probably have to be careful not to singe my eyebrows or something!

Where did you draw your inspiration for *The Last Monster* and Lux's world?

The idea for the world of *The Light Hunters* came when I was walking along an overgrown canal and saw three deer standing in the middle of it. They'd never been there before and I've not seen them since. They looked at me, and I looked at them, then they skittered off into the fields. But I thought afterwards how amazing it would have been if they had been monsters instead. (Scary, actually!) The idea for a world where Monsters roam the lands came from there.

Do you think adding grief to a children's book is important, if so, why?

I think it's important we don't hide the world from children. Part of the reason we read stories is to help us understand life, and if we hide the harder bits then we're not being honest. But, of course, not every children's book requires grief. The story has to come first.

What are the key messages you wanted to get across in this book?

I think belief is the biggest one. The characters in this book have lost belief in themselves a bit, and the story is about them finding it again. Also, there's an element of 'not everything is as it seems.' The Monsters in the first book were thought of as evil. But like evil in real life, we have to look beneath the covers a bit to really understand what's going on.

You go into so much detail within the book which makes you want to turn the page and continue reading, did it take you a long time to come up with the world?

I normally do a bit of planning about the world before I start writing, but most of it comes as I go, scene-to-scene. If a characters comes to a library, you ask yourself as a writer, *What is the library called? Is there anything interesting about it? What is its history?* Same with places, Monters, people. You build the world bit by bit.

What has been the hardest part to write in the books?

The middle is always toughest for me. Beginning a book is easy, as is the end. But keeping the reader interested in the middle without it becoming formulaic and episodic is the hard part. Hopefully I've done well here!

What will you be writing next?

I'm just finishing a book about a magic tree, in a fairy-tale kingdom, which I've had a lot of fun with. I'll be revising that, then the world is my oyster! (If anyone has any good ideas, please send them to my website! :-))

IF YOU LIKE THIS, YOU'LL LOVE...

A. J. HARTLEY

Illustrated by MANUEL ŠUMBERAC

MONSTERS
in the
MIRROR

Where danger and laughter
lurk around every corner . . .

THE
BOOK
OF
SECRETS

PHILIP CAVENEY

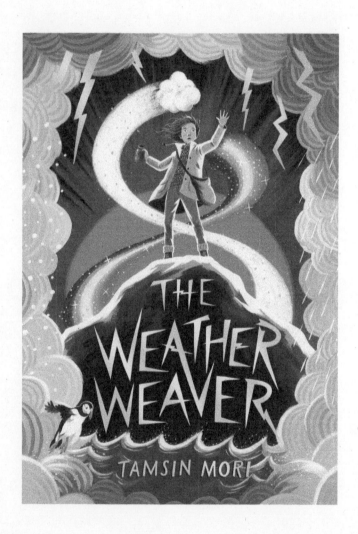